The Seduction of Madalyn

By

Cynthia A Clement

Book Edition
ISBN: 978-0-9920189-3-1

This book is a work of fiction. The characters and incidents are from the author's imagination. Any resemblance to actual incidents or persons, living or dead, is coincidental and unintentional.

Cover Design by Melody Simmons of eBookindiecovers

Dedication

*To my wonderful and talented critique partner, Kim.
You've seen this book through numerous rewrites and
revision, listened to my worries, and helped with the brainstorming.
Through it all, you've been supportive and positive.
Thank you.*

Prologue

The damp night pressed upon Madalyn, her eyes straining in the fog to find the men who had taken her brother. She'd followed them to this pier. Her coachman had refused to go down to the waterfront, so she'd continued on foot, panting now with the exertion and terror.

She must find William.

She must protect her brother.

Those were her mother's last words before she died and Madalyn had lived by that mantra for most of her life. She'd been seven years old when William was born and her mother had put him in her arms. She'd vowed then to keep him safe always. That had been fifteen years ago.

She spied a coach further down the dock and started running toward it. This had to be the one. There was no time to waste. Her breath was coming in gasps as she fought with her long skirts to reach the men.

"Stop!"

The men quickened their steps and before Madalyn reached them, they'd carried her brother aboard the vessel. She arrived just as the gangplank was pulled up. She pulled back from the edge as the sound of the water lapping at the ship's hull paralyzed her.

Madalyn swallowed her fear "You cannot leave." She waved her arms at the ship, but the crew ignored her.

One of the masked thugs turned back at her and shook his head. "Best go home, little lady. He's lost now."

Despair and anger coursed through her. She wasn't going to let them take her brother. She had promised to keep him safe, and no matter what the cost, she would keep her vow. She turned to a stranger standing on the dock.

"Where is the ship sailing for?"

"That's The Magistrate." The man's voice was gruff. "She sails for Charleston."

Chapter 1

May 1824

Madalyn was caught and there was no escape. Not even her worse nightmares came close to her present predicament. She stood atop a scarred, wooden table, in the center of a ship's galley, and was about to be sold. She took a deep breath and stared blankly at the far wall. It was too late for regrets.

"Let the bidding begin!"

Madalyn shook as the voice of the Captain reverberated through the room.

Screaming men surrounded her, their voices full of jeers and taunts. A timber creaked above and the ship swayed violently to the right. Madalyn fell against one of her captors and gagged at the odor of stale sweat.

"More." The men's voices rose in unison. "We need to see what we're buying."

Captain Galer pushed her forward until she tottered on the edge of the table. The ship rocked viciously to the left. She would have fallen into the roaring crowd below if not for the Captain's vice grip on her arm.

"I'll give you more." The Captain spat on the table.

Galer grabbed the neck of her tattered gown, and ripped it from her chest, exposing her chemise. Madalyn clenched her fists, and beat her hands against the man, but he only laughed at her efforts.

"Hold the vixen tight, Lee."

Hands the size of hams encircled her arms, holding her captive. Madalyn struggled to free herself, bucking her body backwards and kicking, but Lee was immoveable. She fought until she was panting for breath, her chest rising and falling rapidly. Her efforts had only incited the men to a feverish pitch.

Captain Galer's dirty face leered in front of her. "A fine beauty we have here."

He stroked a finger down the side of her face. When she twisted away, he held her chin firm and licked her cheek. The smell of alcohol was overpowering, and Madalyn's stomach rolled.

"Imagine taming this in bed."

The crowd roared, almost drowning out the crack of thunder overhead. The ship tossed sideways, sending chairs crashing against each other and lanterns swinging dangerously close to the galley walls. The door slammed shut just as the crowd quieted.

The men turned around, and Madalyn caught a glimpse of a tall, dark-haired man before the crew surged back to her. Another bidder. Her stomach sank.

"I see Mr. Carter's joined us." The Captain's voice was more threat than welcome. "Let's show him what happens to stowaways aboard my ship."

Galer motioned for Lee to move forward and Madalyn was pushed to the edge of the table again. The Captain raised his hand above her head and waited for silence. Within seconds the only sound heard was the deafening roar of the storm that raged outside.

"Let's begin."

Galer's hand dropped and ripped the front of her chemise open as the first man shouted his bid. The crowd surged forward, and Madalyn shut her eyes against the tears that threatened to fall.

Humiliation burned deep within her.

It was soon replaced by anger and pride.

She lifted her head, and stuck her chin out. The sound of the men's frantic bidding disappeared as she took a deep breath and started counting. She mumbled the numbers under her breath. It took her mind away from the horror of her situation.

The bidding seemed to go on for hours, but Madalyn steeled her determination. She'd begun this voyage to find the brother she loved. She would not be defeated.

"Sold." Galer's voice echoed through the galley.

Madalyn tasted bile, and the room swam in front of her. Her captor loosened his grip on her and she twisted one arm free. With head held high, she clasped her torn chemise and gown to her chest. This was only a minor setback. She would find a way to escape and finish her journey.

"Move," Lee growled in her ear.

"This is wrong." She struggled to free her arm, but Lee tightened his grip. "You can't do this."

"It's already done." The beast leered at her.

Madalyn's nose wrinkled in disgust. The room reeked of dirty bodies and smoke, but this man smelled as if he hadn't bathed in over a year. She held her breath and turned away.

"I refuse." Her voice shook.

"You should have thought of that before sneaking aboard Captain Galer's ship." He hoisted her over his shoulder and jumped down from the table.

"Let me go." Madalyn twisted her body, but Lee held firm. When she stopped struggling he dropped her onto the floor. Her legs wobbled as the ship rocked sideways, but before she could find her bearing, Lee grabbed her.

The man spat on the floor. "Yer lucky he didn't give you to the crew."

Madalyn shuddered. The shove at her back forced her to stumble forward. She strained her eyes in the flickering candlelight to see the man who had bought her. The crew jostled her, pinching and fondling, but she was pushed relentlessly toward the rear wall.

A man, elegant in black, stood separate.

Madalyn's heart skipped a beat as she recognized Mr. Carter. He had entered the galley just as the auction began. He was leaning against the wall, his arms crossed. His eyes were indifferent as he stared at her. A shiver of dread ran up her spine.

This was the man who had bought her.

She was pulled in front of him. He was over six feet tall. The top of her head came up to his shoulder. Her eyes were level with the diamond and ruby stickpin in his cravat. Madalyn glanced up. Her stomach knotted, as clear blue eyes searched her face before turning back to her guard.

"Who do I pay?"

"Best give it to the Captain. He don't trust no man."

Mr. Carter motioned to the Captain at the front of the room, and nodded. Carter's acceptance was followed by a jeer from the crowd. Galer made his way over to them.

"She should do you fine." The Captain spoke with a grunt, his breath ragged from fighting the crowd. "A right bargain you have there, Carter."

Carter's eyebrow rose. He pulled out a handful of gold sovereigns from his waistcoat, counted ten and thrust them at Galer. Madalyn closed her eyes, and took a deep breath.

"This is illegal." Her voice wavered.

"I'm the only law aboard this ship." Captain Galer raised his hand and Madalyn cringed. Carter's hand shot out and locked onto Galer's arm. The Captain's eyes widened.

"She is mine." The dark haired man pushed the Captain's arm away. "I will deal with her."

"See that you do." Galer rubbed his sleeve across his nose. "I expect you to pay her passage too."

"Certainly." Mr. Carter's voice had a silky smoothness that was almost hypnotic.

Five more sovereigns changed hands, and then Madalyn was thrust toward the man so quickly that she lost her footing and stumbled. She fell against a wide, firm chest. The scent of soap and pine assailed her nostrils, and she took a deep breath. Memories of the countryside, and the safe life she had left behind, flooded her.

Her reverie was broken by a low voice. "Can you stand?"

She nodded and pushed herself away. At least the man was clean. She forced herself to look up. Amusement twinkled in his blue eyes and Madalyn fought the urge to slap his face.

"You will catch a cold standing like that."

Madalyn looked down. Part of her torn gown had fallen out of her hand. Heat flooded her cheeks, and she scrambled to cover her exposed breast.

"Put this on." Mr. Carter pulled off his jacket, and draped it across her shoulders.

Madalyn kept her head down as she struggled to put her arms into the coat without further embarrassment. Her hands trembled, but she managed to pull the coat close to her body. When she had it buttoned, she lifted her head.

"Come." Mr. Carter took her arm and she gasped at the sudden shock that raced up her arm.

He brought her close to him, sheltering her from the others, as they made their way to the door. Madalyn was surprised at how secure she felt in those arms. A few men tried to touch her, but her protector's glare kept them at a distance.

"Wait." Captain Galer's voice rang out just as they reached the galley door.

Mr. Carter pulled her to a stop and she almost tripped over her feet. His arm tightened around her, bringing her even closer to his chest. His face was expressionless, but she could feel his heartbeat quicken.

"What now, Galer?"

"We're not finished."

The room went silent as the two men glared at each other. Seconds ticked by, and outside the storm still raged. The ship listed from side to side, the swinging lanterns casting eerie shadows across the room. A tremor crawled up Madalyn's spine, and she fought the urge to run.

"Yes we are." Carter's deep voice was heavy with boredom.

Galer snorted. "I just want to give you something to remember me by."

A muscle in Mr. Carter's jaw tightened, and Madalyn held her breath. The animosity between these men was a living, breathing entity. The crew was watching intently, their bodies taut with anticipation. Her eyes darted around for escape, but Carter's hold was firm.

"I doubt I will ever forget this voyage. It's amazing you are able to keep this ship afloat with such a degree of incompetence."

"No one invited you onto the Folly." Galer's eyes narrowed into tiny slits. "Not everyone runs their ships the way you do."

"There is a storm raging outside, and most of your crew is down here tormenting this poor woman." Mr. Carter's voice dripped with loathing. "You should all be hauled to jail for your actions."

"You've never hid your disgust, Carter. You forget I'm the law here."

"You are the one who forgets." Carter tightened his grip on Madalyn's arm, and started to move away from Galer.

"Not so fast." Captain Galer kicked his foot against a table leg. "You've deprived the crew of their fun. You have to give them something in return."

"I'll buy them a night of drinking at the Sailor's inn, when we dock in Charleston."

"Not good enough." Captain Galer motioned for one of his men to block the door. "I've got a better idea. Let's give them a little taste of the wench now."

"No." Carter's voice was low and threatening.

Galer shrugged his shoulders. "Then she stays here."

"I don't recall any conditions on the sale. I paid your price. She is mine."

"The auction was for the crew." Galer spat on the floor. "My rules are different for you."

The crew surged near, and Madalyn's heart began to race. She moved closer to her protector. The hatred between these two men was going to affect her.

"I know you would never have booked passage on my ship if another had been available, but I don't take offense with that."

Galer winked at the crew. A fresh round of heckling greeted Madalyn's ears. Her stomach tightened at the leers from the men. She shifted on her feet, but Carter held steady.

"I don't want any trouble." Carter took a step toward the door. "My business with you is finished. Let us leave."

Galer put his hands on his hips, and leaned forward. "You've interfered for the last time."

"I paid good money for her."

"My men deserve some fun. I won't stop my crew from having her."

"No." The word was out of Madalyn's mouth before she had a chance to think.

"The young lady does not desire it," Carter said with a shrug of his shoulders. "That settles the issue."

"I don't give a damn about her." Galer's voice rose in a snarl. "It's only fair to share one's bounty."

Carter shook his head. "I'm not interested."

"Then the girl stays." Galer motioned for Lee. "The bidding begins again."

A cheer went up from the crew, and Lee grabbed Madalyn's arm. She refused to let go of Carter, clinging to him with the last of her strength. She couldn't bear to be exposed, and auctioned in front of the crew again.

"Enough!" Carter's voice rang out above the shouting men. "I paid a fair price for the chit. I intend to leave with her. Alone."

Captain Galer's mouth dropped open, and he stared at Carter for several seconds. The crew moved back a few paces, and Madalyn tucked herself into the safe haven of Mr. Carter's body. She shook with horror, and Carter rubbed her arm until her shivers subsided.

"There are more of us than you." Galer stuck his chin out. "I only have to give the order."

"Neither you, nor your crew, will ever work again." Mr. Carter's voice was low, each word spoken with menace. "You will spend the rest of your days in prison. You have my word."

The two men glared at each other for several seconds. Galer pursed his lips, and scanned his crew before turning back to Mr. Carter. A slight grin twisted his lips.

"You're signing your own death warrant."

"I think not. My man of business knows I'm on this ship. If I do not turn up alive in Charleston he has instructions to have you all arrested."

Madalyn's stomach tightened at the cold, threatening tone of Carter's voice. Every nerve in her body screamed to run, but she was frozen in place. Terror held her in its grip.

There was no sanctuary.

Either way was danger.

Seconds seemed like hours, as her fate hung in the balance. Madalyn held her breath and waited. Neither man spoke. Their gazes never left each other in their silent duel. Then, beads of sweat appeared on Galer's forehead, glistening in the hazy candlelight. His eyes never left Mr. Carter, but his shoulders seemed to sag.

Galer shrugged. "If you want her so bad, take her."

Madalyn let out the breath she'd been holding, and leaned into Carter. Now she only had to worry about one man, not the whole crew. Carter pulled her close, and took a step toward the door.

Captain Galer moved away, and his crew followed suit. A few of the men spat on the floor as they walked by, but Carter didn't stop. He had turned the door handle when the Captain's voice rang out.

"This isn't the last of it."

Carter turned and bowed his head. "Until next time."

Once the wooden door of the galley was shut behind them, he took his arm away from Madalyn's shoulder. "You should be safe now."

"I would hardly call being bought by a complete stranger, safe." Madalyn shook her tangled hair away from her face. "No gentleman would participate in such an outrageous proceeding."

"I never professed to be a gentleman." Carter's mouth twisted into a grin.

Madalyn inhaled a quick breath under his piercing stare. Her stomach fluttered as his eyes bore into her soul. She tried to hold his gaze, but looked away after a few seconds.

"What are you going to do?" She clasped her hands in front of her.

"I thought that was obvious. Take you to my cabin."

Chapter 2

Strong hands encircled her upper arms. They tightened, and pulled her away from the door. She bit her lower lip, her mind racing for an escape plan. Nothing came, so she refused to move.

Carter leaned close, his voice low and commanding. "It's pointless to delay. At any moment the men will be leaving the galley. I doubt I will be able to hold them off a second time."

Madalyn's eyes widened and she glanced over her shoulder at the battered wooden door. It was the only thing that stood between her and those brutes. Without further protest, she allowed herself to be led away.

They walked down a dimly lit corridor until they reached another door. It led to the ship's deck. Rain pelted them, and the wind whipped her hair around her face. Despite this, she stopped and inhaled deeply.

"Keep moving." Mr. Carter tugged on her arm.

"Just a few more breaths," she begged. "I was in the hold for over four weeks."

"A bit unpleasant?" There was a note of sympathy in his voice.

Madalyn snorted. "You can't imagine how horrible the smell of unwashed bodies and animals was."

Memories of hiding under the straw, beside the pigs, would haunt her the rest of her days. Not only was it uncomfortable and rough, it stunk of urine and feces. She'd never see a barn again without gagging. At least being caught meant she was free of the hold.

"Come." Carter's voice sounded gruff.

They crossed the deck, and stopped at another door. Beside it was a ladder leading to an upper deck. Carter ignored the ladder and opened the door. Madalyn relaxed her tense shoulder muscles once she found herself in a softly lit area of obvious comfort.

On one side was a dining room and small salon. A faint odor of mildew, mingled with tobacco, hung in the air. Threadbare, but tastefully decorated, it was worlds apart from the cargo hold where she'd spent her time aboard ship.

The other side was a series of doors. Mr. Carter led her down the narrow hallway, stopping before the last one on the end. Her captor moved her in front of him, while he pulled a key from his waistcoat pocket. Once the door was opened, she was pushed into darkness.

"Damn. The candle's burnt down."

The faint light from the corridor shone into the room. Madalyn strained her eyes, making out the outline of a small bed against one wall. Everything else was shrouded in black. She turned at the scraping noise behind her. Carter had returned with a lighted candle. He quickly lit two more and then shut the door.

Madalyn glanced around the tiny room. A small table and chair stood beside the bed. A neatly piled stack of papers, a book, inkwell, and pen were all it contained. Against the opposite wall from the bed was a worn leather trunk. Its lid was closed and a smaller box sat atop it. Near the door was a basin and pitcher of water on a small washstand.

"I trust it meets with your approval," a voice drawled into her ear.

Madalyn jumped back and glared at the man. "You frightened me."

"Pity." Carter took one of the lit candles and placed it on the desk. "I was beginning to think nothing could scare you."

"You must think I'm a fool."

She'd never known such fear before. Even now, she was finding it hard to breath. Sheer willpower kept her legs from buckling and her body standing upright.

"The thought had crossed my mind." Mr. Carter pulled out the chair and held his arm out to her. "Sit."

She shook her head, but he only sighed. He took her arm and guided her onto the chair. Madalyn sat with her back erect and her hands clasped in her lap. The dampness of her gown sent a chill up her arm, but she refused to move. It would be a show of weakness.

Her captor stood over her, his arms crossed, his brow furrowed. "You look pale. Do you need anything?"

Everything began to spin. She grabbed the bottom of the chair. Madalyn closed her eyes, waiting for the world to right itself. When she opened them, Mr. Carter was glaring down at her.

"When did you last eat?"

Madalyn shrugged. "I had some cheese a few days ago."

She pushed back the darkness that threatened to swallow her. She needed her wits about her. She could not afford to trust anyone.

"Wait here." Carter turned and left the room, shutting the door softly behind him.

Madalyn put her head in her hands and groaned. The world had righted itself, but the bitter taste of fear was still with her. Her stomach grumbled. She placed a hand over it, but it only protested louder. She didn't have time to worry about food. There was a chance to leave before Mr. Carter returned.

She took a deep breath and started to get up when the door opened again. She slumped back into the chair. She'd been a fool to think she could escape. Even if she made it through the door, there was still a narrow hallway between her and freedom.

A plate was thrust in front of her. "Eat."

Madalyn stared at the roughly sliced piece of bread and chunk of cheese. Relief and disbelief surged through her. She took it with shaking hands and downed the food. She could have eaten more, but at least her stomach had lost the hollow feeling of starvation.

"That's all I could find in the dining room." Mr. Carter took the empty plate from her. "I'll wake the cook."

"No." Madalyn held up her hand. "That was more than I can handle right now."

Mr. Carter nodded. "It's probably best to eat a little at first. I'll get more later."

"Thank you." Madalyn forced the words from her mouth. She didn't want to be beholden to any man.

"I mean you no harm." He walked to the washstand and put the empty plate on it.

"Then why did you buy me?"

Mr. Carter tilted his head. "It amused me?"

"You find owning another human being funny?" Madalyn's jaw tightened painfully.

Mr. Carter turned away from her. He picked up the pitcher of water and poured it into the basin. "Nothing about this situation is humorous."

Madalyn snorted and cringed at how unladylike it sounded. She didn't have time to worry about manners. She needed answers.

"What do you intend to do with me."

The man turned back to her, a wet washcloth in his hands. "I haven't thought that far ahead."

"You must have had some idea when you bid on me?" Madalyn knew her voice had become shrill, but she couldn't control it. The man's casual attitude was irritating.

Mr. Carter shrugged. "There will be plenty of time to consider it later." He handed her the wet cloth. "You need to clean yourself."

Madalyn felt the chill of the cold moist cloth seep through her hand. Everything was wrong. She closed her eyes and tried to remember her life before she had snuck aboard the ship, but to no avail. She had aged years since then.

"Why bother?" Her voice was heavy with weariness.

"You're filthy. Frankly, I find that offensive."

Madalyn's chest rose. Her fist tightened, squeezing water from the still damp cloth. She bunched the cloth in her hand and flung it at him.

He dodged it. The cloth landed with a plop on the door, sliding down with a wet streak to the wooden floor. With a shake of his head, he bent and picked it up. Again, he rinsed it in the basin and handed it to her.

"I'm glad to see there's still some spirit left in you," he said with a slight grin. "I prefer my women a bit lively."

"How dare you." Madalyn fought to control the anger that tightened her chest. She raised the cloth again, but Mr. Carter caught her hand before she could fling it.

"The object is to wash you, not the floor."

"I don't have to do anything you ask." Madalyn clenched her jaw.

"There is no point in arguing," Carter advised. "I'll win."

"You cannot bully me like you did Galer." Madalyn stuck her chin out.

"You like smelling like a sewer?" Carter's face was a mask.

"You're insufferable."

"I speak the truth."

His words stung. Madalyn had to blink back the tears. She knew she stunk, but to have someone point it out, in such a cruel way, was humiliating. She forced herself to remember why she had risked hiding onboard the Folly. Seeing her brother's beloved face again would make everything right.

Madalyn opened the washcloth and started to scrub her face vigorously. It felt refreshing and after a few seconds, her skin began to tingle. She moved her hair away from her neck and scrubbed there also.

"Feel better?"

"Much." Madalyn handed the now black cloth back to Mr. Carter.

Mr. Carter looked down at the cloth and frowned. "What's your name?"

Madalyn hesitated a second. What harm could it do if he knew her name? "Madalyn Montgomery. Who are you?"

"Nathan Carter." He turned back to the washbasin, throwing the soiled cloth into the water.

"Now that we've been properly introduced Mr. Carter, what do you intend?" Madalyn stood away from the chair.

"Nathan, please."

Madalyn's chest constricted as Nathan moved to within a few inches of her. Narrowed eyes perused her body. Her heart beat faster when he lingered on her breasts before moving back to her face.

He brushed a strand of wet hair away from her eyes. Her breath caught in her throat and she licked her dry lips, shivering when his gaze fell to her mouth. His finger tapped her lips and she fought the urge to respond.

"You have beautifully expressive eyes." He took a step back. "Your every emotion is evident."

Madalyn lifted her chin. "Then you must know I am feeling nothing but disdain for you."

"I think not." Nathan turned back to the door and opened it. "Undress."

"What?" Madalyn clutched his jacket closer to her chest.

"Take your clothes off." Nathan enunciated each word in a slow drawl.

Chapter 3

"I can't stand here naked!" Madalyn's voice rose in panic.

Nathan shrugged. "Use a blanket until I return." He turned and left the room, shutting the door with a click.

The distinct sound of a key turning in the lock followed.

Madalyn's heart beat in a frantic tattoo and she stumbled back into the chair. She was trapped. Tremors shook her body and she hugged her arms close. Nathan was too large and powerful for her to fight him off. She must escape and hide.

The only exit was the porthole. She dragged the chair to the small opening and stood on it. She barely reached the tiny window. It was shut tight. Fear gave her strength and she pushed at the latch until it swung open.

A blast of tangy sea air hit her in the face. She pushed her head through and looked out. The blackness of night surrounded everything; rain slashed against her skin and the wind howled in her ears. Waves splashed against the ship, sending it heaving and rolling in all directions. Even if she could fit through the opening, the storm would probably wash her overboard.

There was no escape.

There was no place to hide.

She pulled her head back, slamming the window closed before stepping down from the chair. Her jaw clenched as she glanced at the bed and all it implied. There was no room for regrets now. She couldn't afford to forget why she'd set out on her journey.

She took a deep breath and began to undress. What a fool she'd been to let herself be caught. Danger and hardship she'd expected, but never in her wildest dreams had she imagined this. To be a prisoner and the property of a man was a reality she'd never considered.

Madalyn pulled the front of her tattered gown off and then wrestled with the buttons of the skirt, ripping them in her panic. Once the gown had dropped to the floor, she slipped out of her torn chemise. Shivers racked her body as her bare skin met the cool air of the room.

She needed a way to protect herself. She glanced around the room until her eyes stopped at the small table. A pen meant a penknife. Madalyn felt around the papers, lifting and moving them in her haste. There was nothing.

Steps sounded outside the door and she made a dash for the bed. She unfolded the blanket with trembling hands and threw it about her. She had just tightened it across her breasts when the door opened.

"I see you're ready." Nathan Carter's voice cut through the silence.

Madalyn could only stare at the imposing figure that blocked the faint light from the hallway. He had one hand on the handle and the other rested lightly on the doorjamb. His lips were twisted into a slight grin and he seemed totally at ease.

He walked into the room, leaving the door open behind him. His eyebrow rose when he looked in the direction of the porthole.

"Why is the chair there?"

"I wanted fresh air." She pulled the blanket closer to her body.

"There is no escape." Nathan moved to within a foot of her.

"I know." Madalyn took a step backwards, her legs hitting the edge of the bed.

Nathan put his hands on Madalyn's shoulders and pushed her onto the bed. "I am protecting you. I'm not the enemy."

"How can I trust someone who paid money for me?" Madalyn fought back the tears of panic.

"If I had not," Nathan snarled, "One of the crew would have bought you. When they'd had their fill of you, they would have sold you to another, until each had a turn. Is that what you wanted?"

"You could have stopped it." Her voice cracked with a sob.

Nathan released her shoulders and shook his head. "You can't be that naïve. How old are you?"

"Two and twenty." Madalyn sniffed into the blanket. "I'm not stupid. The captain seemed to fear you. Surely you could have used your influence to stop the auction."

"I did stop it." Nathan's voice was harsh. "Captain Galer only understands money."

Madalyn bit her lip. "I hadn't considered that."

"You haven't given much thought to anything. What could have possessed you to stowaway to begin with?"

"I had no choice." She tossed her hair and glared at Nathan. "Believe it or not, I have as much right to be on this ship as you."

Nathan frowned and took a step closer. Before he could speak, there was a knock at the door.

"This where you want it?"

Nathan nodded at the two men standing in the doorway, motioning with his hand for them to enter. Madalyn brought her legs up onto the bed, hugging them close to her body. A flicker of doubt raced through her. Surely he didn't intend to sell her already?

The men glanced in her direction; the older one winked and blew her a kiss. Madalyn inhaled. She recognized them from the galley.

They had both bid on her.

"Enough," Nathan barked. "Bring in the tub."

"Tub?" Madalyn's voice was a whisper. The words felt like sandpaper leaving her mouth.

"It's the only way to get that filth off you." Nathan turned back to the men. "What are you waiting for?"

The men shrugged their shoulders and went into the hall, returning a few seconds later with a small tin tub. It was half full with water. They put it in the corner of the room, the water swishing side to side before settling back into the tub.

"Anything else?" The older man's voice was low and hoarse.

Nathan shook his head. "I'll have someone else take it away when we're finished."

"See that you do." The man wiped his hand on his black trousers before holding it out to Nathan.

Nathan pulled out several coins and threw them to the man. The men nodded and walked out of the room. The older turned back and blew Madalyn another kiss. She shivered with revulsion, pulling the blanket closer to her body.

Nathan slammed the door shut. "Galer's men have no honor."

"And you do?" Madalyn didn't bother to hide her disbelief."

Nathan's grimaced. "I know it looks bad, but you need to believe I mean you no harm."

Madalyn looked over the edge of her blanket at the giant who stood a few feet away. Hands on his hips, his jaw clamped tight, he looked to be a man used to wielding power. She was no match for him.

"Trust that your intentions are better than all the other men who bid on me?" Madalyn's voice wavered, but she held her head high, her eyes never leaving Nathan Carter.

The left side of his mouth raised into a twisted smile. "Yes. Is that so hard to believe?"

"There is only one man I have faith in," she said in a low voice. "My brother."

Nathan gazed at her, his eyes unwavering. Finally, he nodded his head. "You're right. Trust should be earned."

Madalyn let out the breath she'd been holding and relaxed her grip on the blanket.

Nathan walked over to the tub and flicked his fingers into the water. "It's a good temperature. You'd best get in."

"Not in front of you." Her teeth clamped together.

Nathan shook his head, a slight grin softening his features. "We'll be spending the rest of the journey together in these quarters. You'd better get used to my presence."

"I need privacy."

Nathan glanced around the small cabin, looking up at the wooden plank ceiling and then the floor. He went to his trunks, moving the small one to the floor before opening the large one. He rifled through its contents and pulled out two bed covers.

Even in the dim candlelight Madalyn could see they'd been hand embroidered. Their delicate stitches the work of a master. Nathan moved the chair away from the porthole and placed it near the tub. He shook out the first cover and then wrapped one end around a hook in the ceiling.

Madalyn stood up, the blanket still clasped tightly around her. She went to the half hung drape and fingered its soft silken material. "These are too beautiful to be used in this fashion."

"What would you suggest?" Nathan moved the chair and draped the other end from a hook several feet away on the opposite wall. He stood back from the makeshift curtain.

"Tomorrow I'll make a better privacy screen." Nathan put the chair beside the desk. "This will do for tonight."

Madalyn fingered a perfectly formed red rose, marveling at the detail of the stitches. All her life she'd been taught to do needlework and she'd never achieved anything quite so lovely.

"Where did you get these?"

"My mother."

Madalyn's eyes widened as she looked at Nathan over her shoulder. "They are exquisite."

"You look surprised." Nathan's voice was wry. "Is it because I have a mother, or her workmanship?"

Madalyn glanced away and shrugged. "Neither," she lied. The thought of this man having a mother disturbed her.

Nathan Carter was no longer a nameless stranger, but a man with a family. A mother who showed her love in the bedcovers she'd made for him. Her eyes filled with tears. It was something her mother had done for her.

"Will that do?"

Madalyn jumped at Nathan's words. She brushed a hand across her eyes and cleared her throat. "It's fine."

"You had better get in." Nathan handed her a spluttering candle.

Madalyn nodded and pushed back the curtain. She put the candle on the floor before walking to the tub. A wisp of steam hung over the water. She tested it with her hand and sighed. It was perfect.

"Do you have a change of clothes?"

Madalyn dropped her blanket, turning toward Nathan's voice. "Captain Galer took everything I had."

Nathan cleared his throat. "What did he do with your belongings?"

She pulled her hair to the top of her head and wound it in a loose knot. "He auctioned them."

Her stomach tightened in remembered humiliation. The man had been crude in his remarks as he held up her gowns, toiletries, and unmentionables. He'd waved them about the crew until everything had been sold. A stab of pain twisted in her stomach, as she remembered her mother's necklace. She closed her eyes trying to block out the image of Galer ripping it off her neck. She'd begged him to let her keep it, but he'd ignored her.

"So you have no clothes?" Nathan's voice sounded hollow.

"None." Madalyn paused beside the tub. "Are you alright?"

"Just get in the bath." His voice was sharp.

Madalyn shook her head. She'd never understand men. She tested the water with her foot before stepping in. She sank down into its welcomed warmth, throwing her head back against the tin as she slipped deeper into the water.

"Does it meet with your approval?" Nathan's voice held a hint of sarcasm.

"It's wonderful." Madalyn splashed some water against her neck. "I don't think I have ever felt anything so good."

"Enjoy it because there won't be another until we dock."

"How did you manage this?"

Water was rationed, with most of it being kept for drinking and cooking. Washing was done with seawater hauled over the side of the ship.

"Bribery."

"I'm never going to complain about that again." She sat up in the tub and looked for the soap. "Darn. I have no soap or washcloth."

There was a long silence before she heard the sound of a latch opening. "Cover yourself."

She reached over the side of the tub and grabbed the blanket she had dropped. She draped it over the top rim of her bath, sinking lower until she was shielded completely.

"Ready," she called.

Nathan pulled back the curtain, a cloth and thin sliver of soap in his hand. "This is all I have."

"Put it on the floor." She sunk further into the tub.

Her gaze didn't leave him as he walk toward her. Her heart beat faster when he scanned the bath. Her body tingled with awareness and she fought to breath normally.

Instead of putting the soap on the floor, he handed it to her. Madalyn looked at his outstretched hand and then up to his face. His eyes were half closed and shadows danced across his face giving no indication of his intentions.

"Afraid?" There was a slight inflection to his voice.

She shook her head and pulled her arm out of the blanket. She grabbed the soap and cloth, before pulling her hand back beneath the blanket.

"That wasn't difficult."

"You can go now."

"The bath looks inviting." Nathan leaned toward her.

"Don't" Madalyn's voice held a pleading note. "I want privacy."

"Are you sure?" Nathan tilted his head, his eyes intense with an unspoken invitation.

Madalyn's breath caught in her chest. "You promised." Her voice was low.

Nathan nodded and moved to the curtain. He raised the cloth, but instead of leaving, he turned to her.

"This is made from the finest of silks."

"It looks like it."

He draped the material over his eyes. "Almost see through."

Madalyn frowned. She looked up at the cloth and then at Nathan. His eyebrow was raised quizzically. She pulled the blanket closer to her.

"A candle is a wonderful illumination." Nathan dropped the cover and stepped back.

Her face flared with heat.

"You shouldn't have looked." Her voice quivered. "A true gentleman would have turned away."

"We've already determined that I am no such thing."

"You sound as if you are proud of it." Madalyn threw the blanket off the tub. She grabbed the washcloth and started to rub the soap on it vigorously. She stopped scrubbing when she heard the click of the door latch being lifted.

"I expect you to be finished when I return."

The door closed with a soft thud.

The lock was keyed into place.

Madalyn looked at the soapy cloth in her hand for a few seconds before she started to scrub the dirt from her arm. Nathan Carter was a strange man. One minute thoughtful and the next determined to humiliate her. He might hold her prisoner, but she wasn't going to be defeated.

She had vowed to save her brother.

Escape was her next move.

Chapter 4

Nathan leaned against the wall and let out the breath he'd been holding. He groaned as he remembered Madalyn's near perfect figure getting ready for the bath. The candle had illuminated every delicious curve of her well-proportioned body. He had seldom seen such perfection of form in his thirty-six years of living.

Sheer chance had led him to the auction. He'd gone in search of the Captain to complain. A storm was raging outside, yet no one seemed to be running the ship. Once he opened the galley door, he'd understood why.

His heart had gone out to the young girl balanced so precariously on the table edge. She must have been frightened to death, but she'd stared over all of their heads, defiantly ignoring them. He couldn't walk away and leave her to be brutalized by the crew.

Nathan wiped his hand over his face and pushed away from the wall. Nothing about this situation was easy. He must find a way to get this girl back to her family. He straightened his shoulders and took a deep breath. Standing in a darkened hallway was not going to solve his problem.

Madalyn needed more help than he could give her. His efforts to save her from a cruel situation had only landed them in another predicament. His body hardened as the image of her getting into the bath flashed through his mind. The sooner he put some distance between them, the better.

He should waken one of the ladies on the ship and hand Madalyn over to them. The lateness of the hour made him hesitate. Lady Raglan would not thank him. She'd be inclined to give Madalyn back to the crew.

That left Mrs. Willet. His stomach clenched. The woman was a dragon and a missionary's wife. The combination was overbearing, to say the least. Still, she would know how to protect Madalyn. He'd make sure the chit was presentable and then wake up Mrs. Willet.

He gave Madalyn several minutes of privacy before entering the room again. By that time, his body and thoughts were under control. He cleared his throat as he shut the door behind him.

"Are you finished?"

"I'm rinsing my hair now." Madalyn's voice sounded muffled, but the splashing of water assured him.

Nathan pulled out a clean nightshirt from his trunk. It was miles too long, but would have to do. There was no way he was going to let Mrs. Willet see Madalyn wrapped in a blanket. The woman would draw the wrong conclusion.

"When you're finished, I have one of my shirts for you to wear."

"Close your eyes."

Nathan obeyed. The less he saw of his guest's beautiful form, the better. The sound of Madalyn heaving her body out of the water greeted Nathan's ears. Her manner suggested she was used to being obeyed. He appreciated her courage, yet she wasn't making his life any easier.

"You can open them now."

He turned just as Madalyn stepped from behind the curtain. The blanket was wrapped around her body. Her long light-brown hair hung down her back in a tangled mass of wet curls.

She wasn't a beauty in the conventional sense, but there was a grace and strength to her. Her skin was like flawless porcelain, pale in color except for a hint of roses on her cheeks. Her eyes were large, brown, and expressive. Nathan had to force himself to look away, before he fell into their mesmerizing depths.

"Here." He thrust the nightshirt at her. His voice sounded harsh, but he was past caring. The sooner she was out of his life, the better.

She grabbed the top and walked behind the curtain again. This time when she emerged, she looked like a very young child dressed up in adult clothes. The nightshirt dragged on the floor and billowed out from her body. Three of her could have fit into it.

"Feel better?" Nathan leaned close and inhaled a deep breath. "You smell sweeter."

"At least one of us is happy." She gathered the top about her and sat on the bed. "Are you going to force me to stay here?"

"Where would you go?" Nathan motioned to the door. "Back to the hold? To Captain Galer? Or would you prefer the crew?"

"Then you should leave."

"It's my cabin."

Madalyn sighed. "I appreciate everything you've done Mr. Carter, but surely you can see how wrong this situation is?"

"Do you have a better suggestion?" Nathan leaned against the desk and crossed his arms. "I assume you had a plan when you boarded the ship."

"Well this wasn't part of it." Madalyn bit her lip.

"I did purchase you in good faith." Nathan couldn't resist teasing. "Should I not get something in return?"

Madalyn pulled a blanket around her shoulders. "You told me I could trust you. Are you having second thoughts?"

"No." Nathan sighed, and pushed away from the desk. "I'm going to wake up one of the female passengers. She'll know what needs to be done.

Before Madalyn could answer, there was a loud knocking at the door. Nathan frowned. He moved to open it when the jingling of keys stopped him. Only one person had access to the cabins.

The Captain.

"Get behind me." Nathan stood in front of Madalyn.

The next second the door burst open.

Galer stood there with another person. It was Mrs. Willet. A lace cap hid her hair and her ample figure was covered with an emerald green dressing gown, but there was no mistaking the Reverend Willet's wife.

"What's the meaning of this?" Nathan's voice shook as he swallowed back the anger that tightened his chest.

"I can't believe this of you Mr. Carter." Mrs. Willet clutched her hand to her heaving chest. "I thought you were above reproach."

"I warned you." Galer made a tiny bow to Mrs. Willet before smirking at Nathan. "There are certain things I cannot abide aboard my ship."

Nathan's stomach sank.

Galer was exacting his revenge.

He should have gone to Mrs. Willet immediately. Instead, Galer had filled the woman with lies. The Reverend and Mrs. Willet were religious zealots bent on converting the savages in America. Mrs. Willet wouldn't ignore any perceived improprieties, even amongst strangers.

"This is horrible." Mrs. Willet's voice rose with indignation. "Neither I, nor my husband, will stand for this behavior."

"You don't know all the facts, Mrs. Willet." Nathan forced his voice to remain calm.

"I know enough." Mrs. Willet pulled her lace cap down over her ears. "You have a young lady in your room."

"True." Nathan nodded. "I can explain everything. In fact, I was just about to go and wake you."

Mrs. Willet straightened her back and walked into the room. "Whatever your intentions, I am here for the young lady."

Nathan hesitated a second. Galer had provided him with a solution to his problem. There was no reason for him to explain. Mrs. Willet would take care of Madalyn. He stepped aside and motioned for Madalyn to come forward.

"There, there, child." Mrs. Willet patted Madalyn's hands and then led her to the bed. "You must tell me what happened."

Madalyn looked up at Nathan with a raised eyebrow. He shrugged. There was no reason for him to be involved any longer. He could wash his hands of her.

"I thought better of you Mr. Carter." Mrs. Willet sat beside Madalyn. "What have you done to the poor girl?"

"Nothing." Nathan's tone was defensive. "I gave her some food and a bath."

"Alone?"

"She needed protection." Nathan held his hands up. "I have not touched her."

"He's a scoundrel," Galer piped in. "I wouldn't believe anything he says."

"No need to worry Captain. I am not easily deceived." Mrs. Willet's eyes flicked over Nathan before returning to Galer. "Captain, you have behaved properly in this matter."

The scoundrel had the gall to smile. Nathan only had himself to blame, though. If he'd taken Madalyn to Mrs. Willet first, then Galer wouldn't have been able to spread his lies. Now the woman would never believe the truth.

"I need to talk to the girl." Mrs. Willet pointed to the door. "You gentlemen will have to leave."

"This is my cabin." Nathan crossed his arms.

"You'll have to find someplace else." Mrs. Willet stood and led Nathan to the door. "Give me your key."

He could refuse, but it would get him nowhere. The Mrs. Willet's of the world did not back down. She stood there unmoved, fully expecting him to leave. He glanced at Madalyn, whose lips were twitching. The woman was thoroughly enjoying his discomfort.

Nathan took a large breath and pulled the key from his waistcoat pocket. "I will not be put out of my bed for more than one night."

"No need to worry, Mr. Carter." Mrs. Willet opened the door. "I'll have everything sorted out by tomorrow. Captain Galer, will you kindly wait outside too."

Nathan was pushed from the room before he had a chance to say anything. He stumbled into the hallway, wincing at the sharp click of his door closing.

Galer chuckled beside him. "The tables are turned now. You won't be able to enjoy the spoils either."

"I had no intention of tasting them." Nathan straightened his coat. "Letting Mrs. Willet take care of the girl is the perfect solution."

"We shall see."

The faint light from the salon beckoned. He reached the room before Galer and stretched out on the faded green settee. He might as well be comfortable. Galer leaned against the doorjamb.

"I wouldn't get too cozy. I'm sure Mrs. Willet will have some choice words for you."

"We'll see." Nathan shut his eyes. "Why don't you go and wait for your orders. I'd hate for you to disappoint Mrs. Willet."

Madalyn smiled as Nathan was pushed from the room. He had looked so startled. He didn't deserve to be put out of his cabin, but she had no intention of spending the night with him either.

"You find your situation humorous?" Mrs. Willet's eyebrow was raised, her arms crossed.

Madalyn sighed. "Nothing about this is amusing. All I want is to be left alone."

Mrs. Willet tilted her head. "That's not possible."

Madalyn frowned. "Why?"

"You're a single woman found alone with a man."

"You're here now." Madalyn gathered the extra folds of the linen nightshirt to her chest. Her stomach clenched at the tone of Mrs. Willet's voice.

Mrs. Willet dropped her arms to her side. "You know society will never accept your behavior."

She forced herself to look into Mrs. Willet's eyes. "The only thing that matters is that I reach America."

Mrs. Willet moved to the bed and sat down. "I cannot condone your behavior, but there is no going back. We must move forward.

Madalyn pulled her feet up under her gown. "I thought you were going to help me."

"Your voice is cultured." Mrs. Willet picked up her hand and turned it over. "You've never seen a day's work."

Madalyn lifted her chin. "What difference does that make?"

"It means that you're a gently bred woman." Mrs. Willet's voice softened. "Your actions have put you beyond the pale of society. Is that what you intended?"

"No one need know."

"I know. I cannot ignore the fact that you've been in Mr. Carter's room alone, much less bathed in front of him."

"I had no choice."

"Sneaking aboard a ship is foolhardy. Surely you understood the risks you took."

"I never expected anyone to find me."

"But they did." Mrs. Willet sighed. "What's your name child?"

"Madalyn Montgomery."

"Well Miss Montgomery, you didn't think this through at all." Mrs. Willet patted Madalyn's knee. "You're lucky that the Captain discovered Mr. Carter's deception."

"How can you say that?" Madalyn shivered. "The Captain is a villain. All I want is to be free of these men and the ship."

"The Captain has saved you from a worse fate." Mrs. Willet pursed her lips.

Madalyn frowned. "The Captain is the reason I'm in this situation. He's a fiend and a cheat."

Mrs. Willet pursed her lips. "Perhaps, but that doesn't solve your problem."

"Once I arrive in America, everything will be fine."

"That's a couple of days away. What do you intend to do until then?"

"I can stay with you."

"That might protect you from further shame, but it won't take away the blemish already on your reputation."

Madalyn's breath caught in her throat. "What do you mean?"

"There is only one course of action left open to you."

Madalyn closed her eyes. "No one needs to know what happened if you say nothing."

"The Captain and Mr. Carter already know. Obviously some of the crew brought the bath, so now all of them know. You cannot have men like that disrespect you."

"Nothing has happened." Madalyn swallowed back the fear that was lodged in her throat.

Mrs. Willet gave her a steely look. "I know it will be hard for you to accept, but the sooner we settle this matter the better. You need protection."

"It doesn't matter what others think." Madalyn clenched her teeth. "I know the truth."

"You will care soon enough. The loss of a woman's reputation is beyond repair." Mrs. Willet stood. "Mr. Carter is not innocent in this matter."

"He tried to save me."

"Then he'll do the right thing." She walked to the door. "Sleep now. You'll need your strength tomorrow."

Madalyn's head pounded. The room was tilting, but she wasn't certain if that was her or the sea.

"What's tomorrow?" Madalyn's voice was little more than a whisper. Fear had a firm grip on her heart.

"Your wedding day."

Chapter 5

"Absolutely not!" Nathan pushed himself up from the settee. "I will not marry the girl."

"Think of the young lady." Mrs. Willet sat on the worn wingback chair, her hands resting calmly in her lap.

"I have done enough to protect her." Nathan ran his hands through his hair.

"You've ruined the girl's reputation." Mrs. Willet tilted her head. "Now you must make amends."

"I saved her." Nathan stood and walked to the small chest of drawers near the door. He grabbed the brandy decanter and filled a glass. "You cannot expect me to do more."

"But I do." Mrs. Willet leaned back into the chair. "That girl has been hiding in your cabin. Surely you did not expect to abandon her."

Nathan took a deep gulp of the fiery brandy, savoring its burning descent. It was the only thing that seemed real at this moment. Nothing had been right since Mrs. Willet and Captain Galer had shaken him awake a few moments ago.

"She has only been there for the last few hours." He turned back to Mrs. Willet. "Galer lied to you."

Mrs. Willet pursed her lips. "Whether it's a few hours or days, she's been compromised by you."

"Her reputation was in shatters before I met her thanks to Galer." Nathan took a deep breath. He needed to maintain his calm if he was going to make Mrs. Willet see reason. "The good Captain intended to sell her to the crew."

"See how he lies." Captain Galer shook his head. "I told you he was a wily one."

"So you did, Captain." Mrs. Willet turned her attention back to Nathan. "If you believe her good name has been besmirched then all the more reason for you to step in now."

"I don't need to marry her." Nathan took another sip of the brandy. "I have paid for her passage, so she is free to do as she wishes."

"You only paid after I discovered her." Captain Galer grinned.

"That will not answer." Mrs. Willet cleared her throat. "You have ruined a girl of breeding and education. You have it within your power to rectify this situation."

A brief picture of Madalyn flashed through Nathan's mind. Even with her hair knotted and covered in dirt, her breeding had shown through. She had held her head high, showing nothing but disdain for the auction. It was an expression he recognized. More than one well-born lady had given him the same look.

"She did that herself. No woman of worth would travel unaccompanied."

"True," Mrs. Willet agreed with a sigh. "But you spent time with her alone."

"I tried to protect her." Nathan threw back the last of the liquor and slammed the glass on the table.

"Marriage is the only answer." Mrs. Willet's voice was firm. "Neither I, nor the Captain, will settle for anything less."

Nathan closed his eyes and shook his head. Mrs. Willet seemed determined to see Madalyn married. Nathan was very familiar with the rules of society and only a marriage would erase a soiled reputation.

"I have no wish to marry."

"A man in your situation needs a wife." Captain Galer's pleasant tone was like a razor against Nathan's throat.

"And what situation might that be?" Nathan pushed the words through gritted teeth.

"One of wealth and substance." Mrs. Willet answered. "You have to think of your reputation and station in society as well."

If she hadn't been so serious, Nathan would have laughed at her assumption. Despite his wealth, he was not acknowledged in the polite society of his homeland. The only place that accepted him on his own merits was the United States.

"You're mistaken. I am not a man of family and position." Nathan leaned back against the doorframe, arms crossed on his chest. "Surely a lady of breeding would require that?"

"I don't know your exact circumstances Mr. Carter, but at this moment, Miss Montgomery has no other choice." Mrs. Willet raised her handkerchief to her mouth and took a deep breath. "You are the man who ruined her reputation and only marriage to you will repair it."

Nathan exhaled. "You'd marry Miss Montgomery to the devil, if he were available."

Mrs. Willet straightened her back and glared at him through narrowed eyes. "There is no need to blasphemy. You must protect her with your name."

"I have no wish to help her further." Nathan's voice rose.

"Miss Montgomery must marry." Mrs. Willet enunciated each word carefully. "Even you will admit that."

Nathan threw his head back and groaned. Why had he tried to save the silly girl? It had made sense at the time, just outbid the others and set her free. Now it seemed as if he would never be rid of her.

Did it matter, though? Even knowing the outcome, he would have intervened in the auction. His mother had been a victim of another man's power and he would never have forgiven himself if he'd let Madalyn be abused by the crew. Besides, it had felt good to upset Galer's plans.

"Your argument is sound, but you'll have to find someone else." Nathan pushed away from the door. "I have no desire to marry a woman I do not love."

Mrs. Willet straightened her dressing gown, her chubby fingers patting the fabric calmly before she looked up at him. "Love does not factor into this."

"I will not marry without love." Nathan pulled at his wrinkled his cravat. "There is no point in discussing this further."

"If it's any consolation, Miss Montgomery is not eager to wed either."

"Then there is no need to continue this conversation." Nathan bowed his head to Mrs. Willet.

"Honor demands you marry Miss Montgomery." The Reverend's wife stood.

Nathan looked at Mrs. Willet, her face set in a frown, her eyes narrowed, and his stomach tightened. There was only one woman he had wanted to marry and since her death, he had never loved another. He would not replace her memory with a stranger.

"I have no honor." Nathan's voice was void of emotion.

"I am sorry to hear that." Mrs. Willet nodded to the Galer. "The Captain was afraid you might refuse, so we have come prepared."

Galer pulled out a pistol from his pocket and pointed it at Nathan. "I brought some extra persuasion. I told Mrs. Willet you might be skittish."

"This is your idea of revenge?" Nathan's voice dripped with contempt.

Galer's eyes glinted with a wicked gleam. "You have the right of it. This is my ship and I will not be bested by you."

Despite the untenable demand, the irony of the situation was not lost on Nathan. Captain Galer held the upper hand. Any attempt to explain would be met with disbelief. Mrs. Willet might think him an immoral beast, but society demanded a marriage.

"You cannot force me into this." Nathan clenched his hands at his side.

"I think we just have." Mrs. Willet walked to the doorway. "I will arrange the wedding for tomorrow. See that you are there. I would hate to send the Captain to fetch you."

"You're not doing Miss Montgomery any favors by compelling her to marry me."

"It's your responsibility to make this marriage work."

"And if that isn't possible?" Nathan fought the urge to hit something.

"You must trust in God." Mrs. Willet's eyes hardened. "He has enabled the Captain, and me, to do His work."

Galer and Mrs. Willet left the room

Nathan threw himself down on the settee. He leaned over, blew out the candle, and lay back in the darkness. Even the motion of the ship couldn't relax him. His stomach churned and his brain refused to quiet.

There was no point in fighting it. It was impossible to sleep. Nathan propped against the arm of the settee and clasped his hands behind his head. He needed a solution to this predicament; one that would protect his honor and Madalyn's reputation.

The thin fingers of dawn were creeping along the horizon when he stumbled onto the Folly's deck. The storm had ended in the middle of the night, but dark clouds still hung low in the sky. He rubbed his eyes and brushed his hair back. He looked a mess, but he needed fresh air.

He leaned over the railing and took a deep breath, coughing as the cool salty air hit his lungs. As hard as he'd tried last night, no solution had presented itself to him.

There was only one answer.

He would have to marry Madalyn.

"Had a rough night?"

Nathan turned his head and eyed Captain Galer. The man looked as if he hadn't slept either. His jacket was stained and wrinkled, the buttons stretched across his large bulging midsection. The smell of stale liquor hung in the air.

"No worse than most." Nathan turned back to look at the ocean.

"Liar." Galer spat over the side of the ship. "Did you have dreams of your bride to be?"

Nathan took a deep breath. "You haven't won yet."

Galer clenched his fist on the railing. "Not so smart now. You'll think twice before you ruin someone's fun again. The crew won't forget how you stole her from them."

"She wasn't yours to sell." Nathan pushed away from the railing.

"It's my ship and I'm the law on it."

Nathan glanced up at the menacing clouds. "The storm isn't finished. It won't be your ship much longer if you and your crew don't take care."

"My men do as I ask."

"Unless they're too drunk." Nathan took a step away from Galer.

Galer grabbed his arm. "Not so fast pretty boy. We aren't done with our business."

"And what might that be?"

"Have you forgotten the silly wench sleeping in your room?"

"What of her?"

"I want the woman back."

Nathan clenched his jaw and eyed Galer through narrowed eyes. "Why?"

The Captain rubbed his nose with his sleeve and lowered his voice. "I promised her to the crew and they still want her."

"That's not going to happen."

"I'm willing to forget all of this and tell Mrs. Willet I made a mistake." Galer leaned close. "I want money and the girl."

Nathan heaved a sigh. Most of his life had been spent dealing with men like Galer. The reason he'd built a successful business in shipping and warehouses was because he didn't allow another's greed to thwart his goals.

"I already paid you. You'll get no more from me."

Galer's lip twisted into a sneer. "You forget I can ruin your life."

Nathan poked his finger into Galer's chest. "You've had your fun, but now it stops. I can make certain your ship never sees water again."

Galer stepped back. "My ship sails when I say."

"If word reaches Charleston of your behavior, no one will book passage on your vessel."

"You can't stop my cargo."

"Try me." Nathan's voice was like steel.

Galer clenched his fists at his sides. "I still hold the trump card. You'll regret messing with me."

"I doubt it." Nathan shook his head with disgust. "You're a coward. No respectable captain would have allowed that auction last night."

"I have a right to protect what's mine."

"You also have an obligation to your passengers. Miss Montgomery is now one of them. I expect you to retrieve all of her belongs before noon."

"Everything was sold."

Nathan reached into his pocket and pulled out a gold sovereign. "Now it's bought again." He threw the coin at Galer.

Galer grabbed it out of the air. "This won't cover everything."

"That's your problem.

"You won't escape Mrs. Willet's plans. I'll see to it."

Galer might force him to the altar, but there were ways to escape marriage. He turned to walk away when another voice stopped him. He closed his eyes a second and then turned to greet Reverend Willet.

"Good morning, Mr. Carter, Captain Galer." The reverend's voice was hesitant.

Nathan nodded. "Reverend."

Reverend Willet looked down at his clasped hands. "My wife has made me aware of the goings on last night."

"The truth is not as dire as your wife believes." Nathan kept his voice calm.

Reverend Willet looked up at him. His eyes full of sympathy. "However it came about, the young lady's reputation has been destroyed."

The Captain nodded. "I'm sure Mrs. Willet has the details confused. Isn't that right Mr. Carter?"

"Mrs. Willet was upset last night." Nathan straightened his shoulders. He would not be beholden to a man such as Galer. "I'm certain that morning has made her see how impossible her request is."

Galer's smile faltered and then his eyes narrowed. "Be careful Carter. It's my duty to see justice is done."

Reverend Willet nodded, causing the small wisp of gray hair left on his balding head to be blown into disarray. "My wife is adamant. A wedding is necessary."

Galer swayed back and forth on his feet. "How can I help?"

Reverend Willet's took a deep breath, raising his slightly stooping shoulders. "I need you to assist me this morning with the ceremony."

Galer smiled. "It will be my pleasure."

Reverend Willet nodded and turned back to Nathan. "We will perform the service in an hour's time. Make certain Mr. Carter is present, even if that means using coercion."

Chapter 6

"You can't force me to marry." Madalyn crossed her arms and sat on the bed.

"There's no time to waste." Mrs. Willet put a cream gown over the edge of the bed. "Lady Raglan has kindly agreed to let you wear one of her dresses."

Madalyn's stomach tightened.

Her heart beat at a frantic pace.

She took a deep breath and pushed back her fears. "There is no need to do this."

"We have very little time before the ceremony." Mrs. Willet put her hands on her hips. "Mr. Carter has agreed that marriage is the proper course of action."

"I know nothing about him." Madalyn's voice rose as panic threatened to overwhelm her. "I'm sure he can find someone else to marry."

"He's not the one who needs to wed." Mrs. Willet heaved a sigh. "He's trying to save your reputation."

"I don't need his help."

"Would you rather a life on the streets?" Mrs. Willet lifted her head and pursed her lips. "That is what awaits you unless you marry."

Madalyn's eyes widened. "How can you suggest such a thing?"

"It's the truth." Mrs. Willet pulled Madalyn to her feet and began to undo her nightshirt. "You're lucky the Captain brought your plight to my attention. No one else would have come to your rescue."

"I have thanked you." Madalyn lifted her arms to allow Mrs. Willet to take off her shirt. "But Mr. Carter did not harm me."

"He has to make it right."

"Everything will be fine when I reach Charleston." Madalyn rubbed her arms with her hands. The cabin was cold and damp.

"I would be shirking my Christian duty if I didn't make certain you were safe. Mr. Carter will marry you or pay the consequences." Mrs. Willet threw the nightgown over the trunks in the corner.

Madalyn frowned. Was Nathan not eager to marry either? Some of the heaviness in her chest lifted. She couldn't imagine Nathan being pressured to do anything. He'd stood up to the Captain and the crew. He should have no problem handling Mrs. Willet.

"Mr. Carter has doubts about the marriage?" Madalyn put on the chemise Mrs. Willet handed her.

"The Captain and I have made certain that he has no choice." Mrs. Willet stood with the gown in her arms. "It's time to dress."

Minutes later Mrs. Willet stood back. "You're not much to look at. Your eyes are nice, but your real asset is your figure. This gown shows it to advantage."

Madalyn smoothed down the folds of the cream silk material. She'd never considered her figure an asset. Her uncle had always complained about her lack of looks. Mrs. Willet might have lulled her into getting ready, but that was as far as she was willing to go.

"You have to tell Mr. Carter that I cannot marry him."

Mrs. Willet turned her around and finished fastening the robe. "You can tell him yourself."

A sharp knock at the door interrupted them. There was a short cough and then a hesitant voice.

"We're ready above deck."

Mrs. Willet gave a final pat to the outfit. "Come."

Madalyn was led from the cabin. She should refuse to move, but she needed tell Nathan to his face that she wouldn't marry him. He deserved that much after saving her from the crew.

Once on deck, the fresh air revived her spirits. She'd delayed marriage to her cousin for several years; it should be easy to avoid another one. She quickened her step to match Mrs. Willet. Her stomach lurched though, when she saw the whole crew waiting for them.

Ahead, was Captain Galer and beside him stood a slight man in a dark coat. He was bald except for a small wisp of hair that the wind was blowing into a tangle. His collar proclaimed a minister. Nathan Carter stood in front of the men, his back facing her, straight and rigid.

"Here is the lovely bride," Captain Galer said in a raucous voice.

Her steps faltered at the crew's ribald shouts. She shuddered and then lifted her chin. She looked straight ahead. Humiliation sent the color in her cheeks soaring.

"Enough!" Nathan Carter's deep voice rang out, deafening in its intensity.

Madalyn continued walking until she reached Nathan. Only then did he look at her. His eyes were emotionless and cold, giving no indication of his thoughts. He nodded and then faced forward again. Her stomach tightened.

She leaned close and whispered. "We must speak."

He turned back and raised an eyebrow. "Before the ceremony?"

She nodded. "You have to stop this. I have no wish to marry you."

Nathan's jaw clenched. "Then we are agreed."

He took her hand and placed it on his arm. He led her forward until they stood in front of the minister. She tried to pull her hand away, but he held tight.

"Honor demands a marriage." The intensity of Nathan's gaze caused her stomach to flutter. "We'll discuss what to do afterwards."

"It'll be too late." Madalyn's voice rose in alarm.

"Don't tell me we have an unwilling bride?" Galer opened his jacket to reveal a pistol tucked into his belt. "Perhaps she needs a bit of persuasion."

Madalyn's eyes widened. Her breath caught in her throat and she fought the urge to run. Everything about this ship was crazy. First, Galer had taken her money and refused her passage, then he'd sold her, and now he was forcing her to marry a stranger.

Nathan tightened his grip on her hand. "She's nervous."

A spark of awareness raced up her arm at Nathan's touch. She opened her mouth to refute him, but the words died in her throat. His eyes, hypnotic and intense, held her. She was lost in their dark blue depths.

"We are ready, Reverend Willet." Nathan's voice broke the spell.

Reverend Willet cleared his throat and opened the small black book he held in his hands. "Dearly beloved," he began. The loud laughter from the crew drowned his words.

The Reverend stopped and looked at the men over the top of his wire spectacles. His eyes raked them with a quiet tolerance, until the laughter had ceased.

"We are gathered to see these two joined in marriage," he continued.

Madalyn closed her ears to his words, but the sound of his voice echoed in her head like a dull ache. There couldn't be a worse fate than spending the rest of life with a complete stranger.

The gentle shake of her arm brought Madalyn out of her reverie. Reverend Willet was looking at her expectantly.

"Will you take this man to be your husband?"

Nathan was looking straight ahead, a small nerve twitched near his jaw, but otherwise he could have been made of stone. She opened her mouth, but before she could utter her refusal Nathan squeezed her hand.

"Think carefully." His voice was a whisper. "The marriage can be ended, but your reputation will be lost unless we wed now."

Madalyn glanced back at the minister. His eyes were sympathetic as he gave a nod of agreement. She looked at Captain Galer and a shiver of revulsion shuddered through her. The man's sneer of derision decided her.

"Yes," she said in a loud, firm voice.

One word sealed her fate.

The rest of the ceremony passed in a blur. She heard Nathan agree to the marriage, but the balance of the minister's words and blessing were lost on her. It wasn't until Nathan swung her around to face the spectators that she knew the ordeal was over.

The Captain's voice boomed behind them. "There is a special wedding breakfast being served for the passengers. Extra rations of food and ale for the men."

Nathan cleared his throat. "There is another storm brewing."

The Captain pushed ahead of them. "The men need some recompense after losing such a lovely morsel." His eyes raked Madalyn from top to bottom.

"You will treat my wife with respect." Nathan's voice was low and threatening.

Galer laughed. "You can't expect the crew to forget. You might have prettied it up, but we know what she really is."

Madalyn's stomach heaved at the open derision of the Captain. She would have run and hid if Nathan hadn't held her back.

"Now do you understand why the marriage was necessary?"

Madalyn nodded. Her humiliation was complete. She was numb. She let Nathan lead her to the dining room. He guided her into a chair at the head of the long table and then started to move away.

Madalyn grabbed his arm. "Where are you going?"

"I'm seated at the other end. Mrs. Willet will sit beside you."

Madalyn relaxed her grip and leaned back. She took a deep breath, and forced a smile to her lips. The people seating themselves were strangers, but they seemed civilized. There was no reason to be anxious.

Mrs. Willet patted her hand. "I wish the two of you happiness."

"How is that possible?"

Mrs. Willet shrugged her shoulders. "You'll find a way. It was nice of the Captain to arrange a wedding breakfast."

A slender man dressed in brown tweeds sat across from Mrs. Willet. He combed back his pale blonde hair with his hand and then tugged at his cravat.

"This is Mr. Barnett." Mrs. Willet made the introduction. "It was a surprise to see you at the ceremony, sir."

"I was happy to oblige." Mr. Barnett's voice wavered and he glanced down the table. "Mr. Carter was most insistent."

Madalyn clasped her hands on her lap. "I appreciate your support."

Mr. Barnet's eyes skittering away from her gaze. "You made a lovely bride."

Madalyn smiled. "Thank you."

"I found it a dead bore."

Madalyn glanced up to find a beautiful woman standing beside Mrs. Willet. She waited until Nathan pulled her chair out before sitting down.

"We appreciate your help, Lady Raglan." Nathan's words were clipped and his voice expressionless.

"Most unusual circumstances Mr. Carter." Lady Raglan shook open her napkin. "To have a new passenger appear at the end of our journey is quite remarkable."

"But not inconceivable." Mrs. Willet tapped the table beside her. "You were most kind to lend us a gown."

"Yes." Lady Raglan pierced Madalyn with bright eyes. "I hope it will be returned shortly."

Lady Raglan was the essence of British beauty; porcelain white skin, pale rose cheeks, golden blonde hair, and cornflower blue eyes. Madalyn lifted her chin.

"I will give it back after breakfast."

"I find it difficult to understand the need for such a hasty wedding." Lady Raglan rolled her eyes. "We arrive in Charleston tomorrow."

"It was my wish," Nathan said in a clipped tone.

"Were you a little too eager before the wedding?" Lady Raglan raised one of her delicately shaped eyebrows. "I have heard that people of your station have problems controlling their baser instincts."

Madalyn clenched her fork and fought the urge to throw it at the woman. "I find it seldom wise to listen to rumors."

Lady Raglan's eyes narrowed, but she glanced away and looked down the table at Nathan. "I hope you will not regret your shipboard romance."

Before Nathan could reply, Reverend Willet cleared his throat and stood up. "A toast."

Wine glasses were raised.

"To happiness."

Nathan stood and raised his glass. "To my beautiful bride."

Madalyn's hand shook as she took a small sip. The slam of the deck door followed by loud footsteps prevented any further conversation. Captain Galer entered the room, and laughed.

"Everyone's all polite and proper." He pulled out an empty chair beside Mr. Barnet. "I can see I wasn't expected."

"It's your ship." Nathan gave Galer a faint nod.

"Yes." The Captain lifted a glass and saluted Nathan. "To retribution."

Madalyn watched Nathan pause before he took a sip. He leaned back in his chair as a sailor dressed in a white jacket started to serve the meal. Madalyn grabbed the side of the table as she felt the ship tilt to the right.

"At least there's one man of honor aboard this ship," Mrs. Willet said as she put her wineglass down. "I appreciate your help, Captain."

Captain Galer grinned at Nathan, before turning to Mrs. Willet. "It's always my pleasure to see that justice is done. I hope you are happy with the results?"

Reverend Willet raised his hand. "We are satisfied, aren't we my dear?"

Mrs. Willet nodded. Madalyn watched Nathan grimace and then force a smile to his lips. She released the breath she'd been holding and prayed for the meal to be over. Despite her days of starvation, she barely touched her food. She took a couple of bites of salt pork, but her stomach heaved in protest.

"Your wife seems to have lost her appetite," Captain Galer said with a sneer. "Perhaps she is not accustomed to such a feast?"

Lady Raglan giggled. "I doubt Mrs. Carter knows anything about etiquette."

Madalyn's chest tightened and she put her fork down with a soft click. "Your manners show that you're unfamiliar with any type of society, Lady Raglan."

Nathan cleared his throat and pushed away from the table. "My wife is overcome with emotion."

"How right you are." Mrs. Willet gave Nathan a wide smile and patted Madalyn's hand. "It's time we let the newly married couple have some privacy."

"I'm certain Mr. Carter is anxious to enjoy the charms of his new wife." The Captain slammed his wine glass down on the table.

Nathan stood and went to Madalyn's side. He held out his hand, leaving her no choice, unless she wanted to look the fool. She felt the others watching, but she refused to look back. Instead, she took a deep breath and forced a smile to her lips.

Nathan leaned close, his lips tickling her ears as he whispered, "Ready to consummate the marriage?"

Chapter 7

"How dare you." Madalyn twisted out of Nathan's hold as soon as the cabin door closed behind them.

He moved away and began to loosen his cravat. "Lower your voice. It carries."

"I don't care who hears." Madalyn put her hands on her hips. "That woman was outrageous."

"I suspect Lady Raglan thinks the same of you." Nathan pulled out the chair and sat down.

Madalyn reached her arms behind her back. "Help me out of this dress."

"I didn't realize you were so impatient to share the marriage bed."

Madalyn's words died in her throat, her anger with Lady Raglan momentarily forgotten. She felt her cheeks flush. Heat flooded her body as Nathan leaned back in the chair and smiled at her.

She forced herself to look away. "I have to return the gown."

"You want my aid?" Nathan stood up and touched her back, his fingers caressing down her spine. "Your eagerness is a surprise."

Madalyn fought the lethargy spreading through her body. "I don't want to be beholden to that woman any longer than necessary."

"Ahh," Nathan's voice was little more than a whisper. "I misunderstood."

Madalyn bit the inside of her mouth. The man was insufferable, but he had a hypnotic charm. She must not let him seduce her. The sooner she was free of him, the better. She moved out of his reach.

"I'll do it myself."

"Nonsense." Nathan turned her around and unfastened the gown.

She held it against her shoulders. "You can leave now."

"No." His voice was firm.

Madalyn glanced around the cabin. "I need to put something else on."

Nathan handed her a large floral bag. "I asked Galer to return your things."

She opened the bag and pulled out a pale green muslin gown. It smelt of fish and seawater, but it was better than Nathan's nightshirt. She ruffled through the rest of the clothes and sighed. Her mother's necklace was not there.

"Is something missing?"

"A necklace." Madalyn tried to hide her disappointment. She threw the bag down beside the bed. She'd been a fool to bring it with her, yet she couldn't bear to part with the only thing she had left of her mother.

"Turn around." Her anger made her voice harsher than she intended.

She waited until she was certain Nathan couldn't see her before letting Lady Raglan's gown fall to the floor. She shook out her own dress and was just about to put it over her head when Nathan's voice stopped her.

"Having difficulties?"

Madalyn dropped it over her body. "Could you fasten it?"

She held her breath as his fingers made deft work of the ties. His touch sent tingles of shock down her spine. She was surprised at how pleasant the sensation was. She forced herself to move away once he finished.

"Thank you."

Nathan picked up the discarded robe. "I'll return this to Lady Raglan tomorrow."

"Why not today?"

"Today is our wedding. Even a second apart from you will be agony."

Madalyn sighed. "You don't have to be sarcastic. You can't stay here if we're going to annul the marriage."

"I've already suffered the crew's ridicule once. I won't endure it again." Nathan leaned back against the small table and crossed his arms. "If anyone leaves this room it will be you."

A wave of sympathy softened Madalyn's mood. Nathan had only tried to protect her. She was angered by their predicament, but she needed his help to change things. She took a deep breath and pushed back her frustration.

"I'm being unreasonable."

Nathan bowed his head to her. "The thought had crossed my mind."

"I'm sorry."

"Apology accepted." Nathan uncrossed his arms and motioned for her to sit on the bed.

Madalyn's eyes skittered across the bed before she sat on the chair. "I'll be more comfortable here."

Nathan chuckled. "As you wish." He pushed away from the desk. "We need to talk."

She relaxed. Finally, something she agreed with. "The sooner we end this charade, the better."

"What possessed you to hide aboard ship?"

"I needed to leave in a hurry." Madalyn's eyes darted away from Nathan's gaze.

Nathan tilted his head at her. "What were you running from?"

"It's my problem." Madalyn straightened her shoulders. She didn't want to owe him any more than she already did.

Nathan moved in front of her, imprisoning her by placing both of his hands on the back of the chair. His face was a few inches away and his blue eyes glittered with anger.

"I've been manipulated into marriage, made the laughing stock of a group of men I find despicable, and spent a sleepless night on the salon's settee." Nathan's eyes narrowed. "I saved you from a fate worse than death. My patience is at an end. I expect the complete truth."

Nathan's raised voice reverberated in Madalyn's ears. Her breath caught in her throat as her eyes darted sideways looking for an escape. There was none. Her heart beat in a furious staccato.

She nodded.

The storm passed as quickly as it had come. The muscles in Nathan's face relaxed and he moved his arms away. He still stood in front of her, though.

"What possessed you to board this ship?"

Madalyn twisted her hands in her lap. "My brother."

"Why?"

"Are you sure you want to hear this?" Madalyn's voice was almost a whisper.

Nathan nodded and moved away. "You are my wife. Everything about you concerns me."

Madalyn shrugged her shoulders. "My uncle insisted on taking me to Liverpool. He'd arranged for me to marry my cousin and wanted me to buy my trousseau. William met us there."

Nathan turned back to her. "You desired to wed your cousin?"

Madalyn crossed her arms and heaved a heavy sigh. What difference did it make if Nathan knew the truth? She might need his help to find William.

"I've avoided marriage to him for several years. My uncle wouldn't budge this time." Madalyn lifted her chin. "He said I was getting old and I wasn't pretty enough to attract another man."

Nathan stood staring at her for a few seconds before he sat on the bed. "So you jumped the first ship you saw to escape?"

"I'm not that impulsive." Madalyn shook her head. "I didn't want to marry Horace, but what choice did I have?"

"What about love?" Nathan leaned forward, his elbows on his knees. "Or don't you believe in it?"

"There was a man once." Madalyn smiled. "His name was Bertram. He even proposed, but then he left for America and I never heard from him again."

"He had no honor, but that doesn't mean you won't find love."

"I'm a realist and you don't know my uncle." Madalyn shivered as she remembered the number of arguments they'd had. "He's a cold man."

"So where does your brother fit into this?"

"I hadn't seen him for almost a year." Madalyn looked up at Nathan silently begging him with her eyes to understand. "We'd arranged to see each other once my uncle was in bed."

Nathan frowned. "That doesn't sound terrible."

"Uncle Phillip wouldn't have approved." Madalyn started to shake as the memory of brother washed over her. "I was late. We were to meet in the inn's courtyard, but when I got there all I saw was four men carrying him away."

Nathan sat back. "How?"

"They had some sort of material over his head and they carried him by his arms and legs." Madalyn choked back a sob. "They were kidnapping him."

"What did you do?"

"I followed." Madalyn brought a shaking hand up to her mouth. "I have always protected him. I promised my mother on her death bed."

Nathan cleared his throat. "Where did they take him?"

"To the docks. They boarded a ship called The Magistrate. They took up the gangplank just as I reached it." Madalyn's voice was a whisper. "My brother wasn't moving."

"Your brother struggled and they probably knocked him over the head." Nathan cleared his throat. "What did you do?"

"I asked for the next ship sailing to Charleston and was told it was The Folly."

"So you decided to stowaway?" Nathan's voice was harsh. "You should have told your uncle."

"I did." Madalyn clenched her fists. "You're so quick to judge, but believe me I only stowed aboard this ship when every other option was exhausted."

Nathan rubbed a hand through his hair. "So I guess your uncle refused to help."

"He laughed at me." Madalyn pushed back her rage at the words of derision her uncle had used. "He thought it was about time William learned to be a man. He considered it quite fortuitous that he'd been kidnapped."

Nathan sighed. "I keep jumping to the wrong conclusions."

"You did the same thing last night." Madalyn lips twisted into a grimace. "You think I cheated Galer out of his money, but I didn't. I paid him the full fare for my passage and he refused to let me board."

Nathan frowned. "You paid him?"

"I should have waited. That was my mistake." Madalyn stood and walked to the porthole. "When I came back with my luggage, he refused to let me board. So I decided to hide."

Nathan closed his eyes for a second and then shook his head. "Surely, that told you what kind of man Galer was? Why would you risk it?"

"I had to find my brother." Madalyn walked back to the desk, and leaned against it. "He's only fifteen. He's my responsibility. Imagine how frightened he is."

"It will be worse once he lands in Charleston."

A shiver of dread raced up Madalyn's back. "What will happen?"

"He'll be forced into servitude." Nathan's voice was devoid of emotion. "It's a common practice. Usually men and women chose to spend a number of years as servants to pay for their passage, but unfortunately that is not always the case."

"Is there no way to stop this?"

"His services will be sold once he lands in Charleston."

Madalyn's breath caught in her throat. "But it isn't his choice."

"Kidnapping to sell humans is all too frequent." Nathan rubbed his hand over his face.

"I have to save him."

"We can try." Nathan stood and walked to her. "It'll be difficult. Once we're in Charleston I'll set my man of business to find him."

"Thank you, but I can look for my brother." Madalyn shook her head. "You've done enough."

"A woman cannot search the places I'll need to go." Nathan gripped her shoulders and sat her on the chair.

"There is no choice." Madalyn shook free. "Once I have my brother then we'll return to England."

"You're forgetting the small matter of our marriage."

"We can get it annulled and then I suppose I'll marry Horace like my uncle wants."

"That's assuming he'll still want you after your reputation is in shreds." Nathan's voice was full of doubt. "Men have peculiar ideas of what they expect in a bride."

"You married me." She regretted the words as soon as they were said.

Nathan's eyebrows rose. "Quite right, but unlike most men, I do not need to protect a family name."

Madalyn knew she shouldn't ask, but his words left her curious. "Is there something wrong with your name?"

Nathan smiled slightly. "My parents were not married so I don't have a name to safeguard."

His eyes never wavered from her. She sensed that he was waiting for a reaction. She shrugged her shoulders.

"Is that important?"

Nathan leaned back. "It is to most women."

Madalyn knew that her uncle would never have considered Nathan a respectable man to marry. That didn't sway her. Her uncle had not approved of Bertram either.

"It won't matter to a woman who loves you."

Nathan's eyes narrowed. "We transgress. We were discussing your chances of marriage."

"Horace will understand."

"So certain." Nathan's voice held a hint of sympathy. "You have lived a sheltered life. You'll find that a reputation can never be repaired once it's lost."

Madalyn shrugged her shoulders. "My uncle wants this marriage."

"He may not be so eager when he learns you're already wed and the reason it was necessary."

Madalyn gripped her hands together. "You promised that it would be annulled."

"I hope to prove that the wedding was illegal." Nathan heaved a sigh. "We're both British and can probably annul the marriage on that basis."

"Then we aren't legally married?"

"There were witnesses who signed papers to our union. That is enough in America."

"What will Reverend Willet say?"

Nathan smiled slightly. "We might be able to fight him, but it will take time. Even then the only choice might be divorce."

Madalyn felt a sickening drop in her stomach. The mere thought of divorce seemed too horrible to contemplate, but if it meant being free, then she'd risk further damage to her reputation. Maybe that would force her uncle to reconsider her wedding Horace.

Nathan walked back to the desk. He stood close and Madalyn inhaled the now familiar scent that she associated with him. The hair on the back of her neck tingled with awareness and she forced herself to stay calm.

"Your cousin may not want you afterwards." Nathan's tone was serious.

"Horace does what his father asks." Madalyn sighed. "He would rather marry a book."

"He sounds a safe choice for marriage."

"And boring." Madalyn crossed her arms in front of her. "We hate each other. His idea of an exciting evening is to be locked away in the library researching. He's been writing a critique on King Arthur for over ten years."

Nathan leaned closer, his breath tickling Madalyn's cheek. "Being locked in a library could be romantic."

A twist of excitement stirred in Madalyn's stomach. She moved away from Nathan until her back pressed against the wall. He looked at her through half closed eyes, yet she felt as if he saw into her soul.

"Not with Horace." Madalyn struggled to breath.

"With Bertram perhaps?" Nathan's eyebrows lifted slightly, his voice low and seductive.

She shook her head and her stomach clenched in denial. Never had she thought of Bertram in such a way. Images of her ex-fiancé flitted through her mind, but none of them stirred her body.

"He never suggested such a thing."

"Then he would have made a poor husband." Nathan stepped back from her. "You're well rid of him."

Madalyn eased away from the wall. The ship suddenly lurched sideways and she put her hand out to stop from falling. Books rolled off the table, and she stooped to pick them up.

"The storm is worsening." Nathan took her elbow and helped her up. "Captain Galer will have his hands full today."

Madalyn glanced up at the porthole, her body tensing with fear. "Will we be safe?"

"The ship has weathered worse than this." Nathan led Madalyn over to the bed. "Best get some rest before the sea gets too rough."

"Have you sailed often?" The rocking of the vessel sent her into Nathan's arms. She held onto him until the craft righted and then pushed away.

"It's a family tradition." Nathan moved to the small chest that stood on his trunk, and opened it. He shuffled through some papers, putting a few of them in a small pouch. He added some coins and put the pouch in his coat jacket.

"I thought you had no family."

"No name. Family, I have plenty of." Nathan grinned. "Besides my mother, I have three brothers still living."

"Still living? What happened to the rest?"

"One brother was murdered and my sister committed suicide. My father died over two years ago, but none of us mourned his death."

"Why was your brother murdered?"

Nathan tilted his head. "My sister had a misguided sense of loyalty to her mother, my father's second wife."

Madalyn frowned. "Why would that affect your brother?"

Nathan took a deep breath. "It's complicated."

"I told you about my family." Madalyn crossed her arms across her chest. "I have a right to know about yours."

"My father had two wives. The eldest son of his first wife, my brother Douglas, inherited the title and estate." Nathan hesitated a second before continuing. "My father's second wife wanted her son to inherit, so her daughter killed Douglas. When my younger brother, Alex, who was next in line, discovered what my sister had done, she killed herself."

Madalyn digested this information in silence, before motioning toward the papers. "What are you doing with those?"

Nathan patted his coat. "I don't trust Galer. He has keys to the cabin and I'll feel safer having these with me."

Madalyn was about to ask him why, when the ship sent her back against the bed. She landed with a hard thud. She leaned up on her arm and rubbed her side.

"It's safer in bed." Nathan took off his jacket and started to undo his cravat.

"What are you doing?" Madalyn's voice rose.

Nathan paused in pulling the cravat from his neck. "I thought it was obvious."

"You cannot undress with me in the room."

"We've already discussed this." Nathan threw the wrinkled cravat over his trunk and began to unfasten his shirt. "I did not sleep well last night. I need to lie down."

Madalyn pulled herself upright on the bed. "Then you'll sleep on the floor."

Nathan heaved a heavy sigh and sat on the chair. "I have already endured enough discomfort. I will sleep in the bed I paid for."

"Where will I go?" Madalyn pushed herself back against the narrow bed.

Nathan pulled off his boots and threw them near the trunk. "You are welcome to share my bed."

She watched Nathan stand and tug his shirt off. She blinked her eyes, staring at the wide expanse of muscles on his chest. She'd never seen a man's bare-chest before, and the sight sent a tremor of excitement through her body.

"I hope you like what you see." Nathan's voice held a hint of laughter.

Madalyn turned away. "You should cover yourself."

"Once we're in bed you won't notice." Nathan pulled the covers back from the bed. "Are you going to change?"

"This dress will be comfortable." Madalyn shivered as his eyes rested on her.

Nathan shrugged. "As you wish. Get under the bedding."

Madalyn pushed her body under the sheets, holding her back close to the wall. "Do you have something to put between us?"

"The bed is too small for that." Nathan climbed in beside her. "You're shivering. I can keep you warm."

A surge of heat flooded her body as Nathan moved close. She tried to keep near the wall, but the rocking of the ship made that impossible. She kept rolling into Nathan's arms.

"Close your eyes," Nathan whispered. "You're tense."

"I can't sleep like this." Madalyn tried to sit, but Nathan's arm grabbed her around the waist.

"Relax." He pulled her close to his body. "All I want is sleep, but if you keep moving like that I'll soon want something else."

Madalyn's breath caught in her throat and she held herself rigid. A sensation of warmth flowed from his body and as his breathing slowed into a steady rhythm, Madalyn eased her muscles.

When she was certain he was sleeping, she snuggled deeper into his body's warmth. The rolling motion of the ship seemed to increase. The whistle of the wind was almost deafening.

She'd overheard Galer say that they would reach Charleston tomorrow. Madalyn smiled at the thought of leaving the ship. William would be found and then her marriage could be annulled. The sooner she distanced herself from Nathan, the better.

She was awakened hours later by the sudden lurching of the ship. The roar of crashing timbers and screams from the deck above brought Nathan to full alert. He shook Madalyn and threw the covers aside. She yawned as she watched him grab his shirt and jacket, pulling on his boots as he hopped back to the bed.

"Get up." He tugged on Madalyn's arm. "The ship is sinking."

Chapter 8

Madalyn fought through the fog of sleep. She used her arms to brace herself against the wall, but the minute she let go, she was thrown out of the bed. Nathan plucked her from the floor.

"We have to get on deck." He shrugged into his shirt and then his jacket. "We need to get off the ship."

A wave of nausea rose in her throat. Water terrified her. She'd only boarded the ship because there was no other way to reach Charleston. Even then, it had taken several attempts before she could make her legs obey.

"I can't leave." Madalyn's voice was a whisper compared to the noise on deck.

Nathan gripped her arm and dragged her toward the door. "There's no other choice."

The ship leaned sharply to the left, driving the bed and furniture to the far wall. The sound of running and shouting could be heard above their cabin. The storm roared all around, its fury deafening in its intensity.

Chaos reigned everywhere.

"No time," Nathan shouted as he opened the door and pushed her out into the dark hallway.

Madalyn tripped over something sharp. Pain seared her leg, numbing in intensity. She grabbed her shin, and rubbed it to ease the ache.

"Are you hurt?" Nathan's voice was sharp with concern.

"My leg."

Madalyn bent and patted her hands around the floor to feel what was blocking their exit. Wood and glass shards stung her fingers. Nathan pressed ahead of her, his feet kicking and pushing objects out of the way.

"Give me your hand." The roar of the storm almost drowned out his voice.

Madalyn stumbled in their scramble to freedom, tripping and falling over debris. Nathan knocked and opened the cabin doors they passed, but they were all empty. Everyone else was already on deck.

Seconds stretched into minutes, and time seemed to move backwards as they picked their way blindly to the deck door. Madalyn sighed when they reached it. Safety was just beyond the door. Nathan turned the handle, but it didn't open.

They were trapped.

Panic clawed at her.

The pounding of her heart echoed in her ears and her breath was coming in uneven gasps. A cold wetness sloshed against her ankles and it took a minute to register what it was. Water. It was seeping under the deck door.

"Something has fallen against the door." Nathan shouted. "I'll try to force it open."

Madalyn bit her lip. The inky greyness of the hallway made it impossible to see more than a few inches in front of her, everything else was shadows. She heard the sound of Nathan pushing against the door. It refused to move. He took a couple of steps backwards and ran at it. A slight creaking noise was all Madalyn heard.

"I need something to break it down." Nathan knelt and began to feel along the floor. He stood up with a small chair in his hands. He broke it over his knee and handed Madalyn a spindle.

Nathan leaned close to her, his voice little more than a whisper above the roaring din of the storm. "When I ram the door, I want you to try and wedge that in the opening."

Madalyn felt for the crack of the door opening and fixed her eyes there, never letting them waver. Nathan rammed his shoulder against it two more times.

Nothing happened.

He stopped and threw his head back. His chest was heaving with the exertion of his efforts. Madalyn wondered how long he'd be able to continue. After a couple of seconds rest, Nathan nodded and then took a run at the door again.

It didn't move.

Madalyn clenched her hands tight. Her voice froze in her throat. It was hopeless. The door was wedged shut and there was no escape.

A sharp crack sounded from the deck. The ship shuddered and tilted, throwing Nathan sideways against her. The sound of objects moving across the deck gave her a surge of hope.

"One more time." Nathan pushed away and ran at the door with his shoulder. This time it cracked open a few inches.

"The spindle," Nathan shouted.

Madalyn shoved the wood into the space, ramming it as hard as she could. Nathan grasped it, using it as a lever to pry at the door.

When it was partially open, he gripped Madalyn's arm. "Squeeze yourself through."

Madalyn shook her head, but he pushed her into the opening. Her body was immediately assaulted by piercing stabs of rain. The force of the wind was suffocating. Her chest heaved with the effort it took to breath. She grabbed the door to prevent herself from being blown away.

Nathan thrust his body into the hole, but he didn't fit. He slammed his shoulder against the door trying to make the gap larger. It didn't budge.

"What's blocking it?"

Madalyn looked down at the deck and saw the jagged end of a broken mast beside her. It was massive. She knelt and tried to pull it away. It was immoveable.

She looked back at Nathan. "A mast has broken off." Her words were carried by the wind.

"Find something to use as a lever."

The rain and dark skies made it impossible for her to see, so she patted around the deck for something that might help. Her hands clasped the coarse edge of what felt like a bristle brush. She pulled it toward her.

A rope.

She held it up to Nathan.

"Good." Nathan moved his hand in a circle. "Find something to lift it. Then you can fasten the rope around the mast."

Madalyn scrambled on her knees, until she found a long pole. She handed it to Nathan who pushed it beneath the massive wooden beam and heaved his body down. It moved enough for Madalyn to get the rope under, and knot it about the mast.

"I'll push while you pull on the rope." Nathan heaved his back against the door.

Madalyn yanked on the rope, straining her muscles to the screaming point. When that didn't work, she slung the rope over her shoulder and tried to walk the post aside. Her back and hands stung, but the mast didn't budge. She looked around for another solution, but there was nothing. She looked back at Nathan, her shoulders sagging.

"Go." Nathan's voice held an urgency she'd never heard before. "Save yourself."

Madalyn shook her head. She couldn't leave him to die. She screamed for help, but her words were flung back at her by the wind. No one was in sight.

Nathan was still struggling to push the door open. With a deep breath Madalyn grabbed hold of the rope again, drawing it out to its full length. There was enough length to wrap it around the base of another mast.

She braced her legs against the pole's base and heaved.

The cord cut her hands and her legs burned, but she kept yanking until she felt the mast move slightly. It wasn't much, but she continued to tug until it began to inch away from the door.

"Let go." Nathan screamed from beside her. "I'm free."

Madalyn collapsed against the deck. "Thank God," she whispered.

Nathan dragged her upright. "We have to get off the ship."

He held her close to his body, protecting her from the wind as they avoided the debris that littered the deck. When they reached the side of the ship where the dinghies and row boats were stored, they were in time to see the last one plummeting to the water.

"Damn." Nathan looked over the railing. "Can you swim?"

Madalyn clenched her hands into fists and shook her head. Her chest constricted. She backed away from the edge. She turned to run, but Nathan grasped her waist.

"We have to jump."

"No." Terror seized her. She began to shake and she beat her hands against his chest.

"It's our only hope." Nathan captured her hands before picking her up in his arms. He placed her on the far side of the railing and climbed over to join her.

"Keep hold of my hand. Don't let go."

Madalyn closed her eyes and clasped the railing. The ship lurched and the force of it almost threw her into the water. Nathan's grip on her hand tightened. He pulled her toward him.

"Look at me." He shouted over the pounding storm.

She opened her eyes. They were standing on the outer edge of the ship, the wind buffeting them in all directions. He was right. Their only chance of survival was to jump, but her fear of water had a tighter hold on her body. She was paralyzed.

Nathan pulled her hard against him.

"Keep your head straight." It was the last thing she heard before they plunged through the air.

Darkness overwhelmed her.

Her lungs hurt and her legs refused to move. She was caught by a weight and there was an insistent tug on one arm. She tried to fight it, but the pull was relentless.

She could hold her breath no longer.

She stopped struggling. Her body was weightless, floating in space. A wave of peace spread through her. She was just about to relax and take a breath, when her head was pulled from the water.

"Breathe." Nathan's voice boomed in her ear.

She opened her mouth and gulped. Awareness returned as air filled her aching lungs. She splashed her free arm as she tried to climb out of the water.

"You're safe." Nathan grabbed her flailing arm and held it to her chest. He crossed her other arm over it, and then moved behind her. "Try and float."

"I can't move." Her voice was little more than a sob. Her whole body was a prisoner of Nathan and the sea.

"I can hear voices near." Nathan spoke close to her ear, his tone soothing and confident. "It's probably a boat. Hold on a little longer."

Rescue? A surge of hope rushed through her. Nathan held her firm. She allowed him to steer them toward the voices. Her ears strained to make out the words, but they were too far away.

The water was cold and the salt stung her eyes. The storm made it impossible to see anything, but after ten minutes of swimming, a faint light flickered through the darkness. Nathan's strokes quickened and they were at the boat within a couple of minutes. Nathan grabbed the side, but an oar smacked his hand away.

"Find somewhere else." Madalyn's stomach sank. It was Captain Galer's voice.

"You can't leave us in the water." Nathan grabbed the side of the boat again.

"Watch me." Galer's laugh sent chills through Madalyn's already frozen body.

"At least take my wife." Nathan pushed Madalyn toward the boat. "She can't swim."

"You wanted her." Galer swung the lantern in their direction. "Keep her."

"You're the Captain." Nathan's voice roared above the wind. "It's your responsibility to save your passengers."

"Not this one." Galer peered over the edge of the boat, light from the lantern reflecting in his eyes. "She's a stowaway."

"Her passage was paid." Nathan's voice was a threat. "Twice."

"I don't seem to remember that." Galer grinned.

Nathan took a deep breath. "What do you want?"

Galer pushed away from the side. "To see you drown." Without warning, he slammed an oar down in the water beside them.

"Damn." Nathan's anger rang out. "I won't forget this, Galer."

"You won't live long enough." Galer motioned for his men to move away. "This is your reward for meddling."

Madalyn started to sob. She couldn't stop as she watched the boat move further away. The sea would have them now. Despair filled her soul and she tried to jerk away from Nathan.

"Stay still." His voice was low and urgent.

"Let me go." She struggled to twist free. "Save yourself."

"No." Nathan's arms tightened and held her closer. "We can still make it."

"It's hopeless." Her body shook as the water's coldness seeped further into her bones.

The sound of wood cracking ripped through the storm. Gut wrenching screams for help filled the air. The storm seemed to abate as the Folly heaved its final breath on its decent to its watery grave.

Madalyn listened as the screams faded into the storm. She'd thought they were the last ones on board the ship, but Galer had left others behind. They were lucky to have escaped when they did. Nathan leaned his head back in the water and took another stroke. "Leave me." Her voice was hoarse from screaming. "I'll only slow you down."

"We'll both survive." Nathan moved them through the water.

"I'm tired." She struggled to kick her legs. "All I want is to sleep."

"You must stay awake." Nathan began to rub his free hand down her sides. "Fight."

Tremors shook her body.

Every breath was a struggle.

The cold was unbearable and every inch of her body screamed for relief from the unrelenting water. Rain and wind kept pounding them from above. After minutes of swimming without direction, a jolt of pain seared through her shoulder.

Nathan stopped.

He moved Madalyn into one arm and investigated with his other hand. "It's debris from the Folly, a wooden door."

Nathan hauled the door close to them.

"Can you climb aboard?"

Madalyn's mind was too numb to answer. Nathan shook her. She felt him reach below the water, and grab her body. Her legs were trapped in the skirts of her gown, making it impossible for her to help.

Nathan heaved once and succeeded in getting her halfway onto the door. With another shove, she was out of the water. Nathan grabbed the door with both arms and started to heave himself up.

"Hold on."

She clung as tight as her frozen fingers would allow. Nathan's weight caused the door to bounce in the water and she almost fell off, but he dragged her back.

"It won't hold both of us." Nathan rested both his arms on their makeshift boat. "I'll kick forward."

"You can't stay in the water." Madalyn's teeth chattered. "You'll freeze to death."

"I'm fine." Nathan started to rub her body vigorously. "You're too cold."

A tingle of warmth invaded her body where Nathan had rubbed. She brought her knees up to her chest and used her stiff fingers to pull her dress away from her limbs. Then, she rubbed her legs together until a sharp prickling sensation shot up from her toes.

"Feel better?" Nathan's kicks were gliding the door forward.

Madalyn nodded. She didn't have the energy to speak. Sleep and exhaustion took over until the jolt of a collision shook her awake. Her body was thrown forward and she would have been in the water again if Nathan hadn't grabbed her.

"What happened?" She scrambled back to the center of the door.

"We've hit something." Nathan swam around to the front of the wooden door.

"Land?" Madalyn's voice was a hoarse whisper.

A scraping noise, and then the door stopped moving. She bent forward and felt the object. It was sharp and jagged.

A rock.

"It'll keep us out of the water until daylight." Nathan pulled the door up onto the slippery slope. "Give me your hand."

Madalyn scrambled onto the rock, gripping its jagged edges to stop from sliding back into the water. Nathan gathered her close, rubbing warmth into her body.

"Morning will be here soon. Then, we can see where we are."

She leaned back against him and sighed. "Are we safe?"

"For now."

Nathan's voice sounded confident, but they had no idea how far away land was, or if there was any chance of being rescued.

Chapter 9

Every muscle in her body throbbed. Her bones ached from the cold dampness of her clinging clothes. She tried to stretch out an arm, but it refused to move. Something was blocking it.

"Sore?" Nathan's voice seeped through the nightmares that still clouded her mind.

She opened her eyes and a surge of warmth rushed through her. Nathan was staring down at her, his blue eyes soft with concern. Her heartbeat sped up, and her body tightened in response to his nearness.

They had survived the storm.

"My body doesn't want to move." She grimaced and forced herself to sit.

"We were lucky."

"Thanks to you." She smiled, her eyes shying away from him.

"You deserve credit too. I would have drowned on the ship if you hadn't helped with the door." Nathan shifted his weight and stood, stretching his arms above him. "It's good to be alive."

"Where are we?" Madalyn glanced across the water. Grey wisps of dawn were spreading into the sky. The rain had stopped and the clouds had dispersed, leaving the last remnants of the stars to shine down on them.

"I've been watching lights in the distance for the last hour." Nathan pointed to his right.

Madalyn squinted at the horizon. A minute later a tiny beam of light shone bright and then faded away.

"What is it?"

Nathan shrugged. "I think it might be a lighthouse."

"Land?" Hope began to flicker to life. Land meant the possibility of rescue.

"Probably." Nathan's eyes narrowed as the light shone again. "We just have to get there."

She looked down at the water and shivered. The thought of going back into its murky darkness filled her with panic. "Surely they'll be looking for survivors?"

"We're too far from shore for a search party to find us." Nathan sat beside her. "We'll have to get there ourselves."

Madalyn took a deep breath and tried to calm the anxiety tightening her chest. "How?"

Nathan tilted his head toward the battered wooden door that rested on the rock with them. A tremor raced through her body. What other choice did she have? She closed her eyes and nodded.

Nathan cleared his throat. "I'll steady it so that you can climb onboard."

"It's too far for you to do all the pushing." She stood and shook her long skirts away from her legs.

Nathan eased his body into the water and grabbed hold of the door, pulling it in beside him. "I'll be fine."

"It might be easier if you went on by yourself." Madalyn fought to keep her voice steady. "Then you could send someone back for me."

"No." Nathan shook his head. "We stay together."

Madalyn nodded, and edged toward the door. The rock was slippery and she used her hands to prevent herself from falling into the sea. She leapt to the door with one quick move, bracing herself as it swayed in the water.

"Lie down." Nathan's voice was low, yet insistent.

She scrambled low on the door, her body hugging its splintered surface. She used her hands to help Nathan steer their raft away from the rock and then hung onto the sides.

"How many miles away is it?" Madalyn focused her eyes on the distant light beam.

"Two at the most." Nathan's powerful kicks were propelling them through the water. "Try and relax."

She laid her head on her arm and watched the sky lighten. The sun rose until it was a bright yellow orb in the sky and she could no longer see the light from shore. She found the sound of lapping water mesmerizing and drifted into a state of half sleep until the door stopped moving.

Madalyn looked up to a sea of green grass. Nathan was standing in water that reached his knees. She scrambled off the makeshift raft and waded to the shore beside him. He pulled the door up onto the beach and then lay down beside it.

Madalyn stood at the water's edge. They were on a large beach. The wind was a gentle breeze now, the destruction of the previous night forgotten.

"Where are we?"

Nathan heaved himself upright. "The lighthouse makes me think we're close to Charleston. Perhaps one of the marsh islands along the coast."

"It seems so fresh and clean here." Madalyn took a deep breath of air, her nose twitching as the salt from the ocean mingled with the breeze.

"It's different from England, yet the same in many ways."

She plopped down beside Nathan. "I remember the first time I visited Liverpool as a child. Even then it seemed noisy and crowded. There was no quiet like this."

"You lived near Liverpool?" Nathan's voice seemed to drift off at the end of his question.

She nodded and leaned back on her elbows. "I grew up in a small village outside of the city. When my parents died my uncle moved us closer."

Nathan murmured something that Madalyn didn't understand. When she looked over at him, he was laying back on the ground, his eyes closed, sleeping. Exhaustion had claimed him.

She waited a few minutes before she stood and wandered closer to the shoreline. Nathan deserved a rest, but she wanted to see more of what America had to offer. Now that the fear of drowning was past, she could enjoy the freedom of being on land.

She looked back at Nathan. He was the reason she was still alive. A deep sense of gratitude filled her. He had risked his own life to stay with her and get her to safety. The only other person who had done that before was her father. And he had died saving her life. Her stomach knotted in pain when she remembered her father's sacrifice.

She blinked back tears. To shake off the memories she started to explore, stopping now and then to take a close look at a number of objects that the waves were now washing ashore. She picked up a small glass bottle of perfume and her stomach tightened as she realized where it had come from. This was the debris from the shipwreck.

She threw the bottle back into the water and walked up one of the dunes to get a better look of where they were. The tall grass swayed in the gentle breeze, tickling her hands as she brushed against it. Pale pink flowers dotted the beach and a yellow butterfly fluttered in the distance. A quick movement in the sand caught her attention and she bent closer. Tiny crabs were scurrying away from her and back to the water.

Seagulls squawked above and Madalyn cupped her hands over her eyes to get a better look. They seemed to be laughing at her, circling and dipping closer with each pass. She must look quite a sight, waterlogged and tattered. She turned back to dune and considered the woods beyond it. Perhaps someone lived close by. She started to walk toward it when something pricked her arm.

"Ouch." She swatted at the bug, but it flew off.

The closer she walked to the forest, the worse the bugs were. She waved her hands around, but they still managed to bite her. Madalyn stopped. The pine and oak trees looked forbidding. Something slithered across her foot and she shrieked.

She ran back to the shore, panting for breath when she reached the water. She trembled at the thought of what lay beyond the beach. She wasn't moving away from the water unless Nathan went ahead of her.

She started to turn back to Nathan when a slight movement in the distance stopped her. She squinted and then, her mouth fell open as she realized what she was looking at.

Madalyn cupped her hands over her mouth and shouted. "Nathan."

Silence.

Again she shouted his name. When there was no reply she ran back to where she'd left him. He was still sprawled on his back. A shiver of fear shot through her. Was he alive? She concentrated on his chest until she noticed it rise with a steady breath. Her muscles relaxed. He was sleeping.

She shook his shoulder. "Wake up."

Nathan blinked his eyes and groaned. "What?"

"There are men along the beach."

Nathan sat up so fast he almost hit Madalyn in the head. "Where?"

She pointed in the direction she'd come from. They started to run together, but Nathan outpaced her within seconds. She stumbled over her skirts, but kept moving. When she caught up, Nathan was talking to two men.

The men were younger than Nathan, their attire rough and water stained. They eyed her with a slight leer and Madalyn decided not to move closer. She stood a bit behind Nathan and waited.

"Can you take us into the harbor?"

The dark-haired man nodded. "You be coming off the shipwreck?"

"Yes." Nathan placed his hands on his hips. "The Folly. Are there any other survivors?"

"People been coming in all night long." The other man spit on the ground. His hair was a lighter color at the roots, but it was so dirty that it appeared to be almost black. "Seems strange to find you stranded here."

"We made it to shore on debris." Nathan reached into his damp jacket and pulled out a packet.

Madalyn recognized it from the previous night. Nathan had placed his papers there because he was worried about Galer. Never in her worst nightmares could she have anticipated a shipwreck.

He pulled out a gold coin and held it up. "Can you take us to Charleston?"

The dark haired man reached for the coin first, but Nathan pulled it back. "It's yours when we're safely ashore."

The two men looked at each other and then shrugged. They motioned for Nathan and Madalyn to follow. When they had walked a few minutes, they came upon a small rowboat.

The men were the first to get in. Nathan helped Madalyn aboard before pushing the boat into the water and jumping in.

"Why were you two out here?"

"We've been searching for treasure." The dark haired man nodded at his partner. "Peter here has lots of luck finding stuff after shipwrecks."

Madalyn shivered at the callousness of the man's voice. Nathan put his arm around her shoulder and pulled her close. He looked down at her, his eyes full of warning. She bit her lip and lowered her head. These men were strangers and they were helping them. What right did she have to judge them?

"I'm not sure what the Folly was carrying." Nathan's tone was nonchalant. "Did you find anything yet?"

Peter shook his head. "You two will be our biggest prize. I told you I was lucky, Sam." Peter grinned at his partner.

Nathan's arm tightened around her and she forced herself to keep her eyes on the floor of the boat. There was a small amount of water sloshing from side to side. It added to her already growing fear. The boat rocked and shook with each stroke of the oars. After a while, Madalyn found the motion soothing. The men spotted each other and she clung to the side of the boat when Nathan took his turn at the oars.

She sat silent until the outline of a city began to appear in the distance. The buildings were large, filling the skyline with church towers and massive stone structures. Excitement began to build. Soon she could begin her search for William. That would mean leaving Nathan. An empty, hollow feeling settled in her stomach at the thought.

The tall wooden masts of ships, some with sails billowing, others with flags lowered, filled the harbor. There were huge wharfs where the ships were docked. Warehouses seemed to be everywhere. Wonder filled Madalyn as she gazed at it.

"I thought America was wilderness. I wasn't expecting such a large city."

"Charleston was established over a hundred and fifty years ago." Nathan's voice rang out over the rhythm of the oars. "Most of America is still wilderness, though."

Sam snorted. "You'd have to travel west for that."

"You ain't planning on traveling are you?" Peter looked at Madalyn and winked. "Me and Sam are between jobs right now. We could help you."

"That won't be necessary." Nathan pointed to a group of red-shingled warehouses close to them. "You can tie up there."

"Can't do that." Peter started to steer the boat away to another pier. "That's Carter Holdings and he doesn't take to strangers using his wharf."

"He won't mind." Nathan put his hand over the oars. "There are no ships to the right."

Sam shook his head. "Not now, but most likely one will be here soon."

"Nonsense," Nathan said with a grin.

"Mr. Nathan Carter has the busiest warehouses and pier in Charleston." Sam pushed Nathan's hand off the oars. "We have no need to bother him."

Madalyn's eyes widened. She'd known that he was wealthy, but she hadn't dreamed he was a businessman. His accent and bearing were that of an English gentleman.

The obvious respect and awe in Sam's voice took her by surprise. She looked back at the warehouses and noted how large and well-kept they were. Men were bustling along the pier, carrying cargo to and from several ships that were docked there.

"You have my permission to tie up at the end." Nathan pointed to the edge of the pier where a ladder went down to the water.

"We're not stopping here unless Mr. Carter himself says so." Peter started to pull back on the oars.

"I am Nathan Carter." Nathan's voice was so low that Madalyn didn't think the two men had heard.

Sam squinted at Nathan. "Why didn't you tell us sooner? I thought I'd seen you afore."

Nathan held out his hand. "My apologies."

Sam glanced down at the outstretched hand, hesitating a second before extending his own. "Didn't hear tell you were on The Folly."

"It was a last minute decision."

Peter nodded. "I heard you were in England."

"I had family matters to attend to." Nathan pointed to the pier again. "It would be easier if we could dock there."

Within a few minutes, they were alongside the giant wooden pier. Timber beams were anchored into the water, and a crude ladder was hammered onto the side of one of the uprights. Nathan reached over and grabbed hold of the ladder, pulling the boat closer. He secured a rope from the boat to the beam.

Nathan motioned for Madalyn to stand up. "Can you climb?"

She tilted her head back and looked above her. It was at least ten feet to the top. She took a deep breath and grabbed hold of a rung. Nathan gathered her skirts around her legs and guided her foot to lowest rung. He put his hands around her waist and gave her a boost up. The butterflies in her stomach quietened as his hold on her tightened. He wouldn't let her fall.

Nathan tossed a gold coin into the boat. "Come round to the warehouse and I'll have my foreman find you a job if you're interested."

"I always said you were a decent fellow." Peter gave Nathan a quick salute. "We'd be happy to work for you."

"Tomorrow then." Nathan turned back to Madalyn, and helped her up another rung. Slowly they made the ascent until Madalyn's head rose above the wooden deck of the pier.

A large man, dressed in sweat-stained brown shirt and pants, almost dropped the boxes he was carrying when he saw her. He yelled over his shoulder to another man who came running. This man carried a bundle of papers and was dressed in a loose-fitting jacket.

"What are you doing?" His voice held a note of panic.

Nathan pushed her onto the pier and then climbed up after her. "Calm down Jackson."

"Mr. Carter." Jackson's mouth gaped open. "Where did you come from?"

"The Folly." Nathan stood and helped Madalyn to her feet. "I need transportation."

"Yes sir." Mr. Jackson spun around and shouted at one of the workers. Within minutes, a horse and cart were being led toward them.

Madalyn stood staring about her in disbelief. Nothing was as she'd expected. Instead of wilderness, a bustling city greeted her. The pier was full of activity. Everywhere she looked, there were men carrying boxes or bags, loading them onto carts or ships.

Nathan touched her arm. "Ready?"

She nodded, but her eyes were still focused on the commotion of the wharf. "Where is everything going?"

Nathan took her elbow and led her to the wagon. "England. Some of it is going north to New York."

She stepped up into the cart and sat beside the driver. "It's so busy."

"Charleston is a centre of trade. That's why I stayed here when I first arrived in America." Nathan climbed up beside her.

They moved past the quay and down a road that was lined with warehouses. Then they turned onto an avenue that faced the waterfront. Huge houses lined one side of the street, each one more magnificent than the last.

The wagon pulled up in front of a yellow-stone mansion that was larger than all the rest. It had a huge porch that spanned the front of the house and wrapped around the side.

"Where are we?"

Nathan jumped down and held his hand out to her. "Home."

Chapter 10

Madalyn curled deeper into the soft linen sheets. Her dreams had been a tangle of water and darkness. Nightmares filled with terror and cold had held her in their grip, but the outcome had always been the same.

Nathan had saved her.

A quiet click brought her awake. She opened her eyes and blinked at the soft orange glow of light in the room. It added warmth to the pale yellow walls and blue floral fabric on the windows and bedcovers.

A plump, dark face leaned over her. She wore a red scarf over greying dark hair. Madalyn recognized her as the servant, Annie, who had helped her to bed earlier.

"Did ya have a good sleep?" The voice was pleasant, with an unhurried drawl.

Madalyn stretched her arms over her head. "Is it noon already?"

"It's night." Annie pulled the covers back from the bed. "You slept the whole day through."

Madalyn sat up and rubbed her eyes. "I suppose Mr. Carter slept too."

Annie shook her head. "Mr. Nathan never sleeps much. He's been out all day."

A twinge of guilt pierced her. Nathan had worked so hard to save them and he hadn't even rested. A stab of remorse hit her. Maybe there was someone he had to visit. Someone he cared about.

Her breath caught in her throat as a sense of loss threatened to overwhelm her. It was silly. She and Nathan didn't mean anything to each other. Still, the thought of him with another woman sent a shudder pain through her chest.

There was a quick tap on the bedroom door. Two dark skinned men brought in a tub and placed it by the brick fireplace. They filled it with jugs of water. Madalyn went to the bath. The water was steaming.

"What time is it?"

"Nearly seven." Annie pulled out a pale blue evening gown from the wardrobe at the far end of the room. "Mr. Nathan asks that you dine with him this evening."

"Where did that dress come from?"

"Mr. Nathan had clothes sent over for you." Annie placed the dress on the bed.

Madalyn looked at the gown and felt a bubble of wonder fill her. She'd never had anything so gorgeous. Her uncle had insisted that her dresses were drab in color and style, even when she'd been invited to dinner parties.

"No sense standing round." Annie turned Madalyn and started to unfasten the nightshirt they'd found for her this morning. "Dinner is at eight."

An hour later Madalyn stood in front of the floor-length mirror. Her face was the same, but the gown's color brought life to her skin. The cut of the gown emphasized her figure. It clung to her body, accentuating the curves of her breasts and hips. She twirled around once, glancing over her shoulder to see the effect from behind.

A burst of giddiness raced through her. She'd never be beautiful, but now she was attractive. Her eyes sparkled. A smile danced on her lips. Madalyn took one last look in the mirror and then left the room.

She walked down the hallway. It was lit by wall sconces of candles every ten feet. A rich mahogany balustrade curved around and down the stairway. Madalyn remembered climbing these stairs when they'd arrived this morning, but she'd been too tired to pay attention.

She glanced along the walls and noted the paintings of the English countryside. She tilted her head, and paused before one particularly beautiful landscape by John Constable. It brought back a rush of memories of what she'd left behind.

"Do ya need help?" Annie's soft drawl broke into Madalyn's thoughts.

"I was admiring the paintings."

"Mr. Nathan brings them home when he travels." Annie glanced up at the wall. "It's something you can help him choose now."

Madalyn cleared her throat. "I'm certain he doesn't need my assistance."

Annie patted Madalyn's arm. "Lord child, you're exactly what he needs. It's high time he married. The whole house is celebrating tonight."

"Celebrating?"

"Cook prepared a special meal and Mr. Nathan has given orders for the best wine to be opened for the staff." Annie grinned. "He's making certain none of us will disturb you this evening."

Madalyn watched Annie walk to the end of the hallway where she disappeared through a door. Shock was replaced by confusion. Why was Nathan telling others they were married?

The sooner she saw him, the quicker she'd know what his strategy was. She started down the stairs. Announcing the marriage would make an annulment difficult, but last night she'd learned he was a man to be trusted. She knew he probably had a plan.

Nathan was waiting at the base of the stairs.

She reached out to him. "I apologize for sleeping all day."

He clasped her hand in his. "You had a rough night."

"So did you." A shiver of awareness sparked through her at his touch. "This gown is stunning. Thank you."

Nathan led her into the drawing room. "I'm afraid all your personal belongings were lost in the shipwreck."

The room was enormous with several seating areas arranged around it. Nathan led her to a settee by the fireplace and waited until she sat before he went to a side table.

"Would you care for a glass of sherry?"

"Please."

Madalyn examined the room. It was decorated very much like an English parlor. She felt at ease with the familiarity of the deep red tones and wood of the furniture. The walls were paneled in a dark mahogany. A sense of warmth and security soothed her. Nathan handed her a drink. "Does it meet with your approval?"

"It's lovely." She took a sip of the sherry and relaxed against the settee. "You have a beautiful home."

"It's our home now." He sat in the wing chair opposite her.

"You've told everyone we're married." Madalyn took a deep breath. "Is that wise?"

Nathan tilted his head. "You would rather they thought I had brought a woman of questionable reputation into my house?"

"I hadn't thought of that." Madalyn put her glass down. "A chaperon would have solved the problem."

"There was no time this morning." Nathan leaned forward in his chair. "I have my own reputation to think of as well. This is my home and I won't have my position in society tarnished."

Madalyn took a deep breath and forced a smile to her lips. "What do we do now?"

A knock at the door prevented further conversation. A deep voice announced, "Dinner is served."

"Thank you, Isaac." Nathan stood and held his hand out to her.

The dining room was spacious, with a table that stretched the full length of the room. The table would have comfortably seated forty, but instead, two places were arranged across from each other at one end. It was a romantic and intimate setting. Isaac placed a bowl of clear broth before each of them and then left the room.

"I asked Cook to prepare something light this evening. I thought that after the ordeal of last night, it would be best."

"Actually, I'm quite hungry." Madalyn inhaled the delicious smell of the soup before taking a sip from her spoon. "This is delicious."

The two ate in silence until Isaac removed their bowls and laid out the second course. There was a platter of roasted chicken, a whitefish with a delicate butter sauce and a tray of assorted vegetables. Isaac bowed slightly and then left the room.

"We dine informally tonight." Nathan passed her the platter of chicken. "The servants have the night off."

"That's what Annie said." Madalyn took a small portion of breast meat. "Is that customary?"

"It is if you want privacy." Nathan offered Madalyn the fish, but she waved it aside and took some of the vegetables. "I thought it best so we could discuss our future."

She looked up from her plate. "I need to find my brother. That is the only thing on my mind right now."

"I already have Jackson making enquiries about The Magistrate.

"Has he had any luck?" Madalyn took a bite of her chicken.

"The Magistrate beat us into port by a week."

Madalyn dropped her fork and looked up at Nathan. "That means my brother could be anywhere?"

Nathan nodded and looked down at his plate. "I'm afraid so. Charleston is a large city and they've had a week's head start."

Madalyn narrowed her eyes. "What aren't you telling me?"

"Are you always this suspicious?"

"You won't look me in the eye." Madalyn leaned back in her chair. "How bad is it?"

Nathan cleared his throat. "It seems The Magistrate had problems during her voyage."

The knot tightened in her stomach. "Tell me."

"The ship had an outbreak of Typhus." Nathan's voice was low. "They were carrying a large number of passengers in the hold. Almost half of them died before they reached Charleston."

Madalyn choked back a sob. William was strong, surely he would have survived. He had to be alive. She refused to consider the alternative.

"Do they have a record of those who survived?"

Nathan shook his head. "I doubt they had proper records to begin with. If your brother was taken, he wouldn't have been on their manifest."

"So he's lost?"

Nathan reached over and clasped her hand. "If he is alive, we will find him."

Madalyn blinked back her tears and forced a smile to her lips. "He's strong. He had to survive."

"If he's anything like you, I'm certain of it."

Warmth surged through her. Nathan's confidence and approval gave her renewed faith. No matter how much time it took, she would find out what happened to William.

"So where do we begin our search?"

"Jackson will search the newspaper for advertisements of indentured servant papers for sale. He's also questioning the crew of The Magistrate."

Madalyn sighed. "All this will take time."

"I'm afraid so." Nathan squeezed her hand and then let it go. "We may be married longer than expected."

Madalyn was prevented from answering by Isaac's return to the room. "Cook has prepared a special dessert. May I leave it with you?"

Nathan nodded. "We can fend for ourselves. You go and join the festivities."

Isaac left the room and returned a few minutes later with a white cake decorated with pink flowers. He placed it, along with a couple of plates and a knife, at the end of the table and then left them alone.

"The servants are pleased with my marriage." Nathan's tone was dry. "I didn't realize they thought I was in desperate need of a wife."

"Most men your age are married." Madalyn smiled. "It makes life easier for them."

"You sound like my mother." Nathan shook his head. "Are all women enamoured with wedded bliss?"

"No." Madalyn grimaced. "I'm hardly looking forward to marriage with my cousin."

"That may not be possible now." Nathan sighed and leaned back. "Our marriage and divorce may change his mind."

"Not if my uncle has his way." Madalyn forced a smile to her lips. "Let's talk of more pleasant things. What will your mother think of our predicament?"

"She'd probably think it was fate."

"So she'd want you married no matter the situation?" Madalyn frowned. "That doesn't sound as if she's taking your desires into account."

"She thinks I have a problem making a commitment."

"Is that true?"

Nathan shook his head. "I want love."

"And your mother just wants you to marry?" Madalyn couldn't keep the doubt out of her voice. Her mother wouldn't have forced an unwanted husband on her.

"To marry and move back to England." Nathan reached for the cake. "I have tried to get her to come here, but she refuses."

"You could move to England without marrying. That would keep her happy." Madalyn waved her hand at the room. "You obviously have enough money."

"It will not wipe out the circumstances of my birth." Nathan handed her a piece of cake.

"Once you've settled in an area people will forget your background."

"They always remember."

Madalyn frowned. "Is it that important?"

Nathan looked at her, his blue eyes piercing in their intensity. "I have lived with it my whole life. Whenever I tried to forget, others always threw it back in my face. America is the only place where I am free from stigma."

She took a bite of the cake, savoring its delicious nutty taste. "My uncle hated my mother. He never let me forget that my parents had died and left us alone. It made me detest him."

"So you can understand why I have no desire to return to a place where all I knew was torment."

"It's still hard to leave something you love." Madalyn took another bite of cake. "You at least had your mother's love."

"True, but I have forgotten England. It no longer has a hold on me."

Madalyn shook her head. "That's not true. Every one of your paintings is a reminder of what you left behind."

"That doesn't mean I want to live there."

"Perhaps." Madalyn's eyes narrowed as she noticed the tightening in Nathan's shoulders. "What is there about England that makes you angry?"

"I'm not angry." Nathan sighed and leaned back in his chair. "I've made a life for myself here in Charleston."

"But you've left your family behind."

"They understand." Nathan glanced down at the untouched cake on his plate.

Madalyn frowned. "Surely you could build a business in England?"

Nathan clenched his hands into fists. "I have no wish to discuss this."

Madalyn put her fork down. It was obvious that Nathan harbored resentment toward his birthplace. He might love his mother, but he wasn't prepared to live in England. The pain he'd experienced there went too deep to forget.

She glanced at him, noting the lines of fatigue around his eyes and mouth. While she'd slept, he'd set things in motion to find William. He needed to rest.

"You must be exhausted." Madalyn pushed away from the table. "I'll retire now. Have a good night's rest."

Without a backward glance, she left the room and climbed the stairs. She lingered over the paintings for a few minutes before going to her room. Several lit candles had been left on the night table. She took one and moved it onto the vanity before sitting down.

She reached behind and removed the pins from her hair. She was shaking her hair free when the door opened. It was Nathan. Her heart started to beat faster.

"What are you doing here?" Her voice was a whisper.

Nathan closed the door, the soft click echoing through the silence. With slow, deliberate steps he moved toward her.

"It's customary for a husband to spend his wedding night with his new bride."

Chapter 11

"You can't spend it here." Madalyn pulled her hair behind her neck.

"It's expected." Nathan stood behind her at the vanity.

Her chest tightened as she looked at him in the mirror. For the first time since she'd met him, she realized he was remarkably handsome. Thick black lashes framed his steely blue eyes and added to the air of danger and allure that surrounded him. Her body quivered at his nearness.

She tore her gaze away and picked up her hairbrush. Becoming attracted to Nathan could only mean trouble. She had one purpose in Charleston and she wasn't going to forget it.

"Let me do that." Nathan took the brush from her hand.

"No." Madalyn's voice held a note of panic.

"Afraid?" Nathan drew the brush through her light brown hair once.

A shock of awareness jolted her. Her head tingled from Nathan's touch. How would it feel if he stroked her whole body? A tremor of desire curled deep within her.

Nathan leaned close to her ear. "I need more information about William."

Shivers raced across her skin as Nathan's warm breath tickled her ear. "You could have waited until morning."

"Your room is the only place where we can be private." Nathan eased his fingers through a tangle. "Would you prefer to meet in my room?"

She jerked away, wincing at the sharp pull on her hair. "Ouch." Madalyn rubbed her head.

"Be still. I used to brush my mother's hair when I was a boy." Nathan parted the strands and pulled the brush through.

Within seconds, she was lulled into a state of total relaxation. "She trained you well."

"You have beautiful hair." Nathan's deep voice sent a sensuous shudder through her body. "It was undamaged by our night in the sea."

"What a horrible experience." Madalyn opened her eyes and looked at Nathan in the mirror. "Thank you once again for saving me."

"Unfortunately some crew were lost. Jackson said ten bodies have washed ashore."

Tears prick her eyes. Even though they had threatened and mocked her, she did not wish them dead. Drowning was a horrible end.

"It was the captain's fault." Madalyn's voice quivered.

"I should never have trusted him." Nathan frowned. "Fortunately, I only lost my personal belongings. Many businessmen lost all their cargo."

"What will they do?"

Nathan shrugged. "Some will survive, but others will face bankruptcy."

"You lost your mother's beautiful bed coverings." Her voice was little more than a whisper as she watched for Nathan's reaction in the mirror.

Nathan tilted his head, a grim smile twisting his lips. "My mother will see it for the best."

"Why?"

"She wanted the bed coverings to be a constant reminder of what I'd left behind in England. She was hoping they would convince me to return." Nathan gave a short laugh. "Now I have no choice."

Madalyn frowned. "Why should their loss force your return?"

"She'll insist on replacing them." Nathan shook his head. "And that means giving them to me in person."

"Your mother sounds wonderful." A twinge of envy stabbed Madalyn. "My mother died when I was sixteen."

"I'm sorry." Nathan's voice held a note of compassion.

She forced back her tears. "My father had died years earlier when I was ten. I don't think my mother ever recovered from his death."

Nathan looked at her in the mirror. "How did he die?"

"It was a boating accident." Panic rose in her throat. "He had taken me out on the lake at our home, and the boat capsized. He died saving me."

Nathan paused in his brushing. "That's why you're terrified of water?"

Madalyn nodded. "I keep seeing him struggling to keep me on top of the craft's hull. The last thing he said to me was to be good and help my mother."

"He loved you." Nathan continued to brush her hair.

"And I've tried hard to do what my mother wanted." Madalyn choked back a sob. "That's why I have to find William. It's the one thing she wanted from me."

Madalyn looked down at the vanity. A sense of loss flooded her body. She'd never felt loved by her uncle or her cousin Horace. There was no way she could lose her brother.

Nathan's deep voice interrupted her thoughts. "We need to talk about William. I'm assuming his last name is Montgomery."

"Yes." She sat up. "What do you need to know?"

Nathan cleared his throat. "A description would be a good start."

Madalyn relaxed her shoulders. "He's taller than me, probably almost six feet now. He has dark brown hair, green eyes, and is slightly built."

"How old is he?"

"He's fifteen." Madalyn clenched her hands in her lap. "He's too young to be on his own."

Nathan frowned. "I left home when I was sixteen."

She closed her eyes and tried to calm her breathing. "So you think he'll be safe?"

"It's in the best interest of the men who took him to keep him alive. They'll want their money." Nathan fanned her hair out about her shoulders. "I'll have Jackson look into it."

"Will he have any problems?" She had no idea how large Charleston was.

"If we have no luck with the newspapers, we'll check out the Exchange. A lot of people go through its doors." Nathan put the brush on the vanity. "There's bound to be some trace of him."

Madalyn turned away from the mirror. "I know you think I was crazy to follow him, but I'm his only hope. My uncle would sooner see him dead than help."

Nathan moved to the center of the room. "It may take longer than expected to find him. What if he was moved outside of the city?"

Her stomach dropped. "Is that likely?"

Nathan pushed a hand through his hair. "His contract could have been sold to a plantation."

"How long will it take?"

"Jackson can start his search tomorrow." Nathan turned and looked at her. "We need to make plans in case it takes longer than a couple of days to find him."

She clasped her hands in front of her. "Are you referring to different living arrangements?"

"You needn't worry about being left out on the street. I'll provide you with a generous settlement."

"I don't need your money." Madalyn inhaled. "I have my own."

"Nonsense." Nathan shook his head. "Galer took all your money."

"If there's a way to contact a bank in England I could get funds." Madalyn's tone became apologetic. "My grandmother left me over fifty thousand pounds."

Nathan stared at her and then sighed. "Even more reason to finish this marriage."

"Most men want a wife with a large dowry."

"I have no need of money." Nathan threw his head back and groaned. "The longer we keep up this charade, the harder it will be."

Madalyn bit the bottom of her lip. "What choice do we have?"

Nathan sat on the bed. "I'll have Jackson look into the legality of our marriage, and see what our options are."

An aching emptiness seeped through Madalyn's body at Nathan's rejection. "You can't wait to be rid of me."

Nathan snapped his head up. "You're gently born. Worse, you're an heiress. The last thing you want is a bastard for a husband, no matter how high born his father was."

"I don't want my cousin Horace for a husband either, but I have no choice." She forced back a sob. "My uncle wasn't interested in me before my grandmother left me her money."

"Surely you can find another relative to help you?"

"They're afraid of my uncle." A chill of dread raced up her spine. "No one crosses him."

Nathan rubbed his hand over his eyes. "He won't be pleased to find you've married me. The sooner we end the marriage the better chance we have of him not finding out."

"Then annul it tomorrow."

Nathan shook his head. "Rev. and Mrs. Willet are still in Charleston. It would be best to wait until they're gone."

Madalyn sat beside Nathan. "They can't force us to stay married."

"There'll be hell to pay if Mrs. Willet gets wind of an annulment. She'll not hesitate to ruin both our reputations. We'll wait until they leave Charleston."

"That could be weeks. We might not be able to get it annulled then." She fought back her panic. The longer she stayed with Nathan, the greater her pain would be when she had to leave.

"True." Nathan frowned. "Our other option is divorce."

"Divorce." Madalyn whispered the word. The thought of it was enough to make her cringe. No self-respecting lady would consider it.

"It's not my first option, either." Nathan's jaw was clenched. "Be thankful it is easier to obtain one in America than England."

"What do we do until then?"

"Introduce you to Charleston society." Nathan picked up her hand.

Warmth spread up her arm. "Pretend we are married?"

"We're adults." Nathan weaved his fingers through hers. "There should be some way for us to live together."

Her throat went dry. "Go our separate ways?"

"It's not unusual." Nathan placed a light kiss on her fingers. "We might even become friends."

Madalyn licked her lips. Her stomach tightened with excitement as Nathan's eyes followed her tongue's movement. "Friends trust each other."

"I trust you." The warmth of Nathan's smile tugged at her heart. "Can you trust me?"

"Yes." Her voice was little more than a whisper.

"Shall we seal it with a kiss?"

Nathan's smile widened and her heart lurched. She wanted to feel Nathan's lips against hers. She longed for his kiss.

"You have a beautiful mouth." Nathan's voice was deep and husky as his thumb traced the outline of her lips.

Her head spun. Her mouth went dry. Anticipation throbbed in every nerve of her body. She swayed, moving toward Nathan, drawn to him like a hummingbird to nectar.

Nathan drew near. Madalyn held her breath. A shiver of desire raced through her body, leaving her weak in the knees. His mouth brushed across hers and she closed her eyes, melting into his lips.

He pulled her close, holding her head steady as his lips moved against hers. Nothing in her twenty-two years had prepared her for the onslaught of sensations that poured through her body.

An aching yearning encompassed her. She turned her head to get nearer, and Nathan released her. She fought back a cry as his lips left hers. When she opened her eyelids, she found herself staring deep into Nathan's unblinking eyes.

"More," she whispered.

"This is insanity." Nathan's voice was hoarse.

He looked at her for several seconds before capturing her mouth again. He caressed her lips with his tongue, and then nibbled at them with his teeth. Madalyn gasped at the jolt of sweet pleasure that pierced her.

Nathan plunged his tongue into her mouth. For a brief second she hesitated, unsure, until shivers of delight raced through her body. A soft glide of her tongue against his was rewarded with a groan from Nathan.

She brought her arms up around his neck and twined her body closer. Nathan clasped her tighter, drawing her deeper into his arms, until they fell together upon the bed. Nathan's leg pressed against her body. She savored its weight on her.

A fire sparked within her, its heat increasing with every stroke of Nathan's tongue. Her body pulsed with yearning. She shivered when Nathan moved his hand along her back. Every nerve screamed for more.

Nathan stroked her back and hip, his fingers a light caress that aroused her to a greater pitch. She shivered with need and her body reeled from newly discovered sensations. Reason and time were lost as she let Nathan guide her.

His lips moved down her neck, licking and tasting until she burned with hunger. She spiraled out of control. She moved against Nathan, begging for something just beyond her reach.

He pulled away.

"We need to stop." Nathan's voice shook. "Unless you want to make this a real marriage."

Chapter 12

Nathan held his breath and waited. Madalyn's reaction was not long in coming. Her deep brown eyes widened and then she moved away from him.

"We hardly know each other." Her voice trembled.

"Our bodies would disagree." Nathan smoothed a strand of Madalyn's hair away from her face. "You're a very passionate woman."

Madalyn sat up and straightened the front of her gown. It had become twisted during their embrace. Nathan's body hardened as he let his eyes roam over the fullness of her breasts. She had a body made for love.

"I'm ashamed of my behavior." Madalyn blushed and covered her chest with her arms. "You must think me very forward."

"You have nothing to be embarrassed about." He stood away from the bed. "I kissed you."

Madalyn frowned. "Were you trying to seduce me?"

Nathan sighed. "That wasn't my intention."

"Then why kiss me?"

He raked a hand through his hair. "I couldn't resist."

"So it meant nothing?" Madalyn's voice was hesitant.

"We sealed a pact." Nathan sat on the bed beside her. He was a brute to lead her on. "I can't deny that for a few minutes I forgot our situation, but lust is not a good foundation for a marriage."

"You don't know what I feel." Madalyn looked at him. Her eyes were shining with unshed tears.

"You're too innocent to know the difference between love and lust." Nathan took her hand in his. "If I take you to bed, I want there to be no doubt about what we're doing."

"I know you don't love me." Madalyn sniffed. "I understand we've been forced into a crazy situation. What more is there?"

"If I take you to bed, there will be no undoing our marriage. The vows we took on The Folly will be real and I honor my word."

Nathan watched Madalyn's eyes widen as the meaning of his words sunk in. She was a brave woman. Any man would be proud to call his wife, but he could never love her.

"Do you want the marriage to be real?" Madalyn's voice was low.

"I think it's too early to know what either of us wants." Nathan cleared his throat. "Right now I'm too tired to make any decisions."

She brought her hand to her mouth. "I forgot. You've not slept."

Nathan stood and walked to the door. "I'll have Jackson start his search tomorrow. Goodnight."

When the door was closed behind him, he leaned against it and groaned. He had come so close to throwing caution to the wind and taking what Madalyn had innocently offered him.

His body hardened when he remembered the feel of her in his arms. She was liquid fire. He was still hard with need. The pain was exquisite and he was fighting himself not to go back and finish what the two of them had started. It wouldn't serve, though.

He didn't want to be married without love. Still, the passion Madalyn and him had shared was rare. A part of him hungered to see where it would take them. But he was a man of his word. Once the marriage was consummated, it would be for life. He would never countenance a divorce. Neither he, nor Madalyn, was prepared for that commitment.

He pushed away from the door and walked down the hall to his own room. The servants might wonder at their separate rooms, but he was too tired to care. He had spent the whole day at his business. He wanted to forget everything and go to bed.

Sleep wouldn't come, though. Every time he closed his lids he would see Madalyn's brown eyes glowing back at him. His body hardened with remembered passion and the feel of her lips on his made him long for more. Finally, he sat and punched the pillow into position behind his back.

Madalyn had pushed her way into his life, forcing him to rescue her. Initially, he had done it out of compassion, but now he felt a deep need to protect her. He'd thought there was only one woman in the world that could make him feel that way; his beloved Heloise.

Madalyn was the opposite of Heloise in many ways. Heloise had been quiet and docile. He'd never heard her complain about anything. With a frown, Nathan realized that she'd never expressed an opinion either. Heloise wouldn't have raised her voice, or tried to save her brother.

Nathan closed his eyes and tried to remember what Heloise looked like. It had been almost fifteen years since she'd died and yet his feelings hadn't changed. He still remembered the first day he'd seen her hanging laundry outside. The curve of her neck and the sweet innocence of her eyes had drawn him closer. When she died he'd resigned himself to a life of bachelorhood.

Still, her face eluded him. He didn't even have the memory of holding her. Nathan yawned and pushed the pillow onto the bed. All he saw when he closed his eyes was Madalyn.

Her eyes and lips and taste would haunt him. With a sigh, he tried to focus on Heloise, but she was gone. Madalyn and their kiss was all he could think about. The sooner they annulled the marriage the better. He was only human and he didn't think he would be able to resist the delight of her body for long.

It was Madalyn's plight that stirred him. He needed to find a way to get her brother back. Then he would deal with guarding Madalyn from her uncle. His brain was too foggy with sleep to figure out how he was going to protect her from him.

Madalyn stretched her arms over her head and sighed. Her night had been full of delicious dreams where she'd felt as if she were flying. She felt her lips. They were swollen and tender, but she didn't feel pain. A sense of wonder and discovery filled her. She'd never experienced anything like Nathan's kisses before.

Marriage held unexpected pleasures. It was unfair to keep this a secret. She frowned as she considered kissing other men. Would they make her feel the same way that Nathan had? She doubted it. She trusted and liked Nathan. He was a man worth loving.

Her eyes widened. Had she gone crazy? How could she think about loving a man when her brother's safety should be the only thing on her mind? She forced her mind away from Nathan. Just because he was worthy of love didn't mean she loved him.

"Good day ma'am." Annie's cheerful voice broke into her thoughts.

She sat up in bed and stretched. "Good morning Annie."

"You slept well?" Annie pulled the drapes back from the window.

Madalyn winced at the bright sunlight that flooded the room. "What time is it?"

"It's almost noon." Annie went out the door and came back in with a tray. She set it on the bed in front of her.

There was a cup of hot cocoa, slices of toast and a dish of strawberry preserves. Madalyn's stomach rumbled.

"You shouldn't have to bring my meals to me." She took a sip of the cocoa, savoring the warmth that spread throughout her body. "What will Nathan think?"

"Mr. Nathan has already gone out." Annie pulled a white envelop from her apron pocket. "He left this for you."

She took the note. Her name was written in bold strokes on the front. Inside it read: *I'll be home later to take you to the ball being held for the survivors of the shipwreck. Buy yourself a gown and whatever else you need. Charge it to my account. Nathan.*

"What time did he leave?"

"Mr. Nathan always leaves just after daybreak." Annie opened the wardrobe. "He left instructions for the carriage to be brought round for you."

Madalyn folded the note and put it on the tray. "There's to be a ball tonight."

"At the Exchange." Annie pulled a light green morning dress out of the wardrobe. "It's going to be attended by the very best of Charleston society."

She bit into a piece of toast. "It sounds impressive. Do you know where I can buy a gown?"

"Mr. Nathan has already instructed the coachman." Annie laid the dress over the bottom of the bed. "You'll be the finest dressed woman in Charleston."

A flutter of excitement skipped through her. She'd never been to a large ball before and never had she been considered the finest dressed. Life with Nathan was full of surprises.

When she'd finished breakfast and dressed, it was well past noon. The coachman took her up Market Street, past numerous stores before stopping at a small corner shop. There was a bolt of yellow fabric in the window. Madame Lafitte was printed on a small sign that leaned against the fabric.

Madalyn entered the shop and was immediately greeted by a small, dark-haired woman in her late forties.

"Bonjour Madame." Her voice was soft and lyrical. "How may I help you?"

"I need a gown for this evening." Madalyn looked at the dresses that were displayed throughout the shop. They were beautiful, with a cut that bespoke a designer of worth.

"You're new to Charleston?" Madame spoke with a slight French accent.

"Is it so obvious?"

"I know all the women who come to me."

Madalyn felt her cheeks flush as the dressmaker considered her through narrowed eyes. "My husband sent me here."

The tiny woman clapped her hands and smiled. "You must be Madame Carter."

"How did you know?"

"He sent a message to expect you today." Madame Lafitte winked. "Monsieur Carter's marriage is the talk of Charleston."

Madalyn's stomach tightened and she straightened her shoulders. "I can't understand why?"

Madame Lafitte patted her arm. "There's no need to be offended. Everything Monsieur Carter does interests the ladies of Charleston."

Madalyn relaxed. "I didn't realize."

"He's a man of mystery." Madame led Madalyn into a small room. "No woman can resist that."

Her curiosity was piqued. She hadn't thought of Nathan's past. She knew he was illegitimate, but that wouldn't be something others would discuss. Suddenly, knowing everything about Nathan became an overpowering urge.

"What do they say about him?" She tried to keep her voice casual.

"Ahhh." Madame smiled broadly. "You wish to hear the gossip? No?"

"Yes." Madalyn's voice caught in her throat. "No." Her cheeks reddened and she put her hands to her face.

Madame laughed. "We'll find you a beautiful gown for this evening."

Madalyn nodded. She was desperate to hear about Nathan, but too embarrassed to ask again. It was safer to concentrate on dresses.

Madame led her to a floor length mirror and helped her remove her cloak, and then her dress. She stood in her chemise and drawers as Madame measured her.

"You have a nicely proportioned figure. It'll be a pleasure to dress you." Madame stood back and surveyed her through narrowed eyes. "Betsy, bring in the red satin gown."

Madalyn allowed Madame and Betsy to drop the gown over her shoulders, turning and moving as they requested. The dress was low cut over her bosom and she tugged it up as the two women fastened the back.

"Isn't it too low?"

Madame turned Madalyn to a full-length mirror. "It's perfect."

Madalyn gasped at the effect of the gown. Its dark red color brought out reddish highlights in her brown hair. The gown also provided a starling contrast to her flawless white skin.

"C'est magnifique."

"It's unbelievable." Madalyn spread the folds of the skirt out. "The color is marvellous."

"As is the cut." Madame waved Madalyn's hand away from the bodice. "After tonight, your husband will only have memories of you."

Madalyn's cheeks flushed. "Only beautiful women can do that."

Madame Lafitte made a clucking noise with her tongue. "A pretty face will catch a man's eye, but you need more than that to hold him."

Madame knelt and started turning up the hem of the gown, deftly sewing it with needle and thread. "You have already accomplished more than any other woman."

Madalyn frowned. "What?"

"Many women have thrown their cap at monsieur, but he has ignored all of them. It is said that his heart was broken long ago and that was why he refused to marry, but I think not." Madame motioned for her assistant to take over the sewing.

"I think Monsieur was waiting until he found a lady of breeding and culture." Madame smiled at Madalyn in the mirror. "There is no need to frown. All of Charleston suspects that Monsieur Carter was a noble Englishman before he came to America and you have proved it true."

Madalyn's stomach twisted with guilt. The more she learned about Nathan, the worse she felt about their marriage. The sooner the marriage ended the better.

She took a deep breath. "Marrying me proves nothing."

"Perhaps." Madame shrugged her shoulder. "But Charleston will think as I do once they meet you."

Later that day, when Madalyn stood in front of her own mirror, she remembered Madame Lafitte's words. Speculation about Nathan's background had been very close to the truth. She wondered if the gossip about him suffering a broken heart was also true.

She bit her lip as she tried to imagine what kind of woman could break Nathan Carter's heart. Before last night, she would have sworn that he didn't have a heart, but his kisses gave her pause.

"A penny for your thoughts."

Madalyn jumped at the sound of Nathan's voice. She turned away from the mirror to see him standing at her bedroom door.

Nathan grinned. "I hope your reaction means that you're happy to see me."

"You startled me." Madalyn took a deep breath. "I wasn't expecting you to come in without knocking."

"I thought we had already settled that last night." Nathan shut the door.

"I might have been dressing."

"Annie assured me that you were ready." Nathan leaned against the door. "You look stunning."

Madalyn flushed. There was warmth in his voice and a gleam in his eye that she recognized as admiration. Never had a man looked at her in such a way before. A rush of heat spread through her body.

"Annie insisted on dressing my hair up."

"She knew I had a surprise for you." Nathan reached inside his jacket and pulled out a long thin black velvet box. He walked over to the dressing table.

Madalyn gasped when Nathan opened the box. Inside was a ruby necklace and two matching hair combs. Nathan lifted the necklace and fastened it around her neck. Vibrant stones sparkled within a circlet of gold that surrounded her neck. From this, a spray of larger rubies dropped onto her chest. It was stunning and complimented her gown beautifully.

Madalyn fingers flitted across the necklace. "It's magnificent."

Nathan removed the two combs and placed one on each side of her upturned hair. "They reminded me of you."

"Me?" Her voice was little more than a squeak.

"You're all fire and warmth." Nathan leaned close to her ear. "Passion flickers just below your surface, ready to burst into flames at the slightest provocation."

A shiver of excitement shot through her body. Nathan nibbled at her ear and she quivered in his arms. He tilted her head and captured her lips in a searing kiss. Madalyn lost all sense of time as her body burned with need.

Desire came to life within her, reaching the very depths of her soul. Passion was ignited. A hunger for more sent her into Nathan's arms. She melted against him, the hardness of his body sending tremors to her lower body. A curl of pleasure wrapped itself around Madalyn until she pulsed with need.

"Should we forget the ball?" Nathan's hand held Madalyn against his body, letting her feel the extent of his arousal.

Chapter 13

"Would that be wise?"

Nathan sighed. "We're already causing enough speculation. It wouldn't do to feed the gossip mills with more."

Madalyn wet her lips, shivering at the lingering sensation of pleasure that remained from Nathan's kiss. "You're right of course."

Nathan touched her lips, caressing them lightly with his fingers. "Now you look like a properly loved bride."

"Is that why you kissed me?" She kept her voice light. His rejection hurt, but she refused to dwell on it and spoil the evening.

"No." Nathan released her and walked to the door. He held it open. "We'd best go. It wouldn't do to be late for your presentation to Charleston society."

"Are you certain I need to do this?" Madalyn smoothed the skirt of her gown. "Wouldn't it be easier to annul the marriage, if no one knew about me?"

"They already know. The Willets have made certain of that." Nathan took her arm and led her into the hallway. "Besides, I want to introduce my beautiful wife."

"There's no need to pretend."

Madalyn shook off Nathan's hand, and lifted her gown. She descended the stairs. When they reached the bottom she looked back at him.

"I'm not beautiful."

Nathan raised her hand to his lips. "I say you are."

She pulled her hand away. "That doesn't make it so."

Nathan bowed his head. Isaac held the door open and a footman helped her into the carriage. The drive to the ball was made in silence.

When they reached the Exchange, everything was lit up with candles. The entranceway was decorated with flowers hung from vases on the wall. There was a large banner strung over the balcony. It had the words Victory over Death painted on it. They entered the ballroom and Madalyn stared in awe.

The room was packed. Men and women stood close together, their voices raised in an attempt to be heard above the music. At the far end of the room a small group of musicians was playing a quadrille and quite a number of couples were dancing.

A flicker of excitement mixed with uncertainty settled in her stomach. Madalyn had never been to such a large affair before. She had only attended small hunt balls at the homes of the local gentry. She straightened her shoulders and pushed away any doubts. Tonight, she would enjoy herself and celebrate.

She had lived through a horrendous ordeal and deserved to rejoice with the other survivors. She and Nathan had overcome even greater odds than the rest, arriving on land without a boat. She looked up at Nathan and felt a flutter of joy. His mouth curved into a sensual smile as he squeezed her hand. She relaxed and savored his approval.

Nathan gave their names to the footman and he announced them in a loud booming voice. Silence fell upon the room and a sea of faces turned to them. Nathan took her arm and led her into the ballroom.

Her legs refused to move. So many people watching her threatened to paralyze her. It took several seconds before the buzz of voices returned and people to turn away. She released the breath she'd been holding. Nathan held her steady. They moved forward into the throng.

"Glad to see you survived, Carter," an elderly gentleman with steel gray hair said. "Come see me next week. I have some business I wish to discuss."

"Thank you, Dupuy I will." Nathan shook the gentleman's hand. "May I present my wife?"

Madalyn curtsied, and looked into bright blue eyes that assessed her. A gleam of amusement danced deep within. "It's a pleasure to meet you," she murmured.

Dupuy turned to Nathan and smiled. "Congratulations. I look forward to inviting you both to dinner."

Nathan nodded and then led her toward the dancing. Madalyn glanced back over her shoulder, and flushed when Dupuy winked back at her.

"Who is he?"

Nathan grimaced. "He's a neighbor and a philanderer. Rumor has it that he made his fortune through blackmail. I'm sure he already knows the story of our marriage. You best stay clear of him."

Madalyn shuddered. "Can he hurt us?"

Nathan shrugged. "Only if we let him. Come, let's dance."

Nathan swung her into his arms just as the musicians struck up a waltz. She froze, her feet stumbling as Nathan tried to lead her. She'd never danced this close to a man before.

"Relax," Nathan growled beneath his breath. "You don't want Dupuy believing those rumors."

She bit her lip. "We're getting an annulment as soon as possible."

"Until then, we'll act the happily married couple."

Nathan twirled her around the floor with ease, and soon she found her nervousness leaving. The music and Nathan's arms were soothing. She felt as if she were gliding, her feet no longer touching the ground.

Nathan looked down at her, his eyes hooded, his face expressionless. "You dance wonderfully. Your body moves as if it were part of the music."

She missed a step. "I've never done this before."

Nathan pulled her closer to him. "Then let's enjoy the occasion."

They danced the next two waltzes in silence. She was mesmerized by Nathan's nearness. Her body tingled with awareness and shivers of excitement fluttered across her skin. The world disappeared as they moved across the floor together.

The music ended and Madalyn returned to the present with a start. Nathan was staring down at her. His expression was unfathomable, his eyes a simmering sea of steel blue. Her breath caught in her throat.

"Refreshment?" Nathan's voice was low, sending a quiver of heat through her.

She nodded and allowed him to lead her through the crowd to the refreshment table. He handed her a small glass of champagne, waiting until she had sipped it before drinking his.

"Mr. and Mrs. Carter. You survived." The voice was familiar and Madalyn turned to greet Reverend Willet and his wife.

"No thanks to the Captain." Nathan's voice was calm, but Madalyn felt him stiffen beside her.

Mrs. Willet frowned. "Captain Galer said that he would take care of you."

"He tried to." Nathan took another sip of champagne. "If Madalyn had not been able to fit through the outer door, we would still be on the Folly."

Rev. Willet shook his head. "He assured us that you would be safe."

"Safe at the bottom of the ocean." Nathan gave his empty glass to a footman. "Captain Galer's conduct was despicable."

"He even refused us entry onto his boat." Madalyn's voice shook with remembered terror. "Nathan is the only reason I'm alive."

Nathan shrugged. "We were able to cling to debris and drift to shore."

"How awful." Mrs. Willet patted Madalyn's arm. "You have even more reason to celebrate. We only had to worry about rowing ashore. Mr. Willet was exhausted by the time we saw the lighthouse. Lady Raglan thought we'd never see land again. The exercise did all of us good, though."

"I will share your view when the blisters heal on my hand." Reverend Willet held up his bandaged right hand. "I never knew that a wooden oar could be such a taskmaster."

Mrs. Willet smiled at her husband before turning back to them. "How did you make it into Charleston?"

"We were picked up by some men scavenging for treasure." Nathan shook his head. "It was pure luck."

"It was God's will." Mrs. Willet's eyes softened. "As was your marriage."

Nathan raised one eyebrow. "Perhaps, but I would have preferred not to have been forced."

"There was no choice." Mrs. Willet tapped her husband's arm. "We promised to give the blessing at supper. They're setting up now. Good evening."

Madalyn smiled as she watched them walk away. It felt good to be with people she knew, even if only briefly. Together they'd all survived a harrowing experience. It was truly a reason to celebrate.

"You're happy?"

"Thankful." She looked around the ballroom. "I could almost forgive Captain Galer."

"No." Nathan's reply was a whisper, but there was no mistaking the contempt. "The man is a villain."

"I agree." Madalyn sighed. "I just don't want the evening ruined."

The music started again and Nathan took her arm. "We'll focus on dancing and forget about The Folly."

Madalyn nodded and together, they started to weave their way through the other guests. The crowd had grown to a point where it was impossible not to touch others as they tried to squeeze their way to the dancing. Just as they were in sight of the musicians, an arm reached out and grabbed Madalyn.

"Well my sweets," a voice leered. She recognized the man from the Folly. He had been one of the crew who had bid on her. "All decked out in finery now."

Nathan grabbed the man's hand and pulled it off her. "Touch her again and I'll kill you."

"No cause to get upset," another voice piped in.

Madalyn closed her eyes and shuddered. It was Captain Galer. Nathan pulled her close to his side. She forced herself to look at Galer. She would not let this man, or his crew, ruin her night.

"Roy was just remembering the last time he'd seen the young lady." Galer grinned at the man beside him. "She does do better for dressing."

The men broke out in laughter and Madalyn clenched her hands at her side. Her fingers itched to slap their smug faces, but that would only create a scene and fuel speculation about her. Instead, she lifted her head and glared at them.

"I do not find you amusing."

Captain Galer leaned close to her. "You'd better remember who you're speaking to, sweetie. I knows things about you that would wipe that haughty look from your face."

Nathan grabbed Galer by his shirt, pulling him away from her. "Your behavior is deplorable. Don't think I'll keep quiet about you refusing us entry into your boat. You'll be ruined in this city."

Galer pushed Nathan's hand away. "You're the only one ruined. Taking a whore for a wife."

Nathan's arm shot out with such speed that Madalyn almost missed it when she blinked. Nathan's fist caught Galer on the jaw with a dull thud, and threw the man back against Roy. The two of them landed on the floor.

There was an audible gasp from the people around them. Galer laid sprawled on the floor unconscious as Roy struggled to push the captain off him.

"Take your boss out of here." Nathan's words came out in short spurts, his chest heaving to get air. "This is no place for a spineless coward such as him."

"The captain will want his revenge." Roy stood, his hands balled into fists.

"He's not worth my effort." Nathan straightened his cravat. "Next time he insults me, or my wife, we will meet at dawn."

Madalyn's eyes widened. A duel could be deadly and she had no desire for Nathan to die defending her honor. She pulled on his arm, but he refused to look at her. Instead, he took her elbow and led her to the dance floor.

"You can't fight that man." She hissed between closed teeth. "One of you might die."

"That's the point." Nathan guided her into his arms and began to waltz. "Captain Galer has done enough damage for more than one lifetime."

"But you might die."

Nathan looked down at her, his lips curved in a slight smile. "I thought you'd like that."

She tried to pull her hand out of Nathan's but he held her tight. "I've no wish to see you hurt."

Nathan kept his eyes focused above her head. "It would solve your problem. You wouldn't have to explain a husband to your uncle."

"We have a solution." Her voice shook. "Fighting Galer only brings attention to us."

Nathan sighed. "You're right. I let my anger get the best of me."

Madalyn relaxed and allowed the music to calm her. "Galer is a dangerous man. It's best to forget him."

"Don't underestimate me. I can be dangerous too. I've no patience with men who treat others cruelly." Nathan's voice was harsh. "I have dealt with worse than Galer, and in the end, I'm always successful."

The music stopped and a footman announced that a light supper was now being served. People began to move in the direction of anteroom, where the tables were set up. Nathan took Madalyn's arm and led her off the dance floor. Just as they reached the edge, a man stood in front of them.

"Francois." Nathan clasped the man and hugged him. "You're looking well."

"It has been too long, my friend." Francois smiled and tilted his head toward Madalyn. "Are you not going to introduce me?"

Nathan chuckled. "Francois St. Amand, this is my wife, Madalyn."

Madalyn curtsied and looked up into the green eyes of Mr. St. Amand. They were laughing eyes, with a touch of devilment deep within. He stood a few inches shorter than Nathan and his light blonde hair was a stark contrast to Nathan's dark hair. Madalyn found herself immediately at ease.

"Charleston is all abuzz with the news of your marriage." Francois patted Nathan on the back. "I can understand your haste now that I see your wife."

Madalyn's cheeks redden and she glanced down at the floor. Despite the sincerity of St. Amand's, voice she still couldn't believe men would find her attractive.

"You've done the impossible." Francois' voice held admiration. "I have told Nathan for years that he needed to find a woman and settle down."

A knot of guilt twisted in her stomach. Living a lie was uncomfortable. There were a lot of people in Charleston who would be disappointed, once they ended their marriage. A part of her wished that they were truly married.

"Francois was the first person I met when I arrived in Charleston twenty years ago. We began our first business together."

"We still have that business, although you've branched out further than I."

"I've offered you the same opportunities."

Francois shook his head and leaned toward Madalyn. "I'm not driven like your husband."

"Nonsense." Nathan took her arm and started to walk toward the supper room. Francois followed beside him.

"You're just too comfortable."

"I have more than enough for me and my family."

Nathan tilted his head and nodded. "I'm beginning to realize you're right. A person only needs so much, and family is important."

"Your visit to England has done you good." Francois clasped Nathan's shoulder. "Tell me about it."

"My brother came home from India to claim the title and the family estate, Caldern." Nathan's voice softened, and he smiled at St. Amand. "He left England a few months before I did. We hadn't seen each other in twenty years."

"Did he alter much?"

"He's the same." Nathan stopped walking and turned toward Francois. "He's determined to right my father's wrongs. He offered me an estate near Caldern."

Francois whistled softly. "You're considering moving?"

Nathan shook his head. "My mother is getting older and I miss Caldern, but America accepted me. As much as I miss my family, my life is here."

Madalyn bit her lip. She ached at the loneliness she heard in Nathan's voice. He was a man who deliberately kept separate from his family. She blinked her eyes and looked away. Her eyes scanned the ballroom. There were very few people left, most having gone in for supper. A group of men stood in a corner near the far wall. They were laughing and slapping each other's shoulders.

She froze. The voice of one of the men stilled her heart. She looked back, her eyes hungry for the source. She squinted, until the men's faces became clearer.

Her breath caught in her throat and her heart began to race. She recognized one of the men. It was her ex-fiancé, Bertram.

Chapter 14

The world started to spin. Madalyn took a deep breath as joyful tears filled her eyes. Here was someone she knew and trusted. He might even have news of William.

She rushed over to the group of men. They looked up as she approached. One of them bold enough to hold his quizzing glass to his eye.

"Is there a problem?" The man's eye looked huge behind the glass.

Madalyn ignored him and turned to her ex-fiancé. "Bertram." Her voice was breathless with expectation.

Bertram turned to her and stared. His appearance had changed over the last four years, but his eyes were still the same light green. He was wearing a gold waistcoat embroidered in bright colorful flowers. Instead of a cravat, he wore a loosely tied neck cloth with a large diamond pinned into its knot.

"Yes?" Bertram's voice sounded bored.

Madalyn frowned. "It is I."

"This woman appears to know you," the man with the quizzing glass said. "Perhaps you would like some privacy. These situations can be a bit sticky."

The other men moved away, leaving Madalyn and Bertram alone together. She touched Bertram's arm, but he shook her hand off.

"I don't know what your claim against me is." His lip curled in a sneer. "But this is not the appropriate place to discuss it. You can meet me at my place of business."

The room started to spin again and she put her hand up to her head. "You can't have forgotten. You once swore you loved me."

Bertram flicked a piece of fluff from his coat sleeve. "Are you suggesting we had an intimate relationship?"

Her cheeks reddened at his tone. She lifted her head. "You asked me to marry you once."

Bertram threw back his head and laughed. "Now I know you're lying. I would never dream of getting hitched."

"Four years ago," she said through clenched teeth. "In England."

Bertram frowned, his eyes narrowed and his head tilted. "England?"

"In my Uncle Phillip's garden."

Bertram took a step backward, his eyes widening. "What are you doing here?"

"Looking for William." she clasped her hands in front of her. "He was kidnapped and brought to Charleston."

"You followed him?" Bertram's voice was now little more than a whisper. "Are you crazy?"

"The thought did cross my mind a few times." Madalyn choked back the tears that threatened to overcome her. She knew that Bertram had moved on, but she hadn't expected him to completely forget her.

"I hope you don't expect me to help you?"

Madalyn shook her head. "I wouldn't dream of it."

"Good." Bertram straightened his jacket. "I don't consider us engaged either."

"I'm not stupid, Bertram." Madalyn straightened her shoulders. "I knew you weren't serious when you didn't write."

"Then why bring it up?"

"I suppose I wanted to know if you had any honor." Madalyn shook her head. "I also wondered if you were having difficulties making your fortune."

"Well you can see I'm not." Bertram leaned close. "You can forget about me giving you any money."

"I don't need your money."

"Good." Bertram nodded his head. "There is nothing between us."

She blinked back her tears. What a fool she'd been to ever consider him as a husband. The man was weak. She bit her lip and took a step back from Bertram. She was about to turn away when a voice stopped her.

"Is there a problem here?"

Madalyn turned and looked up at Nathan. His face was expressionless, but a nerve twitched in his jaw. She touched his arm and swallowed past the lump in her throat.

"I was just leaving."

"Mr. Carter." Bertram smiled broadly. "We have not met." He held out his hand. "Bertram Harden."

Nathan ignored the outstretched hand and tilted his head. "I see you and Madalyn know each other."

"We were neighbours in England." Bertram winked at Nathan. "We were great friends at one time."

"I thought you were more than friends." Nathan took her hand and placed it on his arm.

"Only friends." Bertram cleared his throat. "Lady Madalyn lived in the same village where I grew up."

"Lady Madalyn? I had no idea." Nathan's tone was cold and her stomach clenched into a knot.

"We should go into supper." Madalyn tried to turn Nathan away.

"I'm interested in Mr. Harden's recollections." Nathan's eyes narrowed as he continued to stare at Bertram.

"Her father was an Earl. Of course, the title and estate passed to her brother when he died." Bertram tugged at his neck cloth. "I forgot that courtesy titles are seldom used in America."

"Quite so." Nathan turned to her. "Ready?"

She nodded and let out the breath she'd been holding. She sensed Nathan's anger. The sooner they left Bertram, the better. She hadn't been completely truthful about her family, but that wasn't a reason for him to be upset. She'd explain everything once the ball was over. The last thing she wanted was another scene tonight.

Bertram held out his hand. "Perhaps I could meet you to discuss business?" Bertram's voice was hesitant.

Nathan looked down at the hand and shook his head. "We'd have nothing to talk about."

Nathan turned and led her away. She glanced back over her shoulder, and saw Bertram scowling back at them. Pure hatred glared out from his eyes. A shiver of fear ran through her.

"He's angry," she whispered to Nathan.

"Does that matter?" Nathan stopped at the entrance to the supper room. "The man has no honor, but at least I know who and what he is."

"I'm sorry I didn't tell you everything about my family." Her voice shook.

"We will discuss this later." Nathan led her to a table where Francois St. Amand was already seated."

She allowed Nathan to bring her a plate with some cheeses and small biscuits. She didn't think she would be able to eat, but Nathan insisted. After the first bite, she found herself enjoying the repast.

After supper, the musicians struck up again. This time Madalyn found herself partnered with Francois. He was a wonderful dancer.

"You are perfect for Nathan." St. Amand said after a couple of minutes of silence.

Surprise made her look up at him. "Aren't you concerned about the circumstances of our marriage?"

"I was pleased when I heard the news." St. Amand twirled her away from another couple. "If he'd thought about it too long, he'd never have married."

"But how can you know that Nathan and I will suit?"

"Nathan has always been protective of people, especially women. With you, it is more than that." Francois smiled down at her. "You make him nervous."

Madalyn nearly missed a step. "How can that be good?"

"He is very aware of you." Francois lowered his voice. "The second you left his side his eyes followed you."

Madalyn's back stiffened. "Perhaps he doesn't trust me."

Francois shook his head. "Nathan would simply ignore you if that were the case. He's not possessive. You're attracted to him also."

Francois' words brought her to a standstill. He nudged her back into the dance. "Surely that isn't a surprise?"

"I owe him my life." Madalyn shook her head. "I'm grateful and I consider him a friend. There is nothing else to it."

Francois grinned. "Life is full of surprises. You two are a perfect match."

"We hardly know each other."

"What does a man and a woman need to know when they're together?" Francois shrugged his shoulders. "It's about chemistry and a spark of recognition."

She glanced over to where Nathan was standing. He was talking with an older gentleman, but he looked up, his eyes colliding with hers. A shiver of awareness raced up her spine. Nathan smiled, before turning back to his companion.

"Need I say more?" Francois' voice was full of satisfaction.

The music stopped and Francois led her off the floor. Nathan met them just as another waltz was beginning.

"My turn," he said as he took her arm.

They danced in silence. Madalyn was grateful because her thoughts were too confused for conversation. She couldn't shake Francois' comments. It couldn't be true, yet a small doubt niggled at the back of her mind. The kisses they had shared were still vivid in her memory.

"You're very quiet." Nathan's deep voice interrupted as the dance ended.

She rubbed her temple. "My head aches."

"We'll leave."

"You don't have to go. You're enjoying yourself."

"We have things to discuss." Nathan guided her toward the door.

Madalyn sighed. "Could it not wait until morning?"

Nathan looked down at her. "You've had a shock. Perhaps you are right."

The trip home was quick. When they reached the house, Nathan let Madalyn go upstairs alone. Numbly, she let Annie undress her, but she asked her to leave, once her nightgown was on.

When Madalyn was alone, she sat at the vanity and started to pull the brush through her hair. Gone was the woman of glamour and in her place was the face she was familiar with. The drab, lonely woman she'd always been. She was a woman who men rejected. Bertram hadn't even remembered her. Horace was marrying her for money. Nathan was kind, but he did it out of a sense of duty.

Tears began to spill from her eyes. At first it was only a few, but within seconds it was a downpour. She dropped her face into her hands and sobbed. Her chest heaved with the effort and she gulped for air. She had no idea how long she cried, but when her tears began to ease she felt cleansed.

She hiccupped and took a deep breath before raising her head. When she looked into the mirror, Nathan was standing behind her. Intuitively, she'd known he would come to her this evening.

"You didn't hear my knock." Nathan touched her shoulder. "Do you feel better?"

She nodded numbly and pulled a drawer out from the vanity. She started to rifle through its contents, but stopped when Nathan handed her a handkerchief. She took the cloth and wiped her eyes.

"I look a mess," she said with a sniff. "Why are you here?"

"I thought you might need to talk before sleeping." Nathan grimaced. "When you didn't answer, I was worried."

"You don't need to stay." She blew her nose in Nathan's hankie. "I'll be fine now."

Nathan nodded, but instead of leaving, he picked up the brush that she had thrown on the vanity. "Bertram Harden is not worth your tears."

"That's not why I am crying." She closed her eyes, forcing fresh tears back.

Madalyn leaned her head forward and allowed Nathan to pull the brush through her hair. His gentle strokes eased the ache in her head. Her troubles evaporated as she concentrated on the tingling sensation he was creating throughout her body.

"I expected you to berate me for invading your privacy," Nathan said after a few minutes of silence.

"What would be the point?" She sighed and opened her eyes. "You would still come in."

Nathan grinned. "You've learned."

"At least I did one thing right tonight." Madalyn pulled away and stood.

"You're too hard on yourself." Nathan leaned back against the vanity.

She shook her head. "I'm constantly making poor decisions."

Nathan crossed his arms and frowned. "You've had the courage to trust people. There's nothing foolish about that."

She walked over to the window and pulled the curtain back. "He did not even know me." She dropped the curtain and turned back to Nathan. "I know it was finished years ago, but how could I have ever promised him my love?"

"He's an idiot."

Nathan walked to her and gathered her in his arms. Madalyn gulped back a sob and relaxed into the warmth of his body. She leaned her head on his shoulder, and closed her eyes. They stood together for several minutes, before Nathan eased her toward the bed.

"Get some sleep." He pulled the covers down. "We'll talk about what happened in the morning."

She sat on the bed. "I should have told you my brother was the Earl of Fenton. I didn't think it would make a difference, though."

Nathan eased her back against the pillows and tucked the sheets around her. "It doesn't. It just helps me understand the reason for the kidnapping."

"Are you saying it wasn't random?" Madalyn shuddered. "That's too horrible to consider."

Nathan sat on the bed. "I'll need more information about your uncle."

"You think Uncle Phillip is to blame?" Madalyn sat up. "He wouldn't dare. Besides, he can only inherit the estate and title, if William is dead."

Nathan shrugged. "Selling him into servitude might accomplish that."

She leaned forward and touched Nathan's hand. "Tell me there is hope. I need to know that at least my decision to follow William wasn't wrong."

Nathan picked up her hand and kissed it. "You're a strong woman. We'll find your brother."

Madalyn looked into Nathan's eyes, and caught her breath. She felt as if she were drowning in a sea of blue. For the first time, she didn't fight it. She wanted to be lost in those eyes and never surface again. Perhaps Francois was right. It didn't matter how long two people knew each other. All that was important was that they had a connection.

She leaned forward and kissed Nathan. She didn't think about what she was doing. She let herself feel her need and took the risk. The sudden surge of pleasure that racked her body was more than enough reward.

Nathan didn't resist. Instead, he held her close and began to ravish her mouth with his tongue. The sparks flared between them and in seconds they were both on fire with desire.

Chapter 15

Nathan ran his hands down the length of her nightgown and Madalyn trembled at the sensations of pleasure that raced through her body. When he reached the bottom, he lifted the material and touched her leg. She jumped in shock.

"Easy." He soothed before nibbling at her lips until her body relaxed. Nathan's arm pulled her closer to him and he captured her mouth again.

She held nothing back, matching Nathan's hunger with her own. She fell headfirst into passion as the world spiraled out of control. Every touch of his hands, every movement of his tongue, pushed her to heights she'd never known before.

Nathan's mouth left hers and she moaned in protest until she felt his lips on her neck. She arched her head, giving him greater access. His lips moved lower until he reached the opening of her nightgown.

Nathan's fingers shook as he fumbled with the ribbon holding her gown together. "Damn."

"What." She struggled to see what the problem was.

"It's knotted."

"Rip it."

Nathan tore the ribbon with one forceful pull. Within seconds, his mouth had left her neck and reached her breasts. Nathan's tongue flicked against one of her nipples and she cried out at the sudden jolt of ecstasy that shot through her body.

"Did I hurt you?" Nathan's voice was hoarse, his breathing ragged as he looked up at her.

She shook her head. "I've never felt anything so intense before."

Nathan captured her nipple again, stroking it with his tongue, until it was a hard peak. Waves of pleasure rippled throughout her. A swirling sensation of tension built deep within her womb.

"I'm on fire." Her words came out between moans of delight.

Nathan grinned and captured her mouth again. She wrapped her arms around him, and held him close, allowing her senses to carry her away. Nathan continued to kiss her, his tongue plunging deep within her mouth.

Minutes later, Madalyn pulled away, gasping for breath. She stared at him through half-closed eyes, noting every detail of his face. There was no reason for her not to give herself to him. It was what she wanted.

She caressed his jaw, delighting in its slightly rough texture. "I never realized that marriage held such delights."

Nathan groaned. "I should never have let this happen."

"I kissed you." Madalyn moved to capture Nathan's lips again, but he pushed away.

Nathan sat up on the edge of the bed. "I didn't come here to seduce you."

"What if I want to be seduced?"

"You don't know what you are saying." Nathan dropped his head in his hands. "You're vulnerable right now."

"For the first time in my life, I know what I want."

"This isn't right." Nathan raked his hands through his hair. "You're letting yourself be carried away by new sensations. Tomorrow, you'll be angry that I made love to you."

Madalyn pushed herself onto her knees and leaned against him. "I won't regret it."

Nathan pulled away and stood. "You haven't thought about the repercussions if we consummate our marriage."

"You don't want me." Her voice was devoid of emotion.

Humiliation and disappointment warred inside of her. She sat back on her feet. She'd actually thought their desire had been mutual. What a fool she was.

"Of course I do." Nathan's voice rose. "There's a difference between lust and love, though."

She swallowed and blinked back her tears. "I understand." Her voice was stilted. "I'm not beautiful enough."

Nathan grabbed her shoulders and gave a gentle shake. "Don't say that again. I want to spend the night with you, but it would be wrong."

She reached up and pulled him closer. "This cannot be wrong."

Nathan pulled her hands away and walked to the window. "You'll think differently in the morning. You were born into the nobility. I'm a bastard and not fit to be your husband."

Madalyn sniffed and wiped the tears from her cheek. "I should have expected this. No man really wants me. Bertram asked me to marry him and then forgets who I am."

Nathan had started to pace near the window, but at her words he stopped and turned to her. "The man is a scoundrel. No man of breeding would associate with him."

She looked up at the harshness of Nathan's voice. "What do you know about him?" she asked, her tears forgotten.

Nathan threw back his head and exhaled loudly. "I should not have spoken."

She leaned forward. "Tell me."

Nathan groaned. "He's a gambler and a drinker. It has even been suggested that he tricks people out of their money, but that's not proven."

Madalyn dropped back onto the bed. "All men drink and gamble."

Nathan snorted. "I can see you have a high opinion of men."

She started to braid her hair. "They've done nothing to make me think differently."

"Point taken." Nathan sat on the bed beside her. "Let me do that."

Madalyn allowed Nathan to braid her hair, but when he was done, she scrambled to the head of the bed. "What else has he done?"

"Isn't that enough?"

She stared at Nathan with unblinking eyes. "There has to be more for you to condemn him. I want to know what he's accused of."

"Bounty hunting and slavery."

Nathan's words hung in the silence for several seconds. She leaned back against the pillows and took a deep breath. She'd heard whispers of slavery in England, but hadn't thought much about it.

"Are you certain about the slaves?"

"He sells them outside the Exchange with all the other dealers."

"How can this be allowed?"

Nathan shook his head. "It's legal. Most whites own slaves."

"Do you?"

"No." Nathan heaved a sigh. "There's not much difference between being forced to work for a master, or earning a pittance working for the lord of the manor. My mother had no defense against my father when he took a fancy to her. I would never condone it."

Madalyn bit her lip. "You think Bertram is somehow involved in selling slaves."

"I know it."

"Would he also sell indentured servant papers?"

"It's possible." Nathan tried to hold her hand, but she pulled away. "I can ask Jackson to check him out."

Madalyn closed her eyes and tried to remember the boy Bertram had been, but nothing happened. Everything was too confusing and right now the only thing that she could think about was sleep. Too much had happened this evening for her to work out this problem.

"Leave," she whispered. "I'm too tired to think right now."

Nathan stood. "I'll go, but we will talk tomorrow."

Madalyn moved the bedcovers back and climbed under them. The linen felt cool and she closed her eyes. The sound of the bedroom door closing registered, and she yawned. Within seconds, she was fast asleep.

She woke the next morning with the memory of the fire of Nathan's kisses. The feel of his lips still lingered on hers. If only he hadn't stopped. With a moan, she sat up in bed when Annie entered the room and stretched her arms above her.

"Morning, mistress." Annie opened the drapes, flooding the room with golden sunlight.

"Has Nathan been down for breakfast?"

"Mr. Carter left the house hours ago." Annie set a tray of hot cocoa and biscuits with jam on the bed.

"Tsk tsk," she said, reaching out to Madalyn's gown. "How did this happen?"

Madalyn looked down at the ripped fabric. Memories of Nathan's hands on her body came flooding back. Her cheeks flared with heat.

"We'll leave your gown untied tonight." Annie gave her a broad wink. "These ribbons can be too delicate for a man's hand."

Madalyn took a sip of cocoa and almost choked. "Can I ask you a question?" Madalyn put her cup of cocoa back on the tray.

Annie turned away from the wardrobe. "Of course."

"Are you a slave?" she blurted the question out before she could think of a more delicate way of putting it.

Annie's eyes narrowed and she crossed her arms. "Why would a nice lady like you want to know that?"

"I didn't mean to offend you." Madalyn shook her head. "We don't have slaves in England."

Annie's lips twisted into a slight smile. "That would explain Mr. Carter's actions."

"He said that he doesn't believe in owning people." Madalyn felt her face redden.

"Mr. Nathan is a kind man." Annie pulled a rose colored day dress from the wardrobe. "When I came to him, he paid for my freedom."

It took Madalyn a few seconds to understand what Annie meant. "So he bought you first?"

"Yes ma'am." Annie laid the gown over the bottom of the bed. "Then he bought my family's freedom. Ain't no man better than Mr. Nathan."

Annie went to the bedroom door. "Ring when you've finished your breakfast."

Madalyn finished eating and pushed the tray away. Nathan hadn't lied about owning slaves. That meant he'd probably been telling the truth about Bertram. It was hard to believe, though. Bertram belonged to one of the oldest and most respected families in the county. There had never even been a hint of scandal surrounding him.

There was only one thing to do.

She was going to the Exchange.

She couldn't believe that Bertram was a blackguard, until she saw for herself. She rang the bell for Annie. Once she was dressed, she asked for a carriage to be sent around.

The day was sunny. She enjoyed the view of Charleston from the open barouche. George, the coachman took her down Battery Street and along the harbor until the Exchange came in sight. They stopped at the front steps.

"Will you need Tom to accompany you?" George asked as he helped her from the barouche. "The boy can carry parcels."

Tom was sitting on the edge of the driver seat, grinning down at her. He was probably no more than ten years old, but Madalyn couldn't resist his silent plea.

"I'd be honored if Tom came with me." She stepped away from the barouche and waited for the boy to jump down. After getting assurances that the carriage would be waiting for her, she and Tom started toward the Exchange.

"I've never been to the Customs House before." Tom said as he skipped beside her.

"I was here last night for the ball, but we're not going inside today."

"There's not much else here." Tom's voice held a hint of disappointment. "Isaac says that nothing good comes from outside the Exchange."

"Isaac is probably right, but there's someone I must see."

She walked along the outside of the building, pushing past businessmen and sailors alike. Everyone was eager to get inside the Exchange, where they would be allowed to bring their goods in or out of Charleston harbor.

When she turned the corner of the front of the building, she saw a number of men gathered. They were talking and pointing over to the far side. She glanced over and saw Bertram. Her heart beat furiously as she watched Harden talk to one of the men that had been at the ball last night. The two of them seemed to be arguing. Bertram's arms were raised.

She took a deep breath and picked up the skirt of her dress. Water from the storm still gathered in puddles. She threw back her shoulders and marched toward Bertram. The other men seemed surprised to see her, moving out of her way as she approached. When she reached his side, his companion stopped speaking and stared at her.

"Well, it's the little lady from last night." He winked at Bertram. "It's mighty brave of you to come here alone."

Madalyn looked for Tom, but he'd disappeared. She looked back at Bertram. Behind him there were three black men, their legs and hands were in chains, their upper bodies bare, their eyes lowered.

Her chest tightened. Revulsion and disgust overwhelmed her. Memories of her own captivity flooded her mind and she fought back her nausea. If Nathan hadn't stepped in and saved her, where would she be now? She shuddered.

"Women don't come here." Bertram spit on the ground. "Unless you're looking for a black stud to keep you warm at night."

Madalyn's hand shot out and before she could stop herself, she'd slapped Bertram across the face. The sound of it resounded in the air.

Bertram grabbed her hand, pulling her close to him. "You will pay for that," he growled.

Chapter 16

"You're despicable." She twisted her arm free.

Bertram rubbed his cheek. "No real lady would be seen here."

"What about you?"

"Business."

"Does that include selling slaves?" Her voice rose.

Bertram waved his hand around him. "That's the only reason any of us are here."

"How could you sink so low?" She clenched her hands into fists.

"We're providing a necessary service," Bertram's companion said in a conciliatory tone.

"Stay out of this Frank." Bertram growled. "Lady Madalyn needs to learn about life."

"This isn't life." Her voice shook. "You're denying these men their freedom. You're little better than a murderer."

Bertram threw his head back and laughed. "I didn't know you were so dramatic."

"What about indentured servant papers?"

Bertram's eyes narrowed. "What would you know about those?"

"I know my brother William was kidnapped and brought here." Madalyn struggled to control her anger. "Do you know anything about it?"

"If I did, I wouldn't tell you." Bertram crossed his arms. "If I can make money selling something, whether it's papers or people, I will."

Madalyn took a step back. This man was a stranger. How could she ever have believed he was someone decent and honorable? Had he always been cold and calculating, or had something happened to make him this way?

"Don't tell me you're at a loss for words?" Bertram winked at Frank. "I wonder what you'd think if I told you about good old Uncle Phillip."

"What about him?"

"Your uncle is the reason I'm here." Bertram motioned to the men in chains behind him. "He set me up in business in exchange for a cut of the profits."

"No." She shook her head and backed away. "You're lying."

"Slavery financed your fine lifestyle." Bertram sneered."

"My father wouldn't have allowed it."

"Your father's dead. Good old Uncle Phillip made his fortune transporting slaves." Bertram pointed at the harbor. "One of his ships is being unloaded as we speak."

Madalyn looked at the wharves, but all she saw were crates being moved. "There are no slaves on those ships."

Bertram shrugged. "Maybe not today, but that's how all the rich made their money in the beginning."

She shut her eyes and thought about her uncle. He was strict and insistent that she be respectable. He attended church every Sunday. There had never been a breath of scandal associated with him.

"Not so bold now," Bertram taunted.

She took a deep breath. "There are other ways to make money."

"This is the quickest and the easiest." Bertram walked over to the men in chains. "These fine specimens will bring in more money than I could make as a clerk in a bank."

"Let them go," she pleaded. "You can make a fresh start."

Bertram walked back to her, his eyes narrowed and finger pointing at her. "This is my fresh start. I came to America to make my fortune and nothing is going to stop me."

Madalyn moved back a step as Bertram leaned close to her. "What would your family think?"

"Who cares about them?" Bertram stabbed her with his finger. "They sent me away. They said I was no good. Well, I'll prove them wrong."

"This only proves them right."

"What do you know about right and wrong?" Bertram grabbed her arm. "Your whole life has been sheltered."

Madalyn gasped and tried to pull away from him. "If you despise me, why did you ask me to marry you?"

"I wanted a safeguard against your uncle." Bertram's face was close enough she could feel the spittle from his words. "Something I could threaten him with, if he backed out of our agreement."

Revulsion and horror filled her. She turned her head away. "Let me go."

Frank cleared his throat. "Bertram you've had your fun. Let the lady go."

"The fun is just beginning. Lady Madalyn might prove useful." Bertram ran a finger down her cheek and Madalyn shivered with revulsion.

"Her reputation is in shreds." Bertram leered back at his friend. "Her uncle will pay to have someone marry her."

"I am afraid I can't allow it."

Madalyn jumped at the sound of Nathan's voice behind them. Bertram's grip slackened and she pulled free. Relief surged through her body and she ran to Nathan's side.

"Why are you here?" Bertram's tone was full of loathing. "I thought you were too good to come near the slave auctions."

"I deplore what you do." Nathan's tone was cold.

"Then leave." Bertram made a move to grab Madalyn, but Nathan stood in front of her, blocking Bertram's way.

"This is a discussion between two old friends." Bertram motioned to his friend. "Right, Frank?"

"We meant no harm." Frank's voice wavered.

"You threatened the lady." Nathan took her arm. "We're going."

"What gives you the right to spoil a man's fun?" Bertram's tone was belligerent.

"The right of a husband." Nathan clasped her waist.

Madalyn's head spun. She closed her eyes and leaned against Nathan. He pulled her close to his chest. She could hear his heart beating and that gave her courage. She opened her eyes and looked at Bertram.

"You disgust me." She straightened her shoulders.

Nathan walked around Bertram and led Madalyn through the throng of gawking spectators. When they reached the front of the Exchange, Tom was waiting for them.

"Sorry mistress." He grinned at her. "I knew Mr. Carter would be upset if I lets you walk in there alone, but I couldn't chance it."

"You were right to fetch me." Nathan tousled the youngster's hair.

"Thank you." Madalyn smiled and took a deep breath. "I should have listened to what you told me. I didn't realize that it was such an unpleasant place."

"I've noticed that about you." Nathan motioned to George to have the barouche brought up beside the entranceway to the Exchange.

Madalyn's shock was lessening.

"I'm impulsive."

"Yes." Nathan lifted her into the barouche. "You act without considering the consequences."

Tom jumped up into the seat beside George. They set off at a brisk pace and Madalyn leaned back against the cushioned seat.

"What possessed you to go?" Nathan's voice was a growl. "Ladies are never there unattended."

"I know that now." Madalyn straightened out the skirt of her gown and looked at the harbor. She felt empty. "Bertram was hateful."

"I tried to warn you." Nathan leaned back against the carriage cushions and sighed. "I would have accompanied you."

"I'll ask in future." After a few minutes silence, she turned to Nathan. "Thank you for coming to my rescue."

"You're welcome." Nathan took her hand and raised it to his mouth. "Are you convinced now of Bertram's character?"

"The man is without scruples. He was going to use me to blackmail my uncle."

Nathan whistled softly. "He's more despicable than I thought."

"It's worse. My Uncle Phillip is Bertram's partner." She took a deep breath. "Apparently, my Uncle Phillip made his money by transporting slaves."

Nathan's eyes didn't waver from her face. A muscle tightened in his neck, and his lips were a thin line. Madalyn fought back a wave of nausea.

"You knew," she whispered. "All this time you knew about my uncle."

Nathan shook his head. "No. There was a Phillip Montgomery in the slave trade long before I came to Charleston. I wasn't certain he was your uncle, though."

Madalyn forced herself to look at Nathan, even though every nerve in her body was urging her to run away. She couldn't hide from this, though. She needed to know how deep the lies in her life went.

Nathan frowned. "Didn't you wonder where you're uncle's money came from?"

"No." She sniffed and dug in her reticule for a handkerchief. "It was horrible seeing those men in chains."

Nathan's jaw clenched. "You shouldn't have been exposed to something so sordid."

Madalyn wiped her cheeks and straightened her shoulders. "It wasn't just seeing the men. It was remembering how it felt to be standing in their position."

"Forget it." Nathan's voice spat out tersely. "You're safe now."

"I can't. The humiliation of standing in front of the crew and being auctioned off will stay with me forever. That's why I can't allow Bertram to sell those men."

Nathan stiffened beside her. "There's nothing we can do."

Madalyn touched his arm. "You've helped before."

"I'm not a hero." Nathan looked straight ahead. "I took pity on you."

"I'm not talking about me." Her mouth was dry, but she swallowed back her fear. No matter how daring her request she had to try. "Annie told me how you freed her family."

Nathan turned to look at her. "I can't help this time."

"You mean you won't." A surge of anger rushed through her. "Why are these men different?"

"The law is different." Nathan took her hand in his. "I want to help, but the city of Charleston has tied my hands. I can no longer buy slaves and then, set them free."

"Then we must find another way." It couldn't end here. Now that she'd seen the men, she had to try.

The horror of her experience on The Folly would never leave her. She'd been overwhelmed by fear and helplessness. That had changed her. She was no longer a trusting, naïve girl and she couldn't bear to have another soul suffer that indignity.

"Are you sure this isn't just a desire to hurt Bertram and your uncle?" Nathan's hold on her hand tightened. "I won't be part of that."

Madalyn twisted her hand free. "I can't stand by while those men suffer. It's inhuman."

"The men will be sold at auction tomorrow. There's nothing that we can do legally to free them."

"Then we must break the law."

Chapter 17

"You don't know what you're asking." Nathan clenched his fist and pushed back his frustration. "If you did, you wouldn't suggest I risk it."

"If you won't, then I must." Madalyn straightened her shoulders.

There was no way he was going to let her to risk her life again. She'd narrowly escaped Galer and his men. A prison cell was the last place he wanted her to see. They were horrible filthy places, full of disease and parasites. He had no intention of letting her getting near one.

"I won't countenance such behavior from my wife."

"That's not how you felt last night." She turned to Nathan with a raised eyebrow. "We're not really married, so I can do as I please."

Nathan's shook his head. How could she blame him for last night? He'd saved her from the certain regret she'd have felt in the morning. She was too fine a woman to throw her life away on a man like him. He might have money, but he was still a bastard. He wasn't a fit husband for a woman like Lady Madalyn.

"It's dangerous," Nathan said in a harsh tone.

"Then help me." Her voice was soft.

Nathan leaned back and sighed. "I understand your anger, but there are slaves everywhere in Charleston."

"I'm only asking you to free those men."

"So, it is revenge." Nathan looked at her with unblinking eyes.

Madalyn bit her lip and nodded. "Partly," she began. "But it's also because those men need me now. They're going to suffer exactly what I did. I can't stand by and let that happen."

"The penalty is severe for those who help runaway slaves."

"You can't tell me that you condone what Bertram is doing?"

"Of course not." Nathan covered his eyes with one hand. "It's cruel and unnatural."

Madalyn clasped Nathan's arm. "Then you'll help."

Nathan looked off into the distant harbor, his eyes narrowed, his brow furrowed. She wasn't asking for something that he hadn't done in the past, but the law was different now. He understood the desire to help, but the risk was much higher.

"Have you decided?" Madalyn's voice was a soft plea.

The carriage slowed as the house came in view. The barouche stopped and George handed the reins to Tom. When the carriage door was opened, he jumped down and offered Madalyn his hand. They walked in silence until they had started up the stairs to the porch. "I'll help, but aren't you forgetting we still have to find your brother?"

Madalyn stopped on the porch. "Will helping these men interfere?"

"If we're caught, we won't be able to help William." Nathan watched as the emotions played across her face. She had beautifully expressive features and her indecision was plain to see. He'd wanted her to reconsider the risk they'd take by arranging an escape. He'd rescued others before, but he'd always had a plan in place before going out. He'd never done anything on the spur of the moment like this.

"Has Jackson found him?" Madalyn's voice was hesitant. "Is he near?"

Nathan shook his head. "We've found no trace."

"Then we're not risking his life by helping others." Madalyn pursed her lips. "I think we should do it."

Nathan put his hands on his hips. "You will stay home. I won't risk you getting hurt."

"You might need help."

"I can handle it." Nathan narrowed his eyes. "I won't budge on this."

"What if you need help?"

"I know more about this business than you." Nathan's voice held a hint of steel in it.

Madalyn looked down at her feet. "Are you going to lock me in my room?"

Nathan put a finger under her chin and lifted it until her eyes met his. "I'll accept your promise. I don't want you undermining me on this."

She looked at Nathan with unblinking eyes and nodded her head. "If you insist," she said in a quiet voice.

Nathan looked at her for a few more seconds before letting her chin go. "This is far too treacherous for a woman to be involved in."

She glanced away from him and walked into the house. Nathan sensed her disappointment, but he didn't have time to dwell on it. If he was going to free those men tonight, he had arrangements to make. He turned away from the house and went back to the carriage.

"To the docks."

Nathan spent the rest of the day at his warehouses and speaking with several of his ships' captains. He was preparing to go home for the evening when Francois knocked at his office door.

"I came by to toast your wedding." Francois held up a bottle of brandy.

Nathan grinned and pulled out a chair, before getting two glasses from the shelf near his desk. "I thought we did that last night."

"I congratulated you and your bride. Now I want to talk to my friend."

"You want to know why the rush?" Nathan sat down behind his desk.

Francois poured out two generous portions of the amber liquor and handed Nathan one of the glasses. "I'm curious why you didn't wait until you reached Charleston. I always expected to attend your wedding."

Nathan grinned. "There wasn't time."

Francois raised an eyebrow. "So you're not only a husband, but soon to be a father."

"Sorry to disappoint you, but the reason was the gun I had to my head."

Francois had started to sip his brandy, but started choking at Nathan's words. "Don't tell me she trapped you into marriage with her feminine wiles."

Nathan shook his head, a rush of excitement coursing through his veins at the thought of Madalyn seducing him. He almost wished that it were so, but her lips didn't lie. She'd been innocent of a man's touch before they married.

"We've not consummated the marriage."

Francois leaned forward in his chair, his eyes wide with disbelief. "What are you waiting for? I thought this was a love match."

Suddenly, the burden of keeping the secret of his wedding was too much. He trusted Francois as a brother and he desperately needed someone to talk to.

"As I said, we were forced to marry." Nathan cleared his throat.

Francois threw up his hand. "You better start at the beginning."

"Madalyn had snuck aboard the Folly and when Galer found her, he auctioned her to the crew. I outbid the others." Nathan raked a hand through his hair. "I thought it would be a simple matter of setting her free."

Francois whistled. "Why did you have to marry?"

"Her reputation was at stake as was my honor. Reverend and Mrs. Willet, who were also passengers, insisted. They enlisted Galer's help. He was the one with the gun." Nathan looked at his friend with unblinking eyes. "We planned to annul the marriage or divorce once we reached Charleston."

Francois frowned. "Why was Madalyn aboard the Folly?"

Nathan shut his eyes briefly before continuing. "She was trying to follow her brother, William, who'd been kidnapped. His ship left before she could rescue him, so she took the next one to Charleston."

"That's incredible." Francois's loud voice echoed in the room.

Nathan nodded. "I have Jackson searching for him. He came in on The Magistrate. It arrived a week before The Folly. I suspect he's been indentured if he survived the journey."

Francois shrugged. "The answer is obvious."

"The answer to what?"

"To your problems." Francois tone suggested that Nathan was an idiot. "Find her brother and convince her to love you."

"Why the hell would I want her to love me?" Nathan felt his face fill with heat and he looked away from Francois.

"Because you two are good together and you need a wife."

Nathan felt the muscle in his neck twitch. "You're wrong."

"I watched you dancing last night." Francois chuckled. "There's definitely an attraction. What are you afraid of?"

Nathan frowned. "Have you forgotten your sister?"

Francois sighed. "Heloise is dead. Besides, that was different."

"I loved her." The constant ache in his gut at the loss of Heloise twisted into a stab of sharp pain.

"And she chose another." Francois looked down into his brandy.

"I wasn't in a position to offer marriage." Nathan pushed back the familiar grief.

Francois brought his hand down on the chair arm. "You know nothing about my sister's decision to marry."

"I blame myself for her death." Nathan rubbed his face with his hand. "I was still working on the docks, with barely enough money to feed myself."

"Heloise did not wish to marry you." Francois's voice was harsh.

Nathan felt as if he had been punched in the gut. It took a minute for Francois' words to fully register. Even then he thought he'd heard wrong. "Explain."

"You frightened her." Francois softened his tone. "Everything about you was larger than life, your size, your ambition, and most of all, your passion."

"You're lying." Nathan ground out his words between clenched teeth.

"Think back." Francois's eyes never left Nathan. "Heloise always found a reason to leave the room when you arrived."

"She was shy." Nathan voice shook as the first seeds of doubt took root.

"No." Francois shook his head. "She was avoiding you."

"Why didn't she tell me how she felt?" Nathan balled his hands into fists. "Was I such an ogre that she couldn't speak to me?"

"I tried to convince her to tell you, but she refused." Francois sighed. "She was afraid that the sheer power of your personality would convince her to marry you."

Nathan closed his eyes and tried to breath. He'd blamed himself for Heloise's death because he'd been too poor to marry. When she'd married another and worked herself to death, he'd shouldered the guilt.

Nathan's chest constricted with pain. The truth was worse. His love had driven her into the arms of another man. He was responsible for her death as surely as if he had murdered her.

"Heloise married Jamieson to escape my attentions." Nathan's words were barely audible.

"Heloise loved Jamieson." Francois spoke with conviction. "Our father was dead, so she asked my permission to marry. I tried to dissuade her, but she threatened to run off with him."

"He couldn't even support himself, let alone a wife."

"She was happy." Francois leaned over and gripped Nathan's shoulder. "It might not have been wise, but she wanted him."

"You should have told me this before." Nathan was numb.

"I expected you to find someone else." Francois heaved a sigh. "Forgive me, but I thought it best. I couldn't bear to hurt you anymore than you already were."

Nathan clenched his teeth. He'd been betrayed. He'd carried his guilt for years and now he didn't know how the hell he was supposed to feel. Everything he'd believed had been a lie.

"You have a second chance." Francois sat back. "Madalyn is perfect."

"She's the daughter of an Earl." Nathan forced the words from his mouth. "She deserves someone from her own class."

"You're using the same argument you used about Heloise." Francois gulped down the rest of his brandy.

Nathan frowned. "I don't understand."

Francois put his glass on the desk. "You don't think you're good enough to marry."

"That's ridiculous."

"Is it?" Francois picked up the bottle and refilled his glass. "With Heloise you didn't have enough money. Now you have money, but you're not of the same class."

"It's true."

Francois shook his head. "Everyone in Charleston believes you're from a noble family. The fact that you don't talk about it only makes the suspicions real."

"But it's a lie."

"Your father was a Marquess. Your brother is the Marquess of Caldern. In anybody's book that's upper class."

"I'm still a bastard."

"You were raised a gentleman." Francois raised his glass to his lips. "You're the only one who doesn't believe it."

"So what are you suggesting?"

"Seduce your wife."

Nathan took a sip of his brandy. "I don't love Madalyn."

"What does love have to do with marriage?"

"I always thought it'd be part of my life."

"I've plenty of love in my life." Francois drained his glass and grabbed the brandy bottle again. "Nanette and I have an understanding. We live separate lives except for the children."

"And that makes you happy?" Nathan kept his voice neutral.

"I lost my romantic notions years ago. Now I enjoy myself." Francois filled his glass and took a large gulp.

Nathan shook his head. He'd suspected that something was wrong with Francois' marriage, but they'd never spoken of it. Nanette never came to Charleston. She preferred the simpler life at their plantation. Francois was discreet, yet Nathan had heard the rumors of his numerous mistresses.

"Once I'm married I intend to be faithful."

"You always were an idealist." Francois mocked Nathan with a toast.

Nathan looked at his friend over the rim of his glass. "I couldn't abide becoming my father."

Francois shut his eyes briefly as a shudder ran through him. "I forgot," he said in a low tone. "Forgive me."

"My father was a philandering brute. I have no intention of leaving any bastard children to bear the ignominy of knowing they will never be good enough."

"You've done well despite it."

"The accident of my birth has shut many doors." Nathan grimaced as the fiery liquid burned his throat. "My younger brother inherited Caldern and the title, because he was legitimate. I love him dearly, and would never begrudge him what he has, but it still hurts. I refuse to put a wife or a child of mine through such pain."

Francois cleared his throat. "You can still be married without love."

"True," Nathan conceded. "Madalyn would have to agree to it."

"Give her time." Francois pushed himself out of the chair. "You're rich and can provide a secure life."

"She doesn't need a husband for that." Nathan stood and walked over to his friend. "She has money of her own."

Francois clasped Nathan's shoulder. "Marriage will give her the protection of your name. She'll have more freedom than if she were single."

Nathan pondered Francois's advice long after his friend had left. When Heloise had married, he'd given up the thought of a wife and family. Perhaps that had been foolish, especially after Francois' revelation that Heloise had never loved him. Worse, she'd feared him.

He smiled as an image of Madalyn flashed before him. She was one of the bravest people he knew, chasing after her brother without a thought of her own safety. She'd sacrifice everything for the man she loved. His chest tightened at the thought of earning that love.

Madalyn was perfection.

Seducing her would be a pleasure.

She was well educated, of good family, and passionate. His body hardened at the thought of the kisses they'd shared. He burned with desire every time he saw her. He wasn't going to confuse lust with love, but marriage to someone who was sexually compatible sounded wonderful. Now, all he had to do was convince Madalyn.

Chapter 18

After dinner that evening, Madalyn dismissed Annie and changed into a brown day dress. She threw a black hooded cape over her shoulders and blew out her candles before sneaking downstairs and out of the house.

She hid in the shadows of the side porch and waited for Nathan. He'd be angry if he found out that she was going to follow him, but she had to be certain that the men were freed. Besides, she'd be there in case something went wrong.

Time crept by and just when she despaired of him ever leaving the house, she heard a door creak open. The sound came from behind her and Madalyn pulled her cloak close to her body before tip toeing to the back of the house. The floorboards of the porch squeaked a couple of times. She held her breath as she waited to see if anyone had heard, but nothing happened.

When she rounded the back of the house, she saw the figure of a man dressed in black leaving through the rear gate of the garden. She picked up her gown and tailed him.

Madalyn found herself in the mews, and her heart sank. She hadn't considered that Nathan would take a horse or carriage. She bit her fingernails and stood at the side of the stable. What were her options now? A slight shuffle further down the lane caught her attention. A man was hurrying away on foot. The man's height, and the size and breadth of his shoulders gave him away.

It was Nathan.

He moved fast.

She followed in the shadows. The mews ended when they came to a crossroads. Nathan pulled his head down low in his coat and after a quick glance both ways, ran to the opposite side. She waited until he started to disappear into the far laneway before doing the same.

They had walked at least a mile before they reached Broad Street. Nathan took a sharp turn west. Why were they moving away from the Exchange?

When Nathan paused beside a group of low roofed wooden sheds, the reason became clear. They'd worked their way behind the Exchange. This had to be where Bertram housed the men in readiness for the auction the next day. Nathan tried the handle of one of the buildings.

He stopped, tilted his head in her direction.

Madalyn held her breath. She moved closer to the rough wooden shed that hid her. Seconds passed while the thumping of her heart was loud in her ears. The sound of cicadas and the voices of men on the wharfs filled the night. Finally, Nathan's shoulders relaxed and he turned back to the shed handle.

Madalyn fought back the urge to laugh with relief. For the first time since leaving the house, she'd actually doubted her decision to shadow him. Nathan had warned her it was dangerous, but until this moment, she hadn't considered that they might be caught.

He slipped into the shed and she followed a few minutes later. The door was partly ajar. She squeezed through the opening and scuttled along the edge of the building. Leaning back against the wall, she let her eyes adjust to the darkness.

The shed was no better than a stable, with straw strewn everywhere. There were individual cubicles, but instead of animals being kept in them, there were men; four in total. Madalyn clenched her hands close to her body and forced herself to focus on the faint sound coming from the far side of the shed. It was the clink of metal against metal. Nathan was leaning over one of the men that she'd seen earlier that day.

"Sir, you've been followed."

Nathan looked up. "Come out." His voice was a whisper, but Madalyn recognized the suppressed anger.

She took a deep breath and walked toward him. "Where did you learn to do that?" She forced her voice to remain casual.

Nathan glared at her, his nostrils flaring with his heaving breaths. "What the hell do you think you're doing?"

"Making certain you didn't need help." She raised her chin and stared back at Nathan.

"I specifically told you to leave it to me."

"I couldn't let you take all the risk."

"You've no idea of the danger you've put us in." Nathan turned back to the lock.

"I wasn't followed." Madalyn tone was defensive. "What are you using to open it?"

"Skeleton keys and lock picks," Nathan said through clenched teeth. "Quiet before someone hears us."

She walked to Nathan and stood beside him as he worked at the lock holding the chains that bound the man. Within a few seconds, there was a click and it was open.

The large man rubbed his wrists. "Thank you."

Nathan nodded and then knelt to work on the chains around the man's ankles. That lock opened quicker.

"Stand guard." Nathan motioned the freed man to the opening."

"I know you're angry, but I can help." Madalyn leaned close to Nathan, careful to keep her voice low. "It'll go faster with two of us working."

Nathan pointed to the empty cubicle. "Pack the straw up around the chains to make it look as if a man is sleeping under it."

Madalyn went to the stall and bent down to arrange the straw. Nathan might be angry, but at least he was reasonable. She arranged each stall after Nathan freed the men. When she'd finished the last one, she joined Nathan and the men at the door.

"We must get to the pier." Nathan pointed to the first man freed. "What is your name?"

"Jeremiah."

"You'll be in charge."

"What do we do after we're there?" Jeremiah's voice was hesitant.

Nathan leaned closer to the men. "You must leave Charleston."

Jeremiah and the others nodded.

"I have a ship sailing for Halifax in the morning. I've arranged for you to be hired on as hands."

Madalyn looked at the men and a chill went up her spine. Somehow they must survive once they landed. "What happens in Halifax?"

"We can make a life for ourselves there," Jeremiah said in a low voice. "We be free men there."

"I've instructed my captain to give each of you one hundred pounds when you leave the ship."

"That's very generous, Mister Carter."

"You'll need it." Nathan patted the man on the shoulder. "It won't be easy, but you'll be free."

Madalyn blinked back her tears. She'd insisted that Nathan help, but she'd no idea how complicated it would be. She could never have done this on her own.

"I'd heard rumors that you were a good man," Jeremiah whispered. "Even that you might be one of the men behind Denmark Vessey's revolt two years ago."

Nathan looked down. "A lot of people supported Vessey's slave revolt. Not all whites want slavery and many were jailed because of their beliefs."

"Yes sir." Jeremiah's voice quivered. "Thank you. We'll never forget you."

"Don't thank me." Nathan tilted his head toward Madalyn. "My wife is the one who insisted on freeing you tonight."

Madalyn felt her cheeks flush when Jeremiah and the other men looked at her and murmured their thanks. For the first time, she realized the enormity of their actions. Four men would have a chance to live as they chose.

"We must get moving." Nathan opened the door a crack and looked outside. "Captain Randal is waiting. He'll hide you until the ship is at sea. Then you'll take your place as part of the crew."

Nathan took Madalyn's arm. "You stay close by me."

Together, they left the shed and as a group they made their way to the side of the Exchange building. There were still men about on the street and working on the docks. They kept to the shadows and moved to a building that was several hundred feet away from the Exchange.

Nathan motioned for them to be quiet and then he slipped inside. When he returned he had a bundle of clothes in his hands. The men dressed with speed. They pulled their hats low on their faces. It was a perfect disguise.

"You stay here." Nathan took Madalyn's arm and led her inside. "I'll come back as soon as the men are safe."

Nathan pulled a chair forward and pushed her into it. "Don't move until I return."

Madalyn smoothed out her skirt. "Must I stay here?"

Nathan crouched down in front of her. "I need to know you're safe. Promise me you'll stay here. I'll be back in an hour."

Madalyn fought back her urge to follow him. She leaned back in her chair and sighed when he left. Nathan was still angry with her and she couldn't blame him. She'd been of very little help. It was obvious that this wasn't the first time Nathan had helped to free men. He had everything planned, including the change of clothes and a way for them to escape Charleston.

The time moved slowly and it was chilly in the warehouse. After an hour Madalyn couldn't keep her eyes open. She stood and stomped her feet to keep herself awake. Just before she sat down she heard footsteps outside the building. She froze when the door opened.

"You can't even remain sitting on a chair." Nathan's voice echoed in the darkness.

"That's unfair." Madalyn relaxed and rushed to the door. "I was trying to keep awake."

Nathan put his arm around her and led her from the building. "If you'd done what I asked, you would've been warm in your bed."

"I'm sorry." She mumbled her apology into his jacket.

"I could barely hear you." Nathan lifted her head with his finger. "Did you admit that you were wrong?"

"I had to be sure that you'd be safe." Madalyn's voice shook. "If something had happened it would have been my fault."

"How do you think I'd have felt if you'd been hurt?" Nathan's eyes didn't leave her face. "You have to trust that I know what I'm doing."

Madalyn nodded. "Are the men safe?"

"Captain Randal has everything under control." Nathan led them away from the building, keeping to the shadows.

"He didn't mind that there were four instead of three?" Madalyn had to run to keep up with Nathan's pace.

"I had anticipated that." Nathan stopped when they came to the Exchange. "Usually they pack them in tighter."

"How horrid." Madalyn squinted to see in the dark. "Why have we stopped?"

"I asked George to meet me in front of the Exchange. We're early."

"Does he usually pick you up at this hour?"

Nathan nodded. "I frequently work late. The difference tonight is that my wife is accompanying me."

"I already apologized." Madalyn didn't bother to hide her frustration.

"Whisper." Nathan hissed. "We can't be found here."

"Well, then you have a problem," a familiar voice rang out in the darkness.

Madalyn's breath caught in her throat and her stomach clenched in fear. Even before he moved out of the darkness, she recognized the speaker. It was Captain Galer.

Chapter 19

Madalyn's heart skipped a beat when five more men stepped in front of them. Nathan pulled her behind him, using his body as a shield.

"Well it seems the newly married couple is already arguing men." Galer spit on the ground. "Perhaps Mr. Carter needs a lesson in how to treat a woman."

"It is none of your concern." Nathan's tone was icy.

"But it is." Galer snickered. "I introduced you, in a manner of speaking."

"I wouldn't be too vocal about that." Nathan started to move toward the street, but one of Galer's men blocked his exit.

"It's impolite to go without a 'by your leave'."

"And him making out to be a gentleman," another one of Galer's men said as he circled Nathan and Madalyn from the left. "I suppose you can't believe what people tell you about themselves."

"That's right Jock." Galer motioned for his men to spread out. "You can't be too careful. Take the little wife. She looks a proper lady, but we all know that's not true."

"Let us pass." Nathan's voice was quiet, almost calm, but Madalyn could feel the tension in his body.

"No." Galer's voice was harsh. "We've a score to settle."

"This is neither the time, nor the place."

"It's perfect for me." Galer spread his arms out wide. "No one here but us."

"You and your men." Nathan's voice oozed sarcasm. "I hardly call that fair."

"Who said anything about fair?" Galer slapped his thigh and laughed. "I intend to win."

Madalyn gasped and pulled herself tighter against Nathan. Galer's voice was full of hatred. If she hadn't followed Nathan, he would never have been caught behind the warehouse. Once again, her impulsiveness was to blame.

"Six against one?" Nathan raised an eyebrow. "You're a coward."

"Coward?" Galer's voice rose in anger. "I'm a survivor. I do what it takes to keep alive."

"Let us go." Madalyn's voice was shaking, but she had to speak out. "We've done nothing."

"Did you hear that men? The lady thinks we should let them go." Galer moved closer to Nathan. "Maybe I should enlighten her?"

"Keep her out of it."

"The way I see it, she's the problem." Galer paced between his men. "If she hadn't come aboard my ship, there'd have been no auction. No reason for Mr. Carter to interfere."

"Your own actions condemned you Galer." Nathan's eyes narrowed. "She paid you her fare. You refused to let her board. She had a right to be on The Folly."

"It was my ship." Galer punctuated each word with a jab of his finger. "I was the one in charge. My word was law."

Nathan shrugged his shoulders. "I didn't break any of your laws. You held an auction and I outbid everyone."

"You deliberately turned the tables on me."

Galer was screaming. Madalyn looked at the street to see if anyone had heard, but it was empty. She began to pray that George and the coach would appear soon.

"You were paid in full."

"What does that matter?"

Galer took a quick poke at Nathan with his hand and hit him in the chest. Nathan stood firm. Madalyn tried to move from behind Nathan, but his grip on her was strong. His body shielded her from Galer.

"The only thing that matters is my getting my ship back."

"That's impossible." Nathan tilted his head toward the water. "She's at the bottom of the ocean."

"You were bad luck from the beginning." Galer moved within inches of Nathan's face. "You turned your nose up at every order I gave; like you knew better than me. I should have thrown you both overboard."

Madalyn gagged at the strong odor of whiskey that emanated from Galer. She put a hand over her nose. The man smelled as if he had been seeped in liquor for days. No wonder he'd lost all sense of reasoning.

"Go home and sleep it off," Madalyn said.

"Home?" Galer spit the word out as if it were poison. "What home? Your fine husband has made sure that I have nothing left in this world."

She looked up at Nathan, but his tightened jaw and tense shoulders gave nothing away. She tugged on his arm, but he ignored her. His focus did not waver from Galer.

"Your ineptitude is the reason your ship is gone." Nathan enunciated each word slowly. "Look to yourself for your woes."

"What about getting another ship?" Galer swung his arms in the direction of the harbor. "You've made certain that won't happen."

"You cannot expect me to let you captain one of my ships?" Nathan's voice held a note of disgust. "I wouldn't let you swab the decks."

Galer swayed on his feet. "Mighty tough words for a man surrounded."

"I'm not the only ship owner in Charleston. Ask one of them for a job."

Galer leaned forward, his teeth bared like a dog. "You threatened to blacklist me and that's exactly what you've done."

Nathan shook his head. "I don't have time to waste ruining you."

"You're denying that you've stopped me from getting another ship?"

"I am." Nathan glanced around at the men surrounding them. "Do you really think I'd do such a thing?"

"I hear you're a powerful man," Jock said.

"No one is prepared to risk Galer with another ship. They lost money when the Folly went down."

"It wasn't my fault." Galer's voice rose to near screeching.

"You were in charge." Nathan stared at Galer before turning to Jock. "It's Galer's actions before the shipwreck that are at fault."

"It were the storm." Jock rubbed his sleeve across his nose and stuck his chin out.

"There was plenty of warning that a storm was coming." Nathan's eyes narrowed and he swept his gaze over all the crewmen. "You've all sailed for many years. You know I'm right."

"No man could be better than Galer to his crew," Jock said loudly, but Madalyn detected a note of doubt in his voice.

"What about his ability to keep you safe." Nathan raised his eyebrows. "Men lost their lives."

"That's true," another man agreed. "Morty was one of the best and he went down with the ship. Ten men drowned."

"Aye," murmured the other men.

Galer's eyes bulged from his head and he swung around at his crew. His arms flayed in the air and Madalyn hoped that he would be distracted enough to give them a chance to escape. Nathan took a step backward and Madalyn lifted her skirts in preparation for flight. Nathan turned to her and nudged his head in the direction of the street and Madalyn nodded.

"Don't listen to this liar." Galer shouted as he moved from man to man. "He's the reason you're all stranded here."

"You're all free to work on other ships." Nathan eased Madalyn back another step. "You did nothing wrong."

Galer turned back to Nathan so suddenly that Madalyn would have fallen backwards, if Nathan hadn't kept a firm grip on her arm. Galer's eyes looked wild and his teeth were clenched in a grimace.

"You turned my men against me." Galer raised his fists. "No man does that without a fight."

Nathan eased them back another foot. "You give me too much credit."

"You'll fight me, or be branded a coward."

"By you?" Nathan shook his head. "You're beneath my notice."

Galer's hand shot out, hitting Nathan in the jaw with a dull thud. Nathan's head was thrown back. Madalyn missed being hit by a hair's breadth. She covered her mouth with her hand to stifle a scream.

"Stand back." Nathan pushed her away.

Madalyn was grabbed by one of the men. She struggled to get free, but he held her firm. She pushed back with her body and tried to kick him, but he was faster. He lifted her high on his chest and leaned close to her ear.

"Best settle down and leave them at it." Madalyn recognized the voice of Jock. "When Galer is in this mood, there's no talking him out of it."

She tried to twist free. "You have to stop this."

"Neither one wants it stopped now. No man lets another hit him and then walks away." Jock's voice was low and hoarse. "Your husband has his honor to defend."

Madalyn looked to Nathan and watched him move around Galer with raised fists. His jaw was clenched and his eyes narrowed. His focus didn't waver from Galer. The Captain rubbed his nose with his fist and circled Nathan. Both men were totally absorbed in their duel of fists.

Galer's hand shot out first. He aimed for Nathan's face, but Nathan ducked his head. Before Galer had a chance to recover his stride, Nathan punched him in the stomach. Galer jumped back and groaned.

Nathan straightened up. "Had enough?"

Galer spit. "Not until I see you lying on the ground."

Madalyn held her breath. She watched as the two men exchange punches. The sound of Galer's fist connecting with Nathan's body sent shockwaves throughout her, but the fighting continued. The two men battled to exhaustion and yet neither was victor.

Nathan was bleeding from his nose and a cut on his lip. Galer's face was swollen and his one eye was almost closed shut. Neither man seemed to notice their injuries as they continued their brutal assault.

Nathan stumbled backwards and Madalyn held her breath as she waited for him to fall. Instead, he took a gulp of air and then wound up his arm for one final punch. He hit Galer in the abdomen and the man fell back. He lay on the ground, his eyes closed and his battered face barely recognizable.

Nathan leaned over the man. "Enough."

Jock eased his hold on Madalyn and she pushed away from him. She ran to Nathan's side and touched his bleeding lip with the edge of her cloak.

"We need to get you home." She tried to wrap his arm around her shoulder, but he shook free.

"I'm fine." Nathan looked at the men who still surrounded them. "It was a fair fight."

"Yes." Jock nodded. "Galer started it and you had no choice."

"If any of you wants to hire onto one of my ships, see my manager Jackson in the morning. I expect hard work. My captains will not tolerate any of the behavior I saw aboard the Folly."

A murmur of thanks went up from the men and Madalyn breathed a sigh of relief as they started to disperse. Jock walked over to Galer and pulled him upright.

"Now you're stealing my men." Galer's words were slurred and he pushed away from Jock. "I won't have it."

Before they had a chance to move, Galer pulled something out of his coat. Madalyn gasped in horror when a glint of metal reflected in the dim moonlight.

"Put the pistol away." Nathan voice held an edge of steel.

"No!" Galer waved the weapon at Nathan. "This time you'll get what's coming to you."

Nathan and Jock both lunged at Galer. Nathan reached him first. The two men grappled with the weapon. Galer pulled his arm free and pointed the pistol at Nathan.

Nathan pushed Galer's arm into the air, forcing the gun away from his chest. Galer growled; every muscle in his face clenched tight as he fought against Nathan. He edged his arm lower, inch by inch, until he was within range of Nathan's head.

Nathan moved his head to the side and tried to pull the gun upward. Galer's strength seemed to increase with Nathan's efforts. Madalyn stood frozen as she watched the gun move lower until it disappeared between the two men.

Galer grinned. "I will win."

Nathan only clenched his jaw tighter, his muscles straining against the effort of holding the pistol at bay.

A loud shot rang out in the still air.

Both men jumped at the sound, staring at each other with wide eyes.

Madalyn held her breath. Her hands shook as she gripped her cloak. She watched Nathan and Galer back away. Galer's arm dropped limply to his side, the gun still clasped in his hand. Nathan reached out, but stopped when Galer grimaced.

Jock grabbed Galer just as he stumbled backward. He lowered the man to the ground. Madalyn gasped at the bright red stain that spread across his jacket. Nathan leaned over Galer and pressed his hand to the wound. Nathan looked up at one of the other men.

"Go for help."

Before the man could move, there was the sound of running footsteps approaching them. Madalyn strained her eyes in the darkness and saw two men coming from the street.

"We heard a shot." The newcomer gasped for air.

Madalyn immediately recognized the voice of Peter, one of the men who had rescued them from the shipwreck. Within a few seconds his friend Sam joined them.

"Your coachman sent us looking for you." Sam leaned over Galer. "He looks bad."

"Get help." Nathan motioned to Madalyn. "Someone take my wife to the coach."

"I'm not leaving you." Madalyn's voice shook.

Nathan stood away from Galer. "You can't be seen here. Go with Sam to the coach."

"What about you?" Madalyn lowered her voice to a whisper. "I can't let you risk being arrested. I can tell the authorities what happened."

"I won't be arrested." Nathan leaned close to her. "People will question you being found here, more than me fighting with Galer. We don't want people wondering why you were here."

A shiver of fear raced up her spine. She bit her lip and looked deep into Nathan's eyes. He was right. The docks were no place for a lady to be found; neither was a fight. Nathan could explain he was here because of his business. His actions this evening wouldn't be questioned.

She nodded. "Come home soon."

"I'll do my best." Nathan pulled her close and gave her a quick kiss.

He turned back to Galer, but Madalyn kept her eyes fixed on her husband. Her breath caught in her throat. Her heart ached as she allowed Sam to lead her away. They moved down a small walkway that led to the street.

George and the coach were waiting in front of the warehouse. The coach lanterns were burning bright in the darkness. Madalyn was vaguely aware of Sam helping her into the coach. She leaned back against the swabs and closed her eyes. As if in a dream, she heard Sam give instructions to take her home.

Her husband had almost been killed this evening and it was her fault. Galer would never have found Nathan at the warehouse if he hadn't come back for her. Madalyn dropped her head in her hands and gave way to her tears. What if she never saw Nathan again? That was the worst thing imaginable.

Nathan was a man of compassion, strength, and honor. A man a woman would be proud to love. Madalyn quivered as she admitted truth to herself.

She loved Nathan.

Chapter 20

Madalyn watched the slender fingers of dawn creep up the horizon. They lit up the sea, giving it a shimmering beauty. It was lost on her, though. The only thing she could focus on was Nathan. She pulled the drape closed with a sigh and walked to the bed.

Nathan still hadn't returned from the wharf, and she feared the worse. What if they didn't believe the shooting had been an accident? What if they arrested Nathan for murder? Galer's men were witnesses, but could they be trusted to tell the truth?

She sat on the edge of her bed and stifled a yawn. She was exhausted, but sleep refused to come. She'd paced her room all night while her mind had gone over the shooting again and again. The thought of Nathan handling Galer's death alone was more than she could bear. Especially now that she knew she loved him.

The knowledge of her love had come with such blinding certainty that she still couldn't believe it. He'd asked her to trust him and she'd been afraid. She groaned and threw herself down on the bed. If only she'd stayed at home last night.

"I expected you to be asleep," a deep voice said from the doorway.

She jumped up at the sound of Nathan's voice. "How long have you been there? Were you trying to make me mad with worry?"

"I didn't want to disturb your sleep." He shut the door and walked to the bed. "You can't follow even the simplest of instructions."

Her stomach fluttered as Nathan sat down beside her. "I needed to know you were safe first."

He rubbed the back of his neck. "I was never in any real danger."

"What about Galer?"

"He's dead."

Madalyn rolled her eyes. "I knew that. Did the police question you?"

"Jock testified to it being self-defence."

"So you're cleared of his death."

"Yes." He leaned back on his elbow. "Sooner or later the law will wonder what I was doing down at the warehouse so late."

She grimaced and looked down at her hands. "That's my fault. I'm sorry."

He lifted her chin and looked deep into her eyes. "Thank you for that."

Madalyn frowned. "For interfering?"

"For apologizing." Nathan's finger brushed the side of her cheek. "I wish you'd learn to trust me."

"I do." Madalyn's voice trembled. "My foolishness endangered your life. I would never have forgiven myself if something had happened to you."

"Don't be so hard on yourself. Galer has been threatening me since I first set foot on board the Folly." He sighed. "It was bound to happen."

"But not on the same night you were already risking your life." Madalyn choked back a sob. "It was wrong of me to ask you to help."

"No." Nathan tapped his finger over her lips. "Those men had every right to be freed."

Madalyn hiccupped. A flutter of desired curled deep within as Nathan brushed away a tear from her cheek. He continued to look into her eyes and she leaned toward him.

He accepted her wordless invitation and captured her lips. Madalyn gave a small sigh as she melted under his touch. Within seconds, she was laying on the bed beside him, her need for his touch unquenchable.

What started as a tender exploration became a burning hunger. Their tongues curled together, each stroke sending Madalyn to greater heights of pleasure. The world spun away until the only thing that existed was Nathan.

He broke the kiss off and propped his forehead against hers. His chest rose as he panted for air. "You need sleep."

Madalyn took several deep gulps of air. "I thought I'd never see you again."

"I'm not that easy to be rid of."

She kissed his chin. "Don't joke about it."

Nathan leaned back. "Would you have cared?"

Her eyes filled with tears. "More than you know."

Nathan tilted his head, his eyes never leaving hers as he brushed a strand of hair from her face. "I almost believe you." His voice was a hoarse whisper.

"It's true."

Madalyn reached up and claimed his mouth. She poured her heart and soul into the kiss, begging him with her lips to understand the depth of her love for him. Nathan didn't disappoint.

He clasped her close as he rolled her under him. His hands roamed her body, sending shivers of delight throughout her being.

Tremors of desire raced across her skin.

Hunger and need were unleashed.

She moved under Nathan. The feel of his hard body against hers sent a piercing stab of excitement to her inner core. His hands clasped her hips and brought them closer together, until she could feel his hardened manhood through her nightgown. Heat exploded into flames of sensation that seared their way across every inch of her body.

There was only the two of them. Yearning and awareness of each other had been too long denied. There was urgency to their quest for oneness and Madalyn followed where Nathan led. She groaned when his lips left hers.

He trailed kisses down her neck and pushed her nightgown off her shoulder. His lips followed and she was lost in ecstasy as he licked and then suckled her nipple. She burned with the fire that Nathan was building within her.

They were flying, soaring high into the heavens where only the two of them existed, when a loud banging at the door jolted them back to earth.

Nathan shuddered and lifted his head.

The knocking came again and then Annie's voice. "Mr. Carter, the police are downstairs."

"Damn." Nathan rolled away and covered his face with his hands.

"What can they want?" Madalyn pulled her nightgown over her shoulder.

Nathan sat up. "I've no idea."

He stood and walked to the dressing table. He straightened his cravat and pulled his jacket straight. A quick brush of his hands to his hair and he looked every inch the gentleman. The only evidence of their recent lovemaking was the slight flush on his cheeks.

Madalyn walked to her wardrobe. "Wait for me."

"Stay."

Nathan left the room. Madalyn stood at her open wardrobe and bit her lip. She couldn't just stay here and not know what was happening. No matter what Nathan wanted, she needed to be with him. She pulled out a blue gown and began to dress.

It took her ten minutes to get ready, her fingers refusing to do even the simplest of tasks. In the end, she threw a shawl over her shoulders to cover the back of the gown that wasn't fastened. She pulled on the first pair of slippers she could find and then ran out of the room.

She reached the top of the stairs just as Nathan was leaving the drawing room with two men. They stood at the entranceway while Isaac handed them their hats.

"Where are you going?" Madalyn's voice rang down the stairwell. She picked up her skirt and rushed down the stairs.

Nathan turned at the sound of her voice. "These gentlemen would like to ask me some questions."

The two men looked at her and bowed their heads slightly. They were dressed in dark brown coats. The only thing distinguishing them from each other was the color of their hair. One was a dirty blonde and the other black.

"They can do it here." Madalyn tilted her chin up. "This is an outrageous hour to drag a man from his home."

The dark haired man twirled his hat in his hand. "I'm sorry ma'am," he said with a slight cough. "A complaint has been laid against Mr. Carter. He needs to go to the jail with us."

"Nonsense." A note of authority was in her voice. She wasn't an Earl's daughter for nothing. "They're mistaken. My husband was cleared of Captain Galer's death."

The man cleared his throat. "I'm afraid this is something different."

Madalyn looked at Nathan. His face was expressionless, but his eyes burned with intensity. She grabbed his hands, forcing him to look down at her.

"It's nothing." Nathan's voice soothed. "I'll be back shortly."

"Promise?"

Nathan kissed her hands. "Get some sleep."

Madalyn watched the men lead Nathan out the house. She stood there until Isaac closed the door. A chill ran up her spine and she clasped her hands around her arms, rubbing them to keep warm.

"Mr. Carter is a smart man," Isaac said. "He'll be home shortly."

"I pray you're right." Madalyn turned from the door and went up the stairs. When she reached her room, she lay down and pulled the blankets around her. She couldn't shake the chill that pervaded her body.

She snuggled deeper into the warmth of the covers and closed her eyes. There was nothing she could do for Nathan right now. She needed sleep so she could think clearer. There was still a chance that this whole complaint would prove a mistake and Nathan would be home before she was awake.

The sun was low in the sky when she finally woke. She sat up and threw the sheets back. She rang the bell for Annie and started to undo her gown. She struggled with the fastenings until Annie arrived.

"Let me help." Annie had the gown off within seconds. "You must have been uncomfortable sleeping like this."

"I was too tired to care." Madalyn rubbed her arms. "What time is it?"

"Six in the evening."

Horror seeped through her body. She'd slept the whole day away. "Why did no one wake me?"

"We tried, but you were sleeping soundly." Annie brought her a dressing robe to put on.

Remembrance of the previous evening and this morning flooded back. Madalyn's heart started to beat faster. "Is Nathan home yet?"

Annie shook her head. "This is the longest he's been taken for questioning."

Madalyn bit her lip. Panic crept deep inside of her and she trembled with reaction. Why was Nathan being kept so long? What was the complaint that had been registered against him?

"Has there been no word at all?" She tied the belt of the dressing gown.

"Isaac sent George to the jail to ask around. The only news he had was that Mr. Carter was being held in one of the cells."

Madalyn paced in front of her dressing table. "They're holding him in jail?"

Annie nodded. "Some slaves escaped last night and Mr. Carter is the most likely suspect."

Madalyn stopped and turned to Annie. "Why?"

"Ever since Mr. Carter set his slaves free, every slave owner has blamed him for their runaways. Even if he had nothing to do with it, he's set a bad example in their mind."

Madalyn covered her eyes and groaned. It was her fault. Why has she insisted that Nathan help her? Even though she'd no idea that he'd be the first person suspected, but that didn't make her feel better.

"I must do something."

"Mr. Carter would be upset if you got involved." Annie squeezed her arms and led her to the chair. "It's not seemly for a lady to know of such thing."

"I can hardly pretend I'm ignorant."

Madalyn stared at herself in the mirror. There had to be some solution to this problem if only she could think. Her mind was full of cotton wool, though. She straightened her shoulders and tried to focus.

"Who is in charge of the jail?"

"That would be James Roye."

"Bring me a gown," she ordered. "I will see this Mr. Roye."

"He's not an easy man to speak to." Annie pulled out a red gown from the wardrobe. "It'd be best if you went with someone."

Madalyn frowned. Who could she get to help her? The only name that came to mind was Francois St. Amand. Nathan had said they'd been friends for years.

When she was dressed she went down to the parlor and wrote a note to Monsieur St. Amand. She gave it to Isaac to deliver. She walked around the room, pacing and then sitting for a few seconds before standing and moving again. She'd done this for an hour before she heard the knocking at the front door.

Isaac led St. Amand into the parlor. Madalyn motioned him to sit in the settee across from her. She waited until Isaac had shut the door and Francois was seated before speaking. St. Amand might be Nathan's friend, but she wasn't certain how much he knew about Nathan's past activities. She couldn't risk telling him everything, but a partial truth should be enough to convince him to help Nathan.

"Nathan is in the jail."

Francois' eyes narrowed. "When?"

"They took him away for questioning at dawn." Her voice wavered. "When I awoke later today, I was informed that he was being held in a cell."

Francois whistled. "That's not good. Do you know why?"

"They said a complaint had been made against him." She stood and began to pace in front of the fireplace. "It's my fault. I need you to accompany me to the jail."

Francois smiled and shook his head. "You're a woman and delicate. I'll go and arrange Nathan's release."

Madalyn raised an eyebrow. "I'm the reason he's there."

"A woman could never cause such a thing."

She clenched her hand into a fist and fought the urge to scream. She wasn't the helpless, frail creature that St Amand thought. At least Nathan had never doubted her abilities.

"I was angry at Mr. Harden and caused a scene at the Exchange yesterday."

St. Amand frowned. "Did the man insult your honor?"

Madalyn bit her lip. "Yes."

"There's no need to be concerned." Francois reached over and patted her hand. "Nathan will deal with it."

"I fear Mr. Harden may blame Nathan for something that he hasn't done. Mr. Harden isn't an honorable man." Madalyn took a deep breath. "He'll stoop to any means to get his way."

Francois stood. "This must not be allowed to happen. The law is seldom involved in a matter of honor. I'll go and fetch Nathan."

"I must come."

"It's not a place for a lady."

Madalyn opened the door. "You may need me to prove Nathan's innocence."

Francois stared at her for a second and then shrugged. "As you wish."

She was too worried about Nathan to care about his opinion. She was determined to free Nathan from jail, even if that meant confessing to the crime herself.

Chapter 21

Madalyn covered her nose with her handkerchief and tried not to breathe the stale air. The place smelled of unwashed bodies and open latrines. Her stomach was heaving and she didn't know how much longer she could stand the odor.

"I warned you." Francois held onto her arm and led her past several cells. "You should return to the office."

"No." She straightened her shoulder and continued to clutch her skirts high, as she edged her way around the muck on the floor.

"He's down here," the jailer said with a grunt. "I'm not letting him loose until Mr. Roye says so."

"You may bring him to Roye's office." Francois spoke in a crisp firm tone. "I cannot allow the lady to remain here."

The jailor, a short heavyset man looked at Madalyn. His eyes scanned her from head to toe before resting on her chest. "Aye."

Madalyn shivered and stepped closer to St. Amand. He'd been right about the jail being unfit for a woman. The thought of spending another minute in this place was making her weak. She only prayed that she could release Nathan without confessing.

They stopped at the last cell on the left. She gasped at the sight of Nathan sitting on the floor. His back was against the wall, knees bent and his arms draped over them.

Madalyn ran to the cell bars. "Nathan."

He looked up. His expression of surprise and pleasure was quickly replaced by a scowl. "You shouldn't be here."

"When you didn't return, I sent for Monsieur St. Amand." She gripped the bars tightly. "We have come to get you released."

"You know better than to bring her here, St. Amand." Nathan stood and picked up the jacket he'd been sitting on.

Francois raised his hands defensively. "I tried. Your wife can be an extremely difficult person to dissuade."

Nathan brushed off his jacket. "Take her away. Now."

Madalyn's eyes narrowed. "Not until you are released. Mr. Roye has agreed to listen to your statement."

"That's right," the jailer said as he jangled his keys. "I'm here to escort you upstairs."

Madalyn moved back from the bars and waited for the cell door to swing open. Then she rushed into Nathan's arms, burying her face in his chest. He wrapped an arm around her.

"Go upstairs with Francois. I'll be there soon."

She let Nathan nudge her away. She looked back at him, but he was speaking to the jailer. St. Amand took her arm and led her to the door. Within minutes they were standing in James Roye's office.

It was a small room. The walls had been whitewashed at one time, but years of dirt and grime had turned them a dull gray. There was a desk covered with papers and two chairs on either side.

When Nathan joined them his jacket was brushed clean. He looked as if he had just come from home. Madalyn moved to his side and clasped his arm.

"I won't let you take the blame for this," she whispered.

"It won't come to that." Nathan led her to a chair and waited until she'd sat. "At least you were able to convince Roye to meet with me. I think he would've been happy to let me rot in that cell."

Francois chuckled. "You really should stop making enemies. It's time you settled down. It may be dull, but at least it's safe."

Nathan walked to the window and gazed out. "I've had the whole day to think about it."

The door opened and a tall man with greasy dark hair walked in. Some might have described him as handsome except for his heavy black eyebrows that met in the middle of his forehead. Behind him was Bertram Harden. He sauntered in and stopped in the doorway when his eyes fell on its occupants.

"I won't stay in the same room as them." Bertram pointed his finger wildly at Madalyn. "Especially that woman."

Madalyn stood and tilted her head at Bertram. "I should be the one complaining about the company."

"You dare to insult my wife?" Nathan's voice was a growl.

"Enough." James Roye motioned for Bertram to close the door. "I've brought Harden here because he's the man with the complaint against you."

"Speak." Nathan spat the word out before sitting on Roye's desk.

"You set my slaves free."

Bertram's accusation hung in the air.

He'd thrown down the gauntlet. Madalyn held her breath, her heart beating furiously as she waited for a reaction from Nathan.

Nathan crossed his arms. "Why would I do such a thing?"

"Revenge." Bertram was shouting now.

Nathan shook his head. "Waste of my time. You're beneath contempt."

Bertram's eyes bulged and his nostrils flared wide as he pointed at Madalyn. "Then she did it."

Nathan jumped off the desk. "Do not slander my wife."

Francois cleared his throat. "You have gone a bit far. Carter would be within his rights as a gentleman to settle this outside."

"I don't care." Bertram's voice sounded hysterical. "The very day that witch harangues me about selling slaves, they disappear."

Nathan grabbed Bertram by his neck cloth. He banged him up against the wall and shook him. "You will show proper respect for my wife."

"Let him down." Roye's voice rose above Bertram's cries.

"Not until I have an apology." Nathan thrust Bertram higher in the air.

Bertram kicked his feet, struggling for a foothold. Only the tip of his toes touched the ground. He twisted his body, but Nathan's grip did not weaken.

"Alright," Bertram sobbed. "I apologise."

"You best not forget because next time we meet at dawn." Nathan's face was inches away from Bertram. "I won't give you another reprieve."

Nathan released his hold on Bertram, letting him fall to the ground. Bertram lay in a huddle on the floor, rubbing his legs. His face now twisted into an ugly grimace. He glared at Nathan through narrowed eyes.

"You'll still go to prison for stealing my property."

"Prove it." Nathan turned to Roye. "What evidence is there against me?"

Roye cleared his throat. "You were on the docks last night."

"I'm there most nights."

"Your warehouse is close to where Mr. Harden was keeping his slaves. It would've been easy for you to slip in and free them."

"What did I do with them?" Nathan crossed his arms. "Am I a magician?"

"You must admit that your name has come up in connection with this type of thing before." Roye's voice was low and unemotional. "We've been watching you closely since your return."

Madalyn's heart jumped into her throat. She'd no idea that he was being followed. But Nathan must have suspected. That was why he'd been so careful last night, keeping to the shadows and the back alleys. It would've been easier to take the coach.

Nathan shrugged. "Then you must know that I was nowhere near this man's slaves."

"Well," Roye began, his finger loosening his cravat. "My men lost track of you last night."

"So there's no evidence against me."

"Your behavior is suspicious." Roye tapped his finger on his desk. "And you did kill a man last night."

"It was self-defence." Nathan's voice hardened. "Is Galer connected to Harden's complaint?"

"No." Roye sighed heavily. "You've been cleared in that incident."

"Then I am free to leave." Nathan held his hand out to Madalyn.

"You can't let him go." Bertram's voice rose hysterically. "What about my property. I need my slaves back."

"We have no reason to keep him." Roye jerked his head at Nathan. "Go."

Madalyn stood. She glanced up at Nathan and tried to smile. Her body was still frozen with fear and her lips barely tilted up at the edges. Nathan's eyes softened and she took a deep breath. She shook out her skirt and turned to leave the room when the voice of Roye stopped her.

"You are still under suspicion Mr. Carter."

Nathan looked back over his shoulder. "Then let us hope you find the guilty person soon."

"You'd be advised to stay close to home."

"Where would I go?" Nathan opened the door. "I have my business and my wife to keep me occupied."

"This is not over," Bertram shouted. "I will have justice."

Nathan tilted his head at Bertram. "Good day Mr. Harden."

Francois St. Amand made a quick bow to Roye and preceded Nathan and Madalyn out of the office. They walked without speaking until they were outside. Even then, Nathan motioned for silence until they were in the coach.

Madalyn leaned back against the cushioned seat and closed her eyes. She forced back the image of Nathan sitting in that horrid place all day. Every time she thought of it shivers of disgust racked her body. He was free now. That was all that mattered.

"Thank you for coming, Francois." Nathan's deep voice echoed in the quiet of the coach.

"You'll have to thank your wife." Francois chuckled. "She's the one who sent for me."

"Thank you." Nathan picked up her hand and kissed it. "We'll discuss this later."

Madalyn smiled. A wave of weakness kept her from answering his challenge. The after effects of fear were playing havoc with her body. The sooner they were home, the better.

Nathan cleared his throat. "I'll instruct George to take you home Francois."

"I'm not leaving until you tell me what happened last night."

"You heard Roye." Nathan glanced out the window. "There was no evidence that I had anything to do with Harden's missing slaves."

"I'm talking about the dead man."

Nathan sighed. "It was self-defence."

The coach stopped in front of Nathan's residence at that moment. Madalyn waited for Francois and Nathan to jump down, before stepping out. The three of them went into the house. Nathan ordered refreshments to be sent to the parlor. Madalyn sat in a chair by the fireplace and took a deep breath, savoring the feeling of peace that settled deep within her. She felt at home for the first time in years.

Francois waited until Isaac had left their drinks on the table before speaking. "Why did you kill a man last night?"

"Galer and several of his men cornered me as I was leaving the warehouse." Nathan poured himself a glass of brandy. "The man was drunk."

Madalyn shivered. "It was horrible."

Francois looked at her sharply. "You were there?"

"I told her what happened."

"There is no need to lie." Madalyn took a sip of tea, letting its warmth spread throughout her body. "You've already been cleared of his death."

Nathan threw back his brandy. "I had hoped to keep your presence there a secret."

She put her cup down. "I didn't realize that included Monsieur St. Amand."

Francois started toward the door. "Neither did I. If you don't trust me, I'll leave."

"Of course I trust you." Nathan motioned his friend to stop. "I was trying to protect Madalyn."

"I can take care of myself."

Francois moved back into the room and sat across from her. He smiled and lifted his glass in a salute. "After today, I believe you can do anything."

"You shouldn't have brought her there." Nathan poured another brandy. "It was unfit for a woman."

"I couldn't leave you to rot." Madalyn forced her voice to sound strong.

"Francois would've taken care of everything." Nathan took a sip of his drink. "You didn't need to come."

"I'd intended to tell them I was the one responsible, not you." Madalyn held her breath, waiting for Nathan to say something.

Nathan looked at her over the rim of his glass. "Then both of us would've been in jail." Nathan bit his words out. "What purpose would that serve?"

She clasped her hands in her lap. "I was trying to help."

"Eventually Roye would have set me free."

Francois cleared his throat. "What did happen last night? Was there any truth to Harden's accusations?"

"You know better than to ask." Nathan rubbed his face with his hands. "Suffice to say that I am glad Harden did not discover his loss until morning."

Francois whistled. "When the ship had already sailed?"

"Exactly."

Madalyn suddenly remembered Roye's words at the jail. "Why are you being watched?"

"People believe I help slaves escape."

"Do you?"

Nathan shook his head. "I help where I can, but I'm not active in the movement.

"No one accepts that, though." Francois tilted his head. "Why were you freeing slaves last night?"

"I asked him to." Madalyn bit her lip. "I didn't think it would be so dangerous."

Francois looked at her with a raised eyebrow. "I hope you don't intend to make a practice of breaking the law?"

"No. I will make certain of it." Nathan's voice rang out loudly. "It was sheer craziness. I can't trust Madalyn to keep herself safe."

"That's unfair." Her words were barely a whisper. "I did what I thought was right."

"You didn't think before you acted."

"True." Madalyn sniffed. "You were almost put in prison because of me."

Nathan chuckled. "It would never have come to that. This is an old game that Roye and I have played for years. I think you need to get some rest. You're exhausted."

"How was I to know?" Madalyn stood and shook her gown out. "An officer of the law would never have dreamed of coming to my uncle's house."

"You're not in England." Nathan put his empty glass down on his desk before holding his arm out to her.

"Good evening Monsieur St. Amand." Madalyn made a small curtsey. "Thank you for your help."

Francois smiled. "My pleasure."

Madalyn let Nathan lead her to the door. A shiver of awareness raced through her body and her breath caught in her throat. His very nearness made her knees weak. At the base of the stairs, he took her hand and brushed his lips across it. A flame of desire burst to life within her.

"Will I see you tonight?" Madalyn's voice caught in her throat.

"I'll follow shortly."

Chapter 22

Madalyn sat waiting.

Her body was taut with anticipation.

She'd made a decision and now she had to tell Nathan. If she approached him in the right way he might give her what she wanted. These past days with Nathan had shown her what she truly desired.

She wanted a real marriage.

She needed to tell Nathan she loved him.

"Are you fond of sitting in the darkness?"

She jumped and turned at the sound of Nathan's voice. He stood at the door, one hand on the frame, the other on the doorknob.

"I hope you don't mind my intrusion?" Nathan shut the door.

"Francois has gone home?" Madalyn stood and lit the candles by her bed.

Nathan nodded. "He was surprised by your insistence about going to the jail."

"I already explained."

Nathan leaned against her dressing table, his arms crossed. "I thought I told you to wait for me. Will you ever learn to do as I ask?"

She shook her head. As much as she loved Nathan, she couldn't change who she was. She would always be impulsive, acting without thought to the consequences.

"I will listen to your advice, but I'm afraid that I will still do as I think best."

"That's what I thought." Nathan picked up a comb from the vanity and ran a finger across it. "A part of me understands and admires your passion."

"But?" She held her breath as she waited for Nathan's response.

"It will bring you much grief. Once our marriage is ended, you won't have me to rescue you."

"I can take care of myself."

"You need a man's protection." Nathan paused. "You need a husband."

A bubble of hope caught in Madalyn's chest. Was Nathan considering making their marriage real? She inhaled deeply and took a step toward him.

"What are you suggesting?"

"A London season. There you could find a suitable husband."

She stared at Nathan, her mind refusing to believe his words. Did he honestly think that she would consider another husband? She knew deep in her heart that he would be the only man she would ever love.

"I don't wish to marry."

"You'll change your mind once we've found your brother." Nathan threw the comb back on the vanity. "You'll forget about the horrible events of the past days. Then you'll have plenty of time to think about your future."

"I won't let you decide my life." Madalyn didn't conceal her anger.

Nathan sighed. "I had hoped you'd see that it was the right decision. In England, you can have the life that your uncle denied you. You're an earl's daughter with an enviable fortune. You'll have no problem finding a husband."

"Where will you be?"

"I'll escort you to England and leave once the annulment is arranged."

"I don't wish a season in London."

"Then I'll make other arrangements." Nathan pursed his lips. "I could arrange for you to stay with my brother and his wife at Caldern. At least there you'd be safe from your uncle."

"You're sending me away because I didn't follow your orders." Madalyn turned away and walked to the window. "You're punishing me."

Nathan walked up behind her and clasped her shoulders. "This is for the best."

She shook Nathan's hands off and moved away. He wanted to be rid of her. She clenched her hands tight, trying to contain her disappointment, but it didn't work. Tears welled up in her eyes and threatened to spill. She refused to let him see how upset she was. Instead she sat down in a chair and crossed her arms. If he wanted her gone then she'd give him what he wanted.

"I'll leave tomorrow."

Nathan crouched down in front of her. "Don't be foolish. You're still my wife."

She shook her head. "You've been saddled with me long enough. I've brought you nothing but grief."

Nathan took her hands in his. "You're wrong. I've enjoyed every moment. I'm thinking only of you."

She looked at Nathan. Her breath caught in her throat at his nearness. His eyes had softened to a liquid blue and his lips rose in a smile. His thumbs began to caress her hand, sending shivers of pleasure throughout her body.

"I don't understand." Madalyn's voice was a breathless whisper.

"Your uncle denied you the life that you should've had." Nathan squeezed Madalyn's hand. "Now you have a chance to enjoy yourself and take your proper place in society."

"It is too late. I'm not the naïve, trusting girl I was before I boarded The Folly."

"True," Nathan's voice was strong and decisive. "You're so much more than that. Any man would be proud to have you as his wife."

She stared at Nathan in surprise. "You're always angry with me and complaining that I act without thinking."

Nathan kissed her hands. "You had the courage to follow your heart, no matter the risks."

Desire and love overflowed within her.

He thought her courageous. Somehow, she must brave his rejection and find the words to express her love for him. Her heart beat in a furious tattoo, but she knew that she couldn't let him leave her. The words refused to come, though. All that was left was action.

She leaned forward and brushed her mouth across Nathan's. Her lips clung to his. Time stood still as she waited for him to respond. It only took a few seconds and then Nathan moved against her.

His tongue smoothed across the seam of her mouth until she opened for him. She surrendered, savoring the feel of his tongue against hers. Spirals of excitement began to build low in her womb. She was weak with the need to feel him close.

She wrapped her arms around him, throwing him off balance. He dropped to his knees and pulled Madalyn from the chair. Together they clung to each other as the kiss took them to a place where time and thought were impossible. The fire of their passion built until its flames consumed them.

Nathan smoothed his hands across her back and she moaned as tremors of sensation raced across her skin. She moved against him, silently begging for more. He didn't disappoint. He clutched her closer, deepening the kiss until she could barely breathe.

A thrill of pleasure surged through her when she felt Nathan's hard body against her. She let her hands roam across his shoulders. Her fingers fluttered through the tendrils of hair at his neck, gently massaging until Nathan's lips left hers.

Before she could protest, Nathan began to devour her neck with hot, wet kisses. Her body shook with desire, burning with a fever of need. She felt as if she were stretched on a tight wire, her body taut with excitement, ready to break at any moment.

Nathan's lips moved lower, his teeth pulling the material of her nightgown away to expose one breast. Madalyn heard Nathan groan as if from a great distance. He held her close with one arm, letting his other hand gently knead the soft skin of her breast. His fingers fluttered tantalizingly close to her sensitive nipple, teasing her until she was at the point of screaming.

The hot, moist tip of Nathan's tongue raked across her nipple, searing her body with heat. She quivered at the edge of fulfillment. When Nathan took her engorged nipple in his mouth, she gasped as waves of bliss pulsed through her.

Madalyn thought she would die of the pleasure, but she was wrong. Nathan continued to suckle and knead her breast until her whole body quivered uncontrollably in his arms. Only then did his mouth leave her breast and capture her lips again.

This time he drank from her lips, lingering over every sip. His tongue caressed and stroked until she shook with need. Nathan's slow seduction ignited a fire that blazed in every nerve of her body. She knew that only Nathan's touch would ever satisfy her.

The kiss ended with both of them gasping for air. Madalyn rested her forehead against Nathan's and inhaled his cologne. Closing her eyes, she put her hand to his chest. His heart was beating as rapidly as hers.

"You've shown me what I want and need." Madalyn's words were a soft murmur. "I want this marriage to be real. I need you in my life."

Nathan stiffened. Madalyn looked at his face and her heart dropped. His face was devoid of expression and his jaw was tightly clenched.

"I need a marriage based on love, not gratitude." Nathan touched her cheek with a finger, brushing away a strand of hair.

"I love you." Madalyn's voice quivered. Her gaze never left Nathan.

A muscle twitched in Nathan's jaw. He closed his eyes briefly. "You're confused. Too much has happened for you to know your true feelings."

Madalyn shook her head. "Before I met you, I would have settled for the marriage that my uncle wanted. I didn't have the courage to say no because I didn't know what I wanted."

Nathan grimaced. "You need time to heal and space away from me. Then you'll see that I'm right."

Fear gripped her heart. Nathan was speaking to her as if she were a child. "Nothing will change what I feel for you."

Nathan pushed away and stood up. "You're experiencing passion for the first time in your life. It's easy to confuse that with love."

Madalyn sat back on her heels. "I love you. Why will you not believe that?"

Nathan rubbed his eyes with his hand. "It's my fault. I should never have touched you."

"I kissed you."

"I mean before." Nathan threw his head back and exhaled loudly. "You were innocent and I took advantage of that."

Madalyn fought back her tears as the pain of Nathan's rejection settled deep within her heart. "Will nothing convince you of my love?"

Nathan shook his head. "What you're feeling is lust, not love. As much as I want to take you into my arms, I won't tie you to a marriage that will make you unhappy."

Nathan turned and left the room. The click of the closing door echoed in Madalyn's heart. She dropped her head in her hands and began to sob. There was no point in fighting for him. He'd made it quite clear that he didn't want her love. Now she had to pick up the pieces of her life and decide what to do next.

Chapter 23

"I never took you for a fool."

Nathan turned away from the library window and looked at his guest, Monsieur Dupuy. The man's blue eyes held a glint of amusement. Nathan fought back the anger that constricted his chest.

"What have I done to amuse you?"

Dupuy grinned. "I always knew you were hiding something. Never could put my finger on it, though."

Nathan put his hands on the back of his desk chair. "Why would you think that?"

"You were too quiet about your life before you came to Charleston." Dupuy sat down in the wing chair opposite Nathan. "Men like you are always running from something."

"Quite astute," Nathan murmured. "Only you're wrong about me. I have nothing to hide."

"What about your beautiful wife?"

"Careful Dupuy. I don't take kindly to people who slander my wife." Nathan pulled out his chair and sat.

Dupuy's eyebrow rose slightly. "Is that what happened to Galer?"

"He attacked me." Nathan shook his head. "The man was a scoundrel."

Dupuy leaned back in his chair. "Still, he seems to have made your life uncomfortable."

"I wouldn't trust anything that Galer had to say."

"Ahh." Dupuy pursed his lips. "Then he was wrong about you being obliged to marry?"

Nathan almost choked at Dupuy's words, but years of business training came to his rescue. Except for a brief twitch of his eye, his expression remained bland. He picked up a piece of paper and tapped it on his desk.

"I have made no secret about marrying my wife aboard The Folly."

"Interesting." Dupuy crossed one leg over the other. "I never took you for a man to be compelled to do something."

Nathan forced himself to smile. "It was my choice to marry."

"It does surprise me that you would buy a wife, though." Dupuy tapped his fingers on the chair arm. "After all, you were the most eligible bachelor in Charleston."

Nathan's eyes narrowed and he clenched his jaw. Dupuy continued to look at him with amusement. Nathan tilted his head and took a deep breath. Even if the truth about his marriage to Madalyn became known, it wouldn't matter. It might make an annulment easier.

"Where would you hear an ugly rumor like that?"

"It's amazing how angry a downed man can be." Dupuy smirked. "You really shouldn't go about hitting your enemies in public. It makes them thirst for revenge."

"So Galer told you." Nathan shrugged his shoulders. "That doesn't surprise me. The man couldn't be trusted."

"But I can." Dupuy leaned forward. "For a price."

Nathan watched his guest through half-closed eyes. Dupuy repulsed him, yet it would be foolish not to hear him out. "It is your word against mine."

"Not quite." Dupuy pulled a piece of paper from the inside pocket of his jacket. "I made Galer commit the story to paper. The man was bent on destroying you. How could I refuse to help?"

Nathan took the paper that Dupuy held out. It was written in a crude hand, but its words were clear. It outlined what had taken place aboard the Folly and was followed by Galer's signature and the witnessing of two of his crew.

"What do you want?"

"Your plantation, including the land by the river." Dupey's voice sounded casual, but Nathan knew the man was eager to have it.

"It's not for sale."

Dupuy snorted. "I would think that the ownership of this document would have been a small price to pay."

"I won't be blackmailed." Nathan pushed away from the desk and stood up. "Our business is finished."

Dupuy stood up. "One way or another, I will be paid for this information. As a gentleman, I felt honor bound to come to you first."

"Are you threatening me?" Nathan's chest constricted with anger.

"I'm just giving you some friendly advice." Dupuy walked to the door. "I'll give you until tomorrow to decide."

Nathan stayed in the library and let Isaac escort the man from the house. The man was a fool if he thought he could frighten him into paying him for Galer's confession. Even if he did comply, there was no guarantee that it would end there.

Madalyn might not like it that everyone in Charleston knew about their marriage, but it would make it easier to end it. Besides, she'd be in England and the gossip couldn't hurt her there. Nathan sat down at his desk and tried to work on his account books, but with little success. Finally, he pushed the books away. The only thing he could think about was Madalyn.

Her image had been burned into his head since last night when she'd professed her love for him. A part of him wanted to believe that she loved him. Then he would feel less guilty about seducing her.

Thoughts of losing himself in her body had haunted him for days. Even the mention of her name made him hard. His time in the jail cell had been spent fantasying about Madalyn and the feel of her in his arms. When she'd appeared with Francois, he'd thought she was a figment of his imagination until she had spoken.

It would be easy to make her his wife, but it wouldn't be fair to her. All he could offer her was a marriage based on need and friendship, not love. He knew that for most women that would be enough, but not for Madalyn. She'd risked her life and reputation for the brother she loved. She'd expect the same loyalty from the man she'd commit herself to. She deserved no less.

Nathan pushed away from his desk. There was no sense sitting here when there was work to be done at the warehouse. He needed to put some distance between him and his wife before he did something foolish.

Isaac prevented him from leaving, though. "Monsieur St. Amand is here," he said in an even tone. "Shall I send him away?"

Nathan shook his head. "Show him in."

Francois followed seconds later, his boots loud on the wooden floor. Nathan smiled. "Surely you have someplace better to be?"

"Duty calls. I came to say goodbye." Francois glanced around the room before sitting down. "Nanette has sent for me."

Nathan leaned against his desk. "Charleston will be thin of people soon. The hot weather means an exodus to the plantations."

"I'll be leaving sooner than most." Francois rubbed his nose. "Isaac mentioned that Dupuy had visited. I didn't realize you were on intimate terms with him."

Nathan grimaced. "The man tried to blackmail me. When that didn't work, he threatened me."

"With what?"

Nathan went to a side table and held up a decanter of brandy. When Francois nodded, he poured two generous portions. He took a sip of his before sitting across from his friend.

"He had a signed paper from Galer detailing the circumstances of my marriage."

Francois whistled. "I hope you agreed to pay."

Nathan shook his head. "I won't be intimidated. If Dupuy wishes to make the sordid affair public, that's his choice. I'm used to being the brunt of gossip."

"What will Madalyn think?"

"She shouldn't be affected." Nathan winced as the brandy burnt its way down his throat. "She'll be in England."

Francois' jaw dropped open and he stared at his friend for several seconds before speaking. "Why for God's sake?"

"After we find Madalyn's brother, she'll take him back to England. I'll make arrangements so she doesn't have to go back to her uncles' house." Nathan crossed his arms. "In England, she can heal and consider her options. She doesn't have to be tied to a man she didn't chose."

"How does she feel about it?"

"She was unhappy at first, but she has accepted the situation."

Francois flung his arms in the air. "How can you let her go?"

"I can't keep her here."

"But you'll force her to leave?"

"That's not what I am doing." Nathan took a deep breath to quell the ache inside of him. "She needs the freedom to make her own choices."

"And you're making certain she doesn't choose you." Francois took a sip of his drink and then stared at the glass for several seconds. "You're afraid to commit."

"I can't offer her love." Nathan's voice rose in irritation.

"So you're sending her away?" Francois shook his head. "I never took you for a coward."

Nathan forced his voice to remain steady. "I'm doing what is best for Madalyn."

"What if she wants you for her husband?"

"She doesn't know what she wants."

"But you do?"

"She's been isolated her whole life. She needs to meet other men before she can make a decision about love." Nathan cleared his throat. "I'd be taking advantage if I didn't allow her that."

"You're a fool if you let her go." Francois heaved a sigh.

"You're the second person who has called me that today." Nathan said wryly.

"Maybe you should take a closer look at your actions then." Francois took another sip of his drink. "You're throwing away your chance of a wife and family. You'll regret this for the rest of your life."

"What about your marriage to Nanette?" Nathan wished the words back the second they were out of his mouth.

Francois's shoulders drooped and shook his head. "You know I married Nanette for love."

"Yet, even with a wife you love, and children, you aren't happy."

"That's exactly my point." Francois drained his glass and slammed it on Nathan's desk. "It's better to have an understanding with your wife. Love only leads to pain."

Nathan rubbed his neck. "I know." A fleeting vision of Heloise flashed through his mind, but for the first time in years it wasn't accompanied by a piercing stab in his heart.

"Give Madalyn the choice." Francois stood. "She might surprise you. If you're honest with her, then there can be no recriminations later."

"What you're suggesting sounds like a business arrangement?"

"It makes more sense than love." Francois' voice was twisted with bitterness. "Trust me on this."

"I'll give it some thought." Nathan stood. "Remember to ask about Madalyn's brother. Jackson still hasn't had any luck locating him."

"I'll have my overseer look into it. Her brother has to be in the area."

"Give Nanette my best."

"Whatever your decision about Madalyn, you must come and visit us soon." Francois went to the door. "Nanette asks about you often and the boys have grown since you last saw them."

A twinge of guilt gnawed at Nathan. "I'll do my best." He walked Francois from the house and then he ordered his own horse to be brought around.

The sun was bright and warm, but the breeze blowing from the sea made the heat bearable. Nathan turned north and rode to the public cemetery on the outskirts of the city. When he reached the graveyard, he dismounted and tied the reins to a nearby post. He left his horse grazing on the overlong grass and walked down a familiar pathway.

He stopped in front of a weathered gravestone. The words Heloise Jamieson, beloved wife, were engraved. Nathan crouched down and traced Heloise's name with his finger. The stone was rough and gritty against his skin, sending a shiver through him.

"All these years." Nathan sighed. "I was a blind fool."

When Heloise had first died, Nathan had thought her beloved face would remain with him forever. Time had erased most of her image, except the memory of her laugh and her pale blond hair blowing about her face.

Nathan closed his eyes, letting the years vanish as he relived the day he'd known he was in love. She'd been playing a game of tag with the neighbor's child and he'd come around the corner of the house unannounced. For several minutes, he'd stood beside the house, his presence unnoticed. Her every move and every giggle had captivated him. She'd been wildly free and uninhibited. He'd never seen such beauty and joy and in that moment his heart had been lost.

With a grimace, he remembered what had happened when the child had spied him. Heloise had come to an abrupt stop, her laughter silenced, and her smile gone. She'd straightened out her gown and pulled the child to her side.

She'd mumbled an excuse about forgetting the dinner on the stove and disappeared into the house. At the time, Nathan had thought it was her natural shyness that had sent her running, but now he knew differently. She'd been afraid of him and the passion he'd felt for her. His love had frightened her.

Nathan stood and patted the headstone. "Goodbye." His voice was a low whisper. "Forgive me. I won't bother you again." Nathan moved away from the grave, his hands in his pockets, his head down.

With one last look at Heloise's name, he turned and walked back to his horse. He'd wasted enough of his life mourning a woman who'd never returned his love. It was time to move on.

He made the trip to the house in good time, leaving the horse at the stable. He walked to the front of the house, taking stock of everything. So much of his life had been devoted to building a fortune and this house had been the symbol of all he had accomplished. Now he couldn't remember why it had been important.

He climbed the stairs to the front door and turned to look out across the water. It was a beautiful view, with the waves gently rolling in. He took a deep breath of the salt air and exhaled. It was a sight everyone in Charleston wanted for their own, yet he was unmoved by it.

Francois was right.

His life was empty.

The house sounded hollow when he entered. Isaac wasn't there to greet him, so he threw his gloves and hat on a chair in the foyer. He moved toward the library when the sound of footsteps on the stairs stopped him. He looked up and his breath caught in his throat.

It was Madalyn.

She stopped on the last step, her eyes piercing through to his soul. His body shook with a need that was becoming all too familiar. Not an hour went by when he didn't yearn for her. He clenched his hands tightly at his side to prevent him from reaching for her.

"You were out?" Her voice was low.

"I needed to see someone."

"Have you news of my brother?" Madalyn's hand rose toward his arm.

Nathan shook his head. "I was at the cemetery. There was someone I needed to say goodbye to."

"Oh," Madalyn said with a soft exhaled breath.

Nathan forced himself to breath. The soft rise and fall of Madalyn's chest brought back the memory of the last time he'd touched her. He closed his eyes briefly.

"Have you given any thought to what I suggested last night?"

Madalyn had turned to go back up the stairs, but Nathan's question halted her. She turned to look at him, her head tilted slightly. "Have you changed your mind?"

Nathan cleared his throat and looked into her eyes. "I think there is room for some discussion about our marriage."

Chapter 24

Madalyn's heart raced and she gripped the stair rail to prevent herself from falling. After Nathan's rejection last night, she hadn't expected him to change his mind. A small pebble of hope lodged in her heart.

"You believe that I love you." She reached her hand out to him.

Nathan took her arm and led her up the stairs. "I know you think you love me, but that might change when you hear my proposition."

"What is it?" Her voice was hesitant. She couldn't bear it if he wanted things to continue as they were.

Nathan shook his head. "We'll talk after dinner. I won't discuss our future on empty stomachs."

Nathan reached past her and opened her door. "Until then." He smiled as she stepped into the room. "Wear something special."

Madalyn leaned against the door jamb and watch Nathan walk away. He gave her a brief nod before entering his bedchamber. She closed her eyes for a second and then shut her door. Something had changed. She didn't know what, but she wasn't going to question it.

With a quick skip, she ran to her wardrobe and pulled it open. There was an array of silks and cottons in all colors of the rainbow, but an emerald green gown beckoned to her. With a trembling hand, she pulled it out and swung it about her. The gown was perfect.

By the time Annie had finished helping her dress, Madalyn's body was humming with anticipation. It was crazy to hope that Nathan had changed his mind about the marriage, but it was the only thing that explained his actions. Either way, her fate would be decided tonight.

When she reached the head of the stairs, Nathan was waiting. He held out his arm and began to guide her down.

"You look exquisite." Nathan's voice had a husky undertone.

A shiver of delight cascaded down Madalyn's spine. Nathan's voice hinted of stolen kisses and sensual temptations. She leaned over and whispered into his ear.

"So do you."

Nathan smiled. When they reached the bottom of the stairs, he pulled her into his arms and kissed her. His lips soothed and then taunted, teasing her to respond and then moving away when she did.

"Later."

Madalyn flicked her tongue across her lips, smiling when his eyes followed its movement. A sense of power filled her. Nathan wasn't the only one who could play.

Isaac interrupted them with the announcement of dinner. They were again seated at the far end of the table, but this time Nathan was at the head and Madalyn beside him. The room was dimly lit, with candles only at their end.

The footmen brought in the soup, a light broth with delicate shrimp and vegetables. Madalyn ate, but her eyes never left Nathan. He winked at her a couple of times and she almost choked when the soup went down the wrong way.

"I had a visitor today," Nathan began once the soup was removed.

Madalyn's fingers pleated the napkin in her lap and waited until the footmen had left before answering. "Was it important?"

Nathan took a sip of his wine. "It seems Captain Galer put the tale of our marriage to paper before he died."

Madalyn gasped. Horror and shock warred inside her. Before she could reply, the footmen returned with the main course. A platter of roasted pigeons, a venison pastry, new peas, creamed fish, and a plate of sweetmeats were placed in front of them. Nathan dismissed the servants and then they were alone.

"Does one of the crew have it?" Madalyn kept her voice low.

Nathan shook his head. "Worse. Monsieur Dupuy has it and is trying to blackmail us."

"I hope you told him no." Madalyn's hands clenched beside her plate.

"I did, but I had to be certain it was what you wanted." Nathan covered her hand with his, giving it a gentle squeeze. "You'll be more hurt by the gossip than me."

"I refuse to pay someone for their silence."

"As do I, but I have lived many years being the center of vicious tongues. It won't be easy to live this down if the truth is told."

Madalyn picked up her fork. Nathan was right, yet she still couldn't bring herself to deal with a person lost to all honor. It would be better to face the gossip knowing she'd done nothing wrong, than to try and hide from the truth.

"He can't hurt us."

"Dupuy did threaten to do something worse if I didn't comply." Nathan offered Madalyn the plate of fish.

"What did he want?" Madalyn took a small piece of fish and waved aside the pigeon.

"Briars, my plantation." Nathan's voice was devoid of any emotion, but Madalyn sensed an underlying anger.

"That's outrageous." She took a spoonful of the peas before offering them to Nathan.

"He has always wanted it." Nathan took the bowl from her and put it down beside him. "He needs the river frontage."

"When does he intend to make Galer's tale public?" Suddenly the thought of keeping secrets was too much effort. Madalyn didn't care if all of Charleston knew how she and Nathan had met.

"Tomorrow." Nathan's voice was low. "It's not much time to make a decision."

"We have tonight."

Nathan put his fork down and captured her hand. "I wanted you to know everything before we discussed our future."

Madalyn's breath caught in her throat. Nathan's eyes glittered silver blue. She was lost in their mesmerizing depths. He brought her hand to his mouth and the brush of his lips across her skin sent a shiver of excitement through her.

"I have already told you what I want."

"But now there are risks." Nathan picked up the plate of sweetmeats and offered it to her.

Madalyn glanced down at the delicacies and shook her head. "Why is it different now?"

"If you return to England, no one need know about your unfortunate ordeal. If you stay in Charleston, everyone will know." Nathan pushed back from the table. "Shall we retire?"

She accepted Nathan's outstretched hand and let him lead her out of the room. The hallway was empty; the candles trimmed for the night, the wall sconce candles were lit up the length of the stairs and hall above. They walked in silence, their muted footsteps the only accompaniment to their journey.

Madalyn's bedroom was ablaze with candles. Annie had turned down the bed sheets and her night robe was laid across the back of the chair beside her dressing table. Everything was in readiness for her. She waited to see if Nathan would follow her in.

He didn't disappoint. With a soft click, the door was closed and the rest of the world shut out. She walked to her dressing table, her fingers roaming aimlessly over her combs and pins.

"You said you wanted to discuss our future." Her voice trembled. "Have you changed your mind about sending me to England?"

"I still believe that it is in your best interest to forget about this marriage and to find a more suitable husband." Nathan walked over to the window and lifted the curtain before dropping it and turning back to Madalyn. "You need a husband who could return your love."

Madalyn's stomach dropped. She'd hoped he'd come to love her.

At least he was honest.

She'd always know where she stood with him, and that was more than most women had when they entered marriage. She forced a smile to her lips.

"I don't want another husband."

"You shouldn't settle for a man who isn't in love with you."

"Is that what you're offering?"

Nathan rubbed the back of his neck and took a deep breath. "I'm not a young man and I find that after working my whole life to achieve a fortune, I want someone to leave it to. I want children."

"You wish to be free to marry another." Madalyn fought back her tears.

"No." Nathan clenched his hand at his side. "You misunderstand. I'm willing to commit to our marriage, but I cannot promise you love."

Madalyn leaned against her dressing table. Nathan's words were more direct than she'd expected. Her mind told her to run, that only pain could come from a one-sided relationship.

Her heart begged her to stay.

"You want me for a wife?" Madalyn's voice was low and hesitant.

"Yes." Nathan's affirmative echoed between them.

"Why?"

Madalyn bit her lip. She knew that she should accept Nathan's offer, but she needed to understand why he would consider staying with her. There were other women more beautiful than her, who would eagerly accept an arranged marriage with Nathan.

"We enjoy each other's company and even though you have a tendency to ignore my wishes, I find your independence refreshing."

"That will irritate you over time." Madalyn struggled to keep her voice calm, even as Nathan's words destroyed her dreams of love.

"There is more." Nathan straightened his shoulders. "We have a strong sexual attraction."

"Is that enough for a marriage?" Madalyn's voice cracked.

"It's more than most have." Nathan walked to Madalyn and took her hands in his. "I've never met a woman I was more drawn to than you."

"What happens when that fades?"

"You're asking me if I'll be faithful." Nathan squeezed her hands before releasing them. "Marriage is a commitment for life. I've no intention of acting like my father. I'll honor our marriage vows."

Madalyn saw the truth in Nathan's eyes and the knot in her stomach eased. He was offering her a chance to be part of his life, to have his children and perhaps friendship. He was not offering love. Madalyn's heart ached, but it was a beginning.

"You already know how I feel. I love you." Madalyn pushed away from the table and moved to within a few inches of Nathan. She reached out her hand and touched his cheek. "Can you never love me in return?"

Nathan trembled beneath Madalyn's hand and for a split second she thought she had reached him. He tensed his muscles and moved away. Madalyn's shoulders slumped and the tears welled in her eyes.

Nathan clenched and unclenched his hands. "I'm past believing in love. It was wrong of me to suggest that you tie yourself to a marriage with me. Forget that I mentioned it."

Nathan moved to the door.

Madalyn took a deep breath and made her decision.

She had no life without Nathan. If that meant he couldn't love her, it was better than being alone. She'd risked everything for her brother; surely she could gamble her heart on Nathan. Returning to England and marrying her cousin, knowing she'd never see Nathan again, would destroy her.

"I want only you." Her words stopped Nathan.

"You might find a younger man who could offer you the hope of love." Nathan spoke without turning around.

"Marrying my cousin is all that awaits me. He wants my fortune. How can I be certain that isn't the case with any man?" Her voice shook.

"You're a desirable woman. Men would be interested in more than your fortune." Nathan's tone was dry.

"I choose you." Madalyn's voice was a whisper, but Nathan swung his head around as soon as the words were spoken.

He closed his eyes for a few seconds. A tremor shook his body before he sighed. Madalyn braced herself for another rejection, but when he looked at her, his eyes were clear and focused.

Nathan reached for her and joy raced through Madalyn.

His voice was hoarse as he clasped her to him. "God forgive me, but I can't refuse you any longer."

Chapter 25

Nathan captured Madalyn's mouth in a searing kiss of possession. The world spun out of control as she was swept high onto his chest. She clasped her arms tightly around his neck and returned his kiss. His tongue pressed against her lips, demanding entry. She opened, shuddering as he plunged in. He explored her soft inner realm, his tongue gliding and caressing, scorching and branding her with every stroke.

Shivers of excitement raced down her spine as she followed Nathan's lead. Their kiss deepened, their tongues dueling for position, until they found a rhythm. She was repositioned in his arms, but it wasn't until he ended the kiss, that she realized he had laid her on the bed. She clung to his neck, looking up into his eyes, now burning with desire.

"Once I make you mine, I'll never let you go." Nathan's voice was gruff, his body tense with restraint. "Be certain this is what you want."

Madalyn touched his forehead with one hand and brushed back the lock of hair that had fallen to one side. Her heart melted at the intensity of Nathan's gaze.

"I love you," she said in a soft voice. "I only want you."

"Marriage is forever." Nathan's voice was stern, but his gaze had softened.

"So is my love." She reached up and gave Nathan a kiss. "Don't make me wait any longer."

A shudder passed through Nathan's body and he heaved a sigh. His lips twisted into a smile that reached his eyes and sent a flash of heat through Madalyn's body.

"Anticipation enhances the pleasure."

"Don't tease." She squirmed under the roguish glance that he raked over her body.

Nathan ran a finger over her lips. "I've wanted to hold you like this since the first time I saw you."

Nathan claimed her lips and stroked the embers that he had lit earlier. Madalyn's body flared with the heat of passion that scorched within her. He caressed her back as he deepened the kiss. She trembled, savoring the sensations that flamed within her, surrendering to his touch as time ceased.

Nathan moved his lips away from her mouth, softly trailing kisses along her cheek, chin and neck. She squirmed as a delicious tension began to build deep within her.

His teeth nibbled the first button at the front of her dress. Before she could move to unfasten it, Nathan had ripped it off. With continued deftness, he bit off the remaining buttons, his actions slow and deliberate.

A gentle coaxing from his hands and mouth, and Madalyn's dress was peeled away from her chest. His teeth grabbed the white ribbon that held her chemise closed. A quick tug and it fell from her shoulders.

Cool air caressed Madalyn's heated body, causing her already engorged nipples to harden more. She shivered at the heated look in Nathan's eyes as he gazed upon her bare breasts.

"God, you're beautiful." Nathan's voice was hoarse, his breathing ragged.

Nathan's hands caressed the sides of her breasts in slow, rhythmic motions, building a sweet aching need. His finger feathered the tip of a nipple and Madalyn jumped as a shock of molten lava exploded in her womb. His tongue was quick to follow, lathering moist heat across her breast's already swollen peak.

Just as Madalyn thought she could stand no more, Nathan's hand started to tease the nipple of her other breast. Wave upon wave of sensation flooded her body and she lost herself to the excitement building within her.

Madalyn moaned and arched her back. Nathan's hands continued to knead and massage her breasts while his mouth began to kiss, lick, and nip its way down her stomach. His tongue swirled in and around her belly button. Madalyn thought she would scream with the intensity of it.

Her whole body pulsed with need. Her hips moved restlessly beneath Nathan, begging for him to complete their union. Nathan lifted his head from her stomach and she looked at him through half-closed eyes.

"Please," she whispered.

"Soon." Nathan's voice cracked. "This is your first time. Your body needs to be ready."

"I'll explode." She bit her lip. "I can't wait any longer."

"As you wish."

Nathan grinned and sat back on his legs. With a swiftness that took Madalyn by surprise, he tore the crumpled folds of her dress away from her. He threw the ruined gown onto the floor and then turned his attention to her lacy petticoat. He ripped its fastenings and pulled it away. It landed on top of the gown.

The cool air brushed across her exposed body giving her a deliciously wicked thrill. Nathan leaned over her, his eyes slowly raking every inch of her skin. His hand brushed between her thighs, sending a sharp jab of molten heat to her inner core.

"Is that better?" His voice was a low whisper.

She tugged at his waistcoat. "I want to see you."

"But you're the beauty." Nathan captured a nipple and began to suckle.

All thought fled as Nathan's lips and tongue sent sizzling jolts of pleasure throughout her body. She began to vibrate with excitement, her breath coming in gasps as waves of heat pulsed in her womb.

Nathan lifted his mouth and Madalyn fought to capture her breath. "Not fair," she moaned.

"You know what they say about love and war." Nathan bent his head to capture her nipple again, but Madalyn's hand stopped him.

"It's your turn." She pushed herself up on her elbows. "Undress."

Nathan pulled Madalyn to her knees. She reached out a shaking hand and touched his face. There was faint stubble on his chin, sending a tickle of sensation down her arm.

He turned his head and gave her palm a kiss, his lips lingering as their eyes locked. She trembled at the naked emotion that sizzled between them. Nathan's every desire evident in his eyes. His soul was open for inspection.

"I need to feel you against me." His voice was a gravel whisper. He shrugged out of his jacket and tossed it on the floor.

Madalyn's throat was parched, her heart pounded in her chest at the enormity of Nathan's confession. Her hand trembled as she went to untie his cravat, her fingers getting lost in its intricate knots and folds.

"Let me." Nathan gave a sharp tug on the linen and unwound it from his neck. It landed beside his jacket.

Her fingers continued their descent, unbuttoning his waistcoat. He shrugged it off. She reached for his shirt, but he was before her, grasping it in both hands and pulling it over his head. Buttons and shirt flew through the air.

Her breath caught in her throat at the sheer beauty of Nathan. Hard, firm muscles defined his shoulders and arms; his stomach was taut and lean.

He was magnificent.

Madalyn's fingers combed through the light scattering of dark hairs that covered his chest. His breathing was ragged and his heart beat a rapid rhythm under her hand. A shiver of desire shot through her.

Her finger flicked across the nub of one of Nathan's flat nipples. A groan of delight from Nathan sent an answering jolt of heat through her. She leaned forward and stroked his nipple with her tongue, her body flooding with warmth when he shook in response.

She lifted her head away, luxuriating in the feeling of power that Nathan's reaction had given her. He stared down at her through half-closed eyes that simmered with unspoken promises. A quiver of anticipation raced through her veins.

She caressed his chest, kneading its hardness as her hands moved lower. The waistband of his trousers blocked her ministrations. She hesitated only a second before she touched the hard bulge beneath the material. She stroked down its long length.

Nathan jumped as if he'd been burned. He tried to move away, but she stopped him. Pulling on the cloth, she released its fastenings and freed his manhood. Her eyes widened and she gasped when she touched it. It was hot and heavy.

Nathan grabbed her hand away. "Later," he growled. He kicked off his pants and clasped Madalyn to him. "Now it's my turn."

Nathan pushed her back onto the bed. He began kissing her. Her body exploded with desire, shaking as tremors of passion swept through her in waves. His lips moved down her neck, trailing kisses across her breasts and stomach.

His hands eased her legs apart, massaging the sensitive inner skin of her thighs with his thumbs. Madalyn moaned as flutters of pleasure radiated from her womb. Nathan's mouth moved lower, his lips and tongue increasing the intensity of her bliss, as he licked the engorged nub of her inner core. Suddenly, the taut wire of excitement exploded and Madalyn convulsed with wave upon wave of ecstasy.

Nathan continued his caresses until she was exhausted and her body vibrated with bliss. Only then, did he position himself to enter her. He grasped her hips and there was a pressure between her legs.

There was a second of resistance, a sharp stab of pain, and then a sense of fullness and completeness. Nathan leaned over her, both arms on either side of her body, his face tense, perspiration on his forehead. He moved in slow strokes, sending a quiver of delight with every thrust.

Madalyn's hips rose to meet him and they found a rhythm that spiraled their pleasure. All that existed was the joy of loving each other with their bodies. The tight curl of rapture grew with every movement until it exploded. Once again, Madalyn shuddered with ecstasy, but this time Nathan's body pulsed with hers.

It was several minutes before the weight of Nathan's body registered. When she wiggled beneath him, he shifted and stretched out beside her.

"You're shaking. I hurt you." His voice was filled with concern.

She shook her head. "It's chilly in here."

"Damn." Nathan pulled her into his arms and reached for the blanket that had fallen to the floor. With a swift flick of his wrist he covered both their bodies.

Gradually, the warmth began to seep back into Madalyn's body. She snuggled close to Nathan, almost purring her delight at being so near to him.

He brushed her hair away from her face and looked down at her. His gaze was intent. "I've wanted to make love to you since the first moment I saw you."

Heat rose in Madalyn's cheeks. "It was wonderful."

"You're a very sensual woman." Nathan's eyes darkened.

"I've never desired a man's touch before."

"Our bodies recognized each other before our minds did."

"Is that why you saved me from Galer's men?"

"At first, it was because I couldn't stand to see any woman abused in such a way." Nathan's voice softened. "But after I spoke with you, it went deeper than that. I wanted to protect you and keep you safe."

"You didn't want me for your wife though." The pain of Nathan's rejection was too fresh for her to forget it.

"I couldn't trust your feelings." Nathan flung his arm over his head. "You had gone from one trauma to another, first with your brother's kidnapping, then Galer's abuse and our marriage, and lastly, the shipwreck."

"You thought that I might be confused?"

"Yes." Nathan clenched his hand into a fist. "There is also my background. Your family won't approve."

"My uncle never cared about me until I inherited money." Madalyn's voice betrayed her anger. "He has no right to interfere. All I care about is my brother. William will be happy for me."

"As my wife, you may be subjected to snickers and gossip." Nathan turned onto his side and faced her. "I can't keep you safe from ridicule."

Madalyn reached up and smoothed away Nathan's frown. "It doesn't matter."

Nathan grimaced. "Wagging tongues can be hurtful."

"I don't care what others say." Madalyn ran her finger across Nathan's lips, savoring the feel of their moist heat. "Together, we can withstand the gossips."

Nathan's teeth teased Madalyn's finger, sending a shiver of excitement down her arm. "I could always find other things to distract you."

Madalyn trailed a finger across his chest, delighting in the feel of its strength. Nathan's heart was beating rapidly, and his breathing was ragged. A shudder of joy coursed through her veins. No longer did she have to hide her desire.

"Make love to me."

"It's too soon." Nathan kissed her on the forehead. "Your body should heal."

"I ache to feel you inside me again." Madalyn reached under the blanket and caressed Nathan's hardened manhood. "You have the same need."

Nathan groaned as her hand moved down him. She increased her pressure and strokes until he leaned back on the bed, his eyes half-closed with bliss. She kissed him, her tongue dueling with his as her body moved against him, building their desire.

She released his lips and gazed into his eyes. "Please."

"I can't resist you." Nathan's voice was husky.

With a speed that took her breath away, he flipped her onto her back, his leg capturing and holding her body against him. He grinned before his lips softened into a kiss that reached to the depths of her soul. Once again they were lost in a world of passion.

Chapter 26

Madalyn gazed out the library window and hugged her arms close to her. It had been a week since Nathan had first made love to her. She'd never been happier. Long nights of lovemaking, followed by days of anticipation, had left her satiated.

Nathan was a devoted and considerate husband, anticipating her every need. She merely had to mention something for it to appear later that day. She'd never felt so pampered or desired in her whole life.

"A penny for those thoughts." Nathan's whisper tickled her ear.

Madalyn turned and smiled at her husband. "I never knew how wonderful marriage could be."

"It's not always as blissful." Nathan nuzzled Madalyn's neck with his mouth. "We've been lucky to find each other."

"You've made me very happy."

Nathan lifted her hand to his mouth and caressed it with a lingering kiss. Their eyes met and Madalyn's heart leapt into her throat.

"If I didn't have an important meeting I'd carry you upstairs now." Nathan's voice sent shivers of warmth up Madalyn's spine.

Madalyn's eyes darted around the room. "How long do you have?"

"I'm already late." Nathan grinned. "You're insatiable."

Excitement stirred within Madalyn. She moistened her lips and touched Nathan's waistcoat. "It's been hours since you last kissed me."

Nathan's eyes darkened. "What if someone interrupts us?"

Madalyn cleared her throat. "Lock the door."

Nathan's lips twitched. "As you wish."

He walked to the door and the soft click of the lock sent a tremor of joy through her. Nathan came toward her, his steps measured and sure. Her heart pounded in eagerness and she forced herself to breath.

He pulled her into his arms.

His lips possessed hers and all other thoughts fled her mind. The now familiar thrill of pleasure set a fire burning deep within her.

Nathan's lips softened and his tongue stroked and caressed the inner skin of her mouth until her knees weakened. Madalyn would have fallen if Nathan had not held her close. She quivered with need, her whole body humming with blissful anticipation.

Nathan was breathing heavy when he finally ended the kiss. "Satisfied?"

"Never." Her body hungered for more.

She glanced around the library. There were shelves lined with leather bound books, Nathan's large desk and chair, and two wingback chairs in front of it. Nothing looked conducive for lovemaking. She groaned in frustration.

Nathan gave her a quick kiss and then moved them back against the wall. He braced one hand beside her head, while his other reached beneath her skirt and caressed her leg. Molten heat curled in Madalyn's womb and her breathing became ragged.

"This will have to do." His voice was hoarse. "Trust me?"

She nodded, gasping when Nathan's hand pulled her leg high up against his hip. Within seconds, his fingers had reached her moist, inner core, stroking and caressing. Madalyn moaned, surrendering to the sensations that vibrated through her whole being.

She bit her lip, passion and heat threatened to consume her. She trembled as a delicious ache spread throughout her lower body. Nathan's mouth roamed across her lips, face, and neck, coaxing and teasing until her whole body pulsed with yearning.

Nathan pushed her high onto the wall, easing her other leg onto his hip. "Clasp your legs together," he said in a ragged voice.

Madalyn followed Nathan's lead, her body weeping with urgency and desire. She craved the feel of him deep within her. When he finally entered her, Madalyn stifled a scream of satisfaction. Her body hummed with bliss.

She clung to Nathan's shoulders, letting him set the pace of their lovemaking. He held her hips close to him, thrusting rhythmically into her throbbing body. Their bodies swayed, adding to the building tension, until Madalyn felt that she would splinter from the ecstasy.

Nathan shuddered just as Madalyn exploded into a sea of rapture. The world fell away. Their passion carried them to a place where only they existed. Together, they floated back to earth.

Nathan leaned his forehead against her as he gasped for air. "This is insane."

Madalyn chuckled. "Wonderful, though."

Nathan moved away and straightened her skirts. Then he turned and fastened his trousers. Madalyn's legs felt unsteady, so she sat on one of the chairs.

"Are you hurt?" Nathan's voice was soft with concern.

"I need to catch my breath. Your lovemaking leaves me weak."

Nathan grinned. "I'm too old to keep up this pace. You are voracious."

"Is that wrong?" Madalyn frowned. Was her need for Nathan abnormal?

"Every man should be so lucky." Nathan leaned over and kissed Madalyn on the forehead. "I'm a very satisfied man."

Madalyn was comforted by the blaze of approval in Nathan's eyes. "You'll tell me if I overstep the boundaries of acceptable behavior."

"The only rules are the ones we make for ourselves." Nathan helped Madalyn up from the chair. "Your desires match mine perfectly."

Madalyn smiled, savoring the surge of joy that permeated her being. The world glowed brighter and she wondered why she'd been so blessed to find Nathan. He was perfect. She leaned against his arm and let him lead them out of the library.

In the hallway, Nathan picked up his hat and cane. "I have to go. I've been a bit distracted lately, but after today we'll have a chance at a real honeymoon."

"What are you planning?"

"I gave the servants orders to pack the house up. By the end of the week, we'll leave for Briars, my plantation."

"How long will we be there?" This was the first time Nathan had mentioned going to the plantation or a honeymoon.

"The whole summer." Nathan opened the door. "That gives you the rest of the week to gather or purchase anything you might need. I'd rather not have to come back into the city."

"Is there something you need?" Madalyn leaned against the door, inhaling the brisk sea air.

"You." Nathan's eyes smoldered and Madalyn's breath caught in her throat. "I'll have all summer to explore and enjoy my wife."

"Anywhere and everywhere," Madalyn whispered. A surge of delight raced through her as desire flared in Nathan's eyes.

"I've ordered a special dinner for us tonight." Nathan grinned. "The servants will be busy, so we'll serve ourselves."

"I look forward to it." Madalyn watched Nathan stroll down the walkway.

She hummed to herself as she wandered upstairs. She'd ordered some summer gowns from Madame Lafitte, and now would be a good time to pick them up. She'd never been to a plantation before, but she guessed it wouldn't be too different from a country estate in England. She grabbed a hat and went to order the coach.

George drove her to Madame's small corner shop and helped her from the coach. She was just about to enter the shop when a male voice stopped her.

"I see you're finding your way about Charleston."

Madalyn turned and looked into the smirking eyes of Monsieur Dupuy. Her chest constricted in anger, clenching her hands, she forced a smile to her lips. The man was a reptile, but she didn't want to cause a public scene.

"Not for long," she said with a bow of her head. "We leave for Briars tomorrow."

Monsieur Dupuy's eyes narrowed. "Tell your husband it's foolish not to take my advice."

"About being blackmailed?" Madalyn almost laughed at the look of disbelief on Dupuy's face. "You look surprised. I know about your threats. My husband and I discuss everything."

"Then you know that I will have your name ruined." Dupuy stepped in front of her.

"I know you will try." Madalyn shrugged. "We have nothing to hide."

"Galer's own words will hang you."

"I doubt it." She turned back to the shop, but Dupuy's arm stopped her.

"There are worse things than gossip." Dupuy's voice held a note of menace.

A shiver of fear gripped her. Dupuy leaned toward her, his eyes filled with venom, one hand clenched his cane like a claw, and the other pointed at her. Madalyn inhaled a quick breath and tried to ignore the hatred emanating from the man.

"Your threats are useless." She took a step back. "You'll have to find another way to finance you lifestyle."

"You go too far." Dupuy spat the words. "It will be a pleasure to bring you down."

Dupuy turned and walked away. Madalyn shook off the feeling of doom that settled on her shoulders. The man was angry because someone had finally stood up to him. There was nothing he could do to harm her. If Nathan was prepared to live with the gossip, then so was she.

After gathering her purchases from Madame Lafitte, Madalyn bought a few toiletries and then headed back to the house. Everything was upside down, with dustsheets covering the furniture in the dining room and the drawing room.

Annie was busy folding her gowns and packing them away in two large trunks.

"Master has ordered everything be ready, but I'll keep the trunks open until the last minute."

Madalyn handed Annie the new gowns and put her other purchases on her dressing table, before going to her wardrobe to help Annie.

The afternoon sped by quickly and once everything had been sorted it was almost time for dinner. Annie helped her dress and then went off to assist in the kitchen. A few servants would be staying in Charleston, but most would travel with them.

She dressed for dinner and went down to the library to wait for Nathan. It would be the last room the servants closed up. Beside the fireplace a small table had been set for two. Candles burned on the mantle, shining an ethereal glow down on the crystal stemware and china.

"Does it meet with your approval?"

Madalyn turned and smiled at Nathan. "Did you order this?"

"I thought it would be the perfect way to start our official honeymoon."

Madalyn walked to Nathan and ran her fingers down his brocade waistcoat. A feeling of peace settled as she gazed up into her husband's eyes. Nathan seemed to know what she needed even when she did not.

Isaac entered the room at that moment, followed by two footmen. They placed a number of covered dishes on the table. Isaac gave a slight bowed before leaving, closing the door behind him. Now they were truly alone.

Nathan wrapped his arms around Madalyn. "You're looking exquisite this evening."

Madalyn reached up to kiss Nathan, but he pulled away. "We have all evening. I want to savor every moment."

He guided her to the table. "Dinner first."

She sat across from Nathan, her body tingling with awareness. His eyes simmered with passion making it impossible to concentrate on dinner. The meal was a blur as her body pulsed in anticipation of promised ecstasy.

When they finished eating, Nathan led her from the parlor and upstairs to her bedchamber. The trunks stood on one side and her dressing table was bare except for one brush. Only then, did he pull her into his arms.

His lips brushed across hers, sending a jolt of need to every nerve in her body. Madalyn gazed up at Nathan's beloved face, her breath catching in her throat at the naked yearning burning in his eyes. She stood on tiptoes, eager to feel his lips again.

Nathan shook his head, his finger tapping her lips. "There's no rush."

A shiver of excitement raced through her veins. His finger traced the outline of her lips then moved across her cheek and down her chin. He spread his hand across her neck, and let his thumb continue to caress her lower lip.

"I intend to enjoy every inch of your body." Nathan's smoldering eyes dropped to her mouth. "The taste and smell of you haunts me. It consumes my every thought, until nothing remains but you."

Chapter 27

Madalyn's mouth went dry, her breathing slowed as Nathan's words sang to her soul. Never before had he admitted to needing her. Hope sprang to life. Surely love would follow soon.

She moistened her lips with her tongue, surprised by the groan it elicited from Nathan. Before she had a chance to respond, Nathan's mouth covered hers. He nibbled at her lips, then let his tongue soothe them with moist heat before capturing them in a kiss.

Madalyn was lost in the feel and taste of Nathan. His tongue dueled with hers, sending a shock of sensation to the very tips of her toes. Her knees weakened and she leaned into him, moving against him.

He clasped her to him. A swell of feminine power rushed through Madalyn when she felt the extent of his arousal. She reached down and captured him in one hand, squeezing and rubbing until Nathan trembled with need.

"Later," he growled, picking her up in his arms and walking to the bed. "Tonight, I do the feasting."

Nathan tumbled her onto the bed. Tendrils of heat shot through Madalyn, as she watched him pull off his boots and cravat, before he knelt on the bed beside her. He leaned over and ran his hand down the length of her body.

"You have too many clothes on." Nathan's voice was low.

Madalyn savored the fire that was building within her. Nathan's eyes promised sensual delights. His hand's tender ministrations left her begging for more. Through half-closed lids, she followed the slow movement of his fingers as they explored the lace edging of her dress's bodice. Her breath caught in her throat.

"Turn over."

She reached for Nathan, but he evaded her. He motioned for her to turn onto her stomach. She hesitated for a second, but she could never deny him. With deft fingers, he unfastened her gown and pulled it from her. Her chemise and drawers were disposed of just as quickly.

She lay across the bed, luxuriating in the feel of Nathan's firm hands kneading and massaging her back. She floated in a sea of bliss.

Nathan's lips followed his fingers, each kiss more searing than the last, as he made his way from her shoulders to the tips of her toes. She was boneless, completely in thrall of Nathan's lovemaking. Only then, did he ease her onto her back.

His fingers moved with feathering lightness over the whole of her body. His kisses followed the same journey, lingering and teasing until Madalyn's body pulsed with need. She moved against the bed, wordlessly begging Nathan to end the sweet torment.

He ignored her plea.

His hands and lips moved to focus on her breasts.

He cradled each one in a hand, kneading and fondling until Madalyn was mindless with pleasure. His thumbs rubbed across her engorged nipples, sending jolts of moist lava to her lower body.

"Now," Madalyn begged in a breathless voice.

Nathan shook his head before lowering it to her breasts. His lips continued the onslaught, sucking and nibbling until Madalyn was panting with yearning. His mouth left her breasts and trail kisses down her stomach. His tongue swirled moist heat, lathering and soothing until pleasure diffused throughout her.

When he reached her center, his mouth caressed the tender skin of her inner thighs. His tongue darted out, teasing her pulsing inner core, until she was stretched to the breaking point. Her hands twisted in the bedcovers and she bit her lower lip to stop herself screaming.

Madalyn splintered with ecstasy.

It was several moments before she came back to earth. Nathan was leaning beside her, a satisfied grin on his face. He pulled his shirt over his head and her body began to stir again. The beauty of his tightly honed muscles and wide chest sparked a renewed stab of longing in her womb. She went to touch him, but he dodged her hand.

"I've haven't finished." Nathan leaned over and kissed Madalyn, his lips demanding and enticing.

She melted as he began his sweet torment again.

Nathan's lovemaking lasted throughout the night, as over and over again, he gave her unimagined sensual delights and rapture. Only when she was exhausted from his lovemaking did he enter her. She quivered with the beauty of their joining. Each thrust of his body sent a shiver of rapture through her. They moved as one. Their souls and bodies joined as they reached a shattering peak of ecstasy. Together, they collapsed into a contented sleep.

The next morning, Madalyn was woken by Nathan's kiss. She looked up to see him standing beside her, fully clothed.

"I've received an urgent letter from Francois." Nathan sat on the bed, his fingers brushing her cheek. "I may be away for a day, but I'll be back to escort you to Briars."

She yawned and sat up. "Is it serious?"

Nathan hesitated and then shook his head. "It's nothing to concern you."

"I'll go with you." She flung back the covers and reached for her dressing gown. "Wait until I get ready."

"Relax. I want you rested for our move to Briars." Nathan pulled the blankets back over her. "I've ordered you breakfast and a bath. You must stay in Charleston until I know what Francois desires. I'll send you word."

Madalyn leaned back against her pillows. Her heart was bursting with love for Nathan. He showed he cared in so many ways. It was hard to trust that it was real, impossible to believe that she deserved such a wonderful man.

After Nathan left, she ate her breakfast in bed, and waited until the bath was brought to her room. When the servants had left, she walked over to the tin tub and checked the temperature. Steam rose from the water. She threw a handful of rose petals into the bath.

Humming to herself, she picked up her brush and was about to pull it through her hair when the bedroom door opened.

"Did you forget something…?" The words died in her throat when she turned around and saw who had entered the room.

Her heart beat in a furious staccato as fear raced up her spine.

The quiet click of the door closing echoed through the still air.

"Expecting someone else?" The voice boomed loudly into the silence.

"Uncle Phillip?" Madalyn stumbled over her words, her mind refusing to believe her eyes.

"You sound surprised." Her uncle moved his large bulk into the room, his breathing heavy from exertion. "Surely you didn't think that I would let you disobey me?"

Her fingers shook as she pulled her dressing robe closer to her body. Her mouth was dry, but she forced herself to take a deep breath. Her uncle could no longer touch her. She was safely married.

"You've no right to be here." Madalyn's voice cracked, but she forced herself to continue. "Leave."

Her uncle grinned, his eyes a steely gray. "You are under my care. I have every right."

"I'm married." Madalyn straightened her shoulders. "You can't touch me."

"Ahh yes… your marriage." Lord Phillip tilted his head. "I ran into an old friend last week. It seems Lady Raglan was witness to a trumped up wedding aboard a ship."

Madalyn recalled the lovely, but rude Lady Raglan with revulsion. "How long have you been in Charleston?"

Lord Phillip's eyes narrowed. "I know that your husband has been foolish in the enemies he's made. Hoping to escape Charleston before I could find you?"

For a fleeting second, the image of Monsieur Dupuy flashed into Madalyn's mind. He wasn't the only person who knew that they were leaving Charleston, but he'd threatened her. Now his words made sense. He'd known that her uncle was in Charleston.

"The marriage is legal." She lifted her chin. "The captain and a minister oversaw it."

"I've already taken steps to have it annulled." Lord Phillip moved into the room. "Get your clothes. We're leaving."

Madalyn stood her ground. "I'll never leave with you."

Lord Phillip shrugged. "Have it your way."

He moved with swiftness.

He smacked the side of her face with an open hand.

Her head wrenched back from the impact and her teeth felt as if they'd been jarred from her mouth. She raised her hands to protect herself from another blow.

Lord Phillip took advantage of her defenseless body and grabbed the neckline of her dressing gown. He yanked on it. The sound of tearing material was deafening. Cold air brushed against her skin.

She covered her breasts with her arms, but once again the horror and shame of being exposed flooded her. She clutched the remnants of her robe, her hands grasping at the ruined material in a vain attempt to recover her dignity.

Her uncle marched across the room and flung back the lid of one of the trunks. With rough hands, he mauled through the contents, flinging articles of clothing over his shoulder.

"Get dressed."

Madalyn knelt on the floor, reaching for the gown and chemise her uncle had tossed to her. She clasped them close to her and stood.

"I need privacy."

Her uncle's lip lifted in an ugly sneer. "And give you a chance to escape? Never."

"Turn around then." Madalyn's could barely speak the words, her voice thick with unshed tears.

"I've seen it all before." Her uncle's voice dripped sarcasm. "A girl that would run away and marry a stranger deserves to be treated like a whore."

"Why bother with me then?"

"Don't act the fool." Lord Phillip's face twisted with anger. "The money."

"You can have it. Just leave me be."

"It's not that easy." Lord Phillip shook his hand at Madalyn. "Until your marriage is annulled, you have no control over the monies."

Madalyn's breath caught in her throat. She had forgotten that a woman lost control of her money. "Nathan will give it to you."

Her uncle grabbed her, his fingers biting into her arm. "He'll be happy to be rid of you, but the money is another thing."

Madalyn winced at the pain, forcing herself to look into her uncle's eyes. "You never cared for me. Why force me to go with you?"

"I want you nearby until this matter is settled." Lord Phillip gave her a shake. "You'll be under lock and key."

"I won't fight you on the money." Madalyn heard the fear in her voice. "You don't have to take me with you."

"You forget that you're engaged to Horace."

Madalyn gasped. "You can't still expect me to marry him."

"There's no other way." Lord Phillip released her arm. "Once I have my hands on the money, I don't give a damn what happens to you. Get dressed or I'll drag you out naked."

Madalyn pulled the clothes on. Her hands shook so badly she couldn't fasten the gown. Her uncle lost his patience. With a snort, he spun her around and did the dress up. Then he grabbed her arm, and pulled her from the room.

"The servants won't let you take me." Madalyn's voice rose.

"They're busy closing the house. It's amazing how safe people feel inside their homes."

Her uncle clasped his hand over her mouth and kept her close to him. She tried to wiggle away, but his other hand tightened on her throat.

"One more move and I'll strangle you."

Madalyn shivered with terror. Her uncle's voice was devoid of emotion, cold and icy in its bluntness. She tried to control the tremors that racked her body, but that only made it worse. Her uncle lifted her against his chest and then walked down the stairs.

She tried to twist her head around to see if anyone had seen them, but Lord Phillip's hands held her firm. Outside, a closed carriage was waiting. She was thrown in, her body slamming against the velvet squabs. She struggled to catch her breath.

"This is insane. You can't expect to kidnap me in broad daylight." Madalyn's words came out between gulps of air.

"I just did." Her uncle settled himself back against the seat and stretched his legs out. "Don't get too comfortable. We'll be stopping shortly."

The noise outside the carriage got louder and Madalyn strained her ears for a clue of their whereabouts. There were men shouting and the sound of horses and carts moving on wood. The coach stopped suddenly, throwing her against her uncle.

He draped a black cape around her shoulders and pulled the hood over her head. After tying the hood, he lifted Madalyn against him.

"Not a word," he hissed as his hand wrapped around her throat.

"Where are you taking me?" Madalyn's voice shook with renewed fear.

"Home."

Chapter 28

Nathan stood at the pier watching the seagulls circle the ships. The cool morning breeze was refreshing. He took a deep breath of the salt air, and stomped his feet. He couldn't remember ever feeling so alive before. He owed that to Madalyn.

Just the thought of her made his body harden in anticipation. Soon they'd be at Briars, where the rest of the world couldn't touch them. The worries about gossip and business would fade away. All that would exist was Madalyn.

"Madalyn." Nathan's voice was more a sigh than sound.

"Did you say something, sir?"

Nathan turned around, clearing his throat, when he saw Jackson standing behind him expectantly.

"I've a letter from St. Amand. He needs me at his plantation so I am leaving today. You will have control of the operation." Nathan started to walk away from the pier. "After I return, my wife and I will be going directly to Briars."

"Of course." Jackson fell in step with Nathan. "You will be at Briars, if I need you, though."

"Only in an emergency." Nathan flagged down his coach. "I promised my wife a honeymoon."

Jackson's smile widened. "Excellent, sir."

Nathan pulled the carriage door open. "Anything else I should know before I leave?"

Jackson pulled at his collar and looked down at his feet. "Monsieur Dupuy left a message."

Nathan paused in getting into the vehicle. He looked at Jackson with a raised eyebrow. "Yes?"

"He said to tell you that no man crosses him." Jackson swallowed hard. "He has taken his revenge."

Nathan clenched his jaw. "Is that all?"

"He said that you would understand." Jackson rubbed his nose. "There's also the matter you asked me to look into."

"Dupuy's finances?"

Jackson nodded. "It seems he's mortgaged to the hilt. The bank is holding notes on all his property."

Nathan nodded and jumped into the carriage. "Buy up all the notes you can. That should give me the leverage I need."

Nathan sat back in the coach and swore. He'd hoped to call Dupuy's bluff, but obviously the man was quicker than him. No matter, he thought with a shrug. He and Madalyn would be at Briars when the gossip about their marriage made the rounds. By the time they returned, it would be old news.

Nathan still had Dupuy's financial situation to consider. He frowned at the implications of Jackson's words. Buying Dupuy's notes would give him total control of the man's future. He was a fool to let his position become so precarious. One word from him and Dupuy would be ruined. Nathan dismissed it from his mind. There would be plenty of time to deal with the leech after his honeymoon.

The sun was high in the sky when he pulled into St. Amand's plantation, Rosewood. He jumped down from the carriage just as two boys flew out the front door. They crashed into Nathan before he took a step closer to Rosewood's pillared entryway. He picked them up in his arms and swung them around before letting them down.

"You've grown."

Daniel, the shorter of the two was the exact image of his father. He was four. His green eyes danced with devilment and his hair was a silver white. Pierre was two years older and taller. He was closer in looks to his mother, with serious brown eyes and hair the color of wheat. His smile was all Francois, though.

"Uncle Nathan, we haven't seen you in ages." Daniel grabbed his hand and pulled him toward the house. "Mother says that you're very busy in the city."

"She's right." Nathan reached out and ruffled Pierre's hair. "That's no excuse for not visiting sooner, though."

"Father says you were in England for several months." Pierre looked up at him with interest. "We have a visitor from there."

Nathan's chest tightened with anticipation. He'd been reluctant to tell Madalyn that her beloved William may have been found. Until he'd seen the boy with his own eyes, he refused to get her hopes up. She'd gone through too much to find her brother to give her another disappointment.

"That's why your Father sent for me." Nathan allowed the boys to drag him up the stairs and through the front door.

"Nathan!" Nanette's musical voice greeted him. "Boys, go get your father.

Nathan enfolded her in a hug and breathed in the sweet floral smell that he always associated with Nanette. She'd been born at Rosewood. It was her family's plantation. She'd inherited it when her father and brother had been killed in a carriage accident. Her mother had died giving birth to her.

"It's so good to see you." Nanette stood back from him and gave him a long assessing look. "You look happy."

Nathan grinned. She was right. He was content for the first time in years and there was only one reason for that. Madalyn.

"Marriage suits you." Nanette nodded and then clasped his arm to lead him to the front parlor. "Francois told me that you met your wife on your last crossing from England. I understand she's British."

"Yes." Nathan glanced around the richly decorated parlor. Everything was the same as his last visit. He was about to take a seat just as the boys returned with their father.

"Nathan." Francois shook his hand. "You came quickly."

"Your note seemed urgent." Nathan inhaled a quick breath. "Have you found him?"

Francois nodded. "It's him. I'm certain."

A surge of relief rushed through Nathan. "Madalyn will be ecstatic."

"My overseer found him on Ashton Grove. It's a plantation in the next county. His papers had been bought before he'd even left the ship."

"That's why there was no record of the sale in Charleston." Nathan rubbed his nose. "That suggests a connection with his abductors."

"Not necessarily." Francois motioned to Daniel and Pierre. "Ask William to join us."

When the boys had left the parlor Francois cleared his throat. "I know the owner of Ashton Grove and he wasn't involved in the abduction. He was approached by a Bertram Harden with the papers long before the ship landed."

"So it was no coincidence that William was taken."

Francois shook his head. "You'd guessed that already."

"When Madalyn told me her brother was the Earl of Fenton, I'd suspected it had been deliberate."

"It's a miracle he survived."

"That was the intention." Nathan's voice was dry. "How bad was he treated?"

"Fenton was ill on the ship, starved, and beaten. When they arrived at Charleston, he was given up for dead."

Nathan pushed back his rage. Anger would not change what had happened to the Earl. Thankfully, the boy had survived. He didn't want to think about how devastated Madalyn would have been if her brother had died.

"He must have a strong will to live."

"Luck had more to do with it. He was sent to Ashton Grove. Ben Harington is tough, but fair." Francois gave Nathan a penetrating look. "He gave him medical care and then put him to work."

Nathan clenched his fists. "How bad?"

Francois pursed his lips. "I doubt he's the same boy Madalyn remembers."

Nathan nodded. He understood better than most what it meant to have everything taken away without warning. His father's remarriage had done that to him. One moment living at Caldern and the next relegated to a small cottage. Only his brothers' love had saved him. William didn't even have that.

Just then, a young man entered the parlor. Nanette went to him and led him over to Nathan and Francois. He was little more than a boy, but the wariness in his eyes touched Nathan. He had the same brown curls and straight nose as Madalyn. There was no doubting the family resemblance.

"Lord Fenton." Nathan bowed his head slightly. "I'm Nathan Carter, your brother-in-law."

William's brown eyes narrowed. "My sister isn't married."

"A lot has happened since your abduction." Nathan gestured to a chair. "Perhaps we should discuss it."

Francois sat on a settee and out of the corner of Nathan's eye he watched as Nanette took a chair at the opposite side of the room. Francois gave a slight grimace and then turned back to Nathan.

"I haven't explained anything to William. He only knows that you asked me to find him."

Nathan raised an eyebrow. Trust Francois to leave the tricky stuff to him. Nathan sat and leaned forward, resting his elbows on his knees. William was seated with his back stiff, hands clenched on the chair arms.

"Madalyn saw your kidnapping."

"You lie." William's voice was gruff. "It was too dark and I was alone."

"Nevertheless, your sister went to meet you. She arrived just as the men grabbed you." Nathan paused to let his words penetrate William's defences. "She followed you to the dock and tried to stop the ship from leaving."

William shook his head. "She could have been harmed."

"She knows it was foolish, but she took the next ship sailing for Charleston."

"Why didn't she tell my Uncle what had happened?"

"She did."

Nathan watched as William absorbed the information. He frowned and his eyes were clouded with confusion. It took a couple of seconds before the enormity of Nathan's words registered. At that moment, it seemed as if the boy became a man.

"So my uncle was responsible for the kidnapping."

"I'm afraid that's probably the case." Nathan leaned back in his seat. "When Madalyn asked for help, he laughed."

William's lips twisted into a grimace. "So much for family love. You can't trust anyone."

A surge of sympathy raced through Nathan. "If that were the case, you wouldn't be free now."

William's shoulders sagged. "You're right. I have to thank you and Monsieur St. Amand."

"Don't forget your sister. She risked her life to save you."

"Where is Madalyn?"

"In Charleston." Nathan stood "I wanted to be certain you were found before I told her. Now, if you're feeling up to travel, I suggest we go to meet her."

"Of course." William stood and turned to Francois. "Thank you for setting me free."

"I was glad to help." Francois gave a slight bow of his head. "I hope this doesn't give you a distaste for America."

William shook his head. "On the contrary. Everyone here has helped me. My real issues are with those in England. I hope I can repay your kindness in the future."

"No need." Francois cleared his throat. "You really have your sister to thank. She's a remarkable woman."

William grinned and then turned to Nanette. "Thank you for your kind hospitality."

Nanette gave him a hug. "We were happy to help. The housekeeper has your belongings packed in your room."

Francois patted William on the back. "I'll go with you."

William nodded and then looked at Nathan. "We'll be right back."

Nanette's shoulders drooped when Francois and William left the room. She stumbled back into her seat and sighed. Nathan didn't know what had caused the rift in his friends' marriage, but seeing Nanette in such obvious distress was the breaking point. He was going to get to the bottom of this.

"How long have you been unhappy?"

Nanette jumped at Nathan's words. "I'd forgotten you were still here."

"That's obvious." Nathan sat in the seat beside her. "I don't know what the problem between you and Francois is, but it has to end. You can't live the rest of your lives ignoring each other."

Nanette gave a wan smile. "Francois thinks it's the perfect solution. The only problem is when I ask him to come home."

Nathan clasped her hand. "When did it start?"

"Before Daniel was born." Nanette shuddered. "Francois doesn't believe Daniel is his son."

It took Nathan a second to digest Nanette's meaning. There was no doubt that the boy was his, but for some reason Francois doubted.

"Why would he suspect that?"

Nanette's eyes began to fill with tears. "Do you remember John Calvert?"

"He lives on the next plantation."

Nathan eyes narrowed as he remembered the handsome scoundrel. He had a reputation with women and a devil may care attitude. He'd inherited his father's property in his early twenties and had since tripled his land holdings and wealth. He was sought after by mothers for their daughters, but had so far escaped marriage.

"He's older than you, and not one of your particular friends."

"That's not entirely true." Nanette took a deep breath. "Before I met Francois, John was a frequent visitor. He asked me to marry him."

"Obviously you refused him."

"Yes, but I was wrong not tell Francois." Nanette straightened her shoulders. "John swore that he would never get over me, and he took every opportunity to corner me. At first, I thought it was flattering, but after a while…" Nanette stopped speaking.

"It was harassing," Nathan finished.

Nanette nodded. "I refused to go places where he was, and for a time that worked. Then he started dropping in at Rosewood unannounced."

"That's when Francois took notice."

Nathan's voice was grim. He could see the situation all too clearly. If he'd found another man sniffing around Madalyn, he would have shot him. It must have cut Francois to the core to think that Nanette was entertaining the neighbor. Still, it was a far stretch from visiting to an affair. Something else must have happened.

"Francois was livid. He refused to let me explain and that made it worse."

"What made him think it was an affair?"

"John came over uninvited late one afternoon. Francois was coming in from the fields and John must have spied him through the window." Nanette caught back a sob. "John grabbed me and kissed me. I struggled and beat at him with my hands, but it didn't help. He only released me when Francois roared."

"Why didn't I hear about a duel?" Nathan frowned. Francois hadn't mentioned any of this to him, and he was his closest friend. Surely, he would have been asked to act as his second?

"Francois refused. He said my behavior was indefensible." Nanette buried her face in her hands. "It was for the best. I'm certain John's plan was to kill Francois."

"So Calvert walked away?"

"He has never returned." Nanette looked up. "He got his revenge. Shortly after, I discovered I was with child, but Francois refused to believe it was his. Instead, he left for Charleston and other women."

"Haven't you tried to make him understand?" Nathan's jaw clenched. To show such a lack of trust in his wife was horrific, but to deny his own son was sinful.

"He's seldom here and when he is, he refuses to acknowledge my presence." Nanette sighed. "It has become unbearable. He insists I am dead to him. If there was a way to end the marriage, I would."

"Is there a chance for forgiveness?"

"I asked Francois to forgive me." Nanette's lips trembled. "I've done nothing wrong, but I tried, hoping that would end the silence. He refused. If I didn't still love him I could probably find a way to tolerate our separation."

"I'm truly sorry Nanette." Nathan squeezed her hand. "If there is something I can do, let me know."

Nanette gave him a watery smile. "You're a good friend."

Just then Francois walked in. Nathan watched as his friend's eyes and lips narrowed. Francois wasn't quite as indifferent as he let on. Instead of releasing Nanette, he raised her hand to his lips and kissed it.

"I'll take my leave now." Nathan stood. "I must make haste to Charleston."

He walked out of the room and waited on the front porch for his friend. William was already at the carriage and looked up at him. Nathan nodded and turned to Francois.

"Thank you for finding Madalyn's brother."

"I'm glad the boy was alive." Francois's words were clipped.

Nathan inhaled the sweet perfume of the roses that surrounded the house. "I'd like to return the favor and give something back to you."

"I haven't lost anything."

"Then you're a fool." Nathan slapped his gloves against his hand. "I've known you since I arrived in America, almost twenty years ago. I've never interfered in your personal life before, but there's a first time for everything."

"I don't need your meddling."

Nathan tilted his head. "Someone needs to make you see the truth. Nanette has never been unfaithful to you. Daniel is the spitting image of you. There can be no doubt he is your son."

"You don't know anything about it."

"I know Nanette. She loves you."

Francois gave a harsh laugh. "What do you know about love?"

"I know it can hurt, but it can also heal." Nathan pulled on his gloves. "I'll admit I wanted to push love away, but thankfully a good friend convinced me to let it into my life."

"She betrayed me."

"You're the one guilty of that particular sin." Nathan's voice was harsh and low. "When she needed your help and understanding, you walked out on her. Instead of defending her, you turned your back."

"You would have done the same."

Nathan shook his head. "I understand your anger, but to refuse to listen and then to insult the woman you professed to love, is inexcusable. Your words and deeds have betrayed her far worse than any imagined embrace you saw."

"She was in his arms." Francois spoke through clenched teeth.

"Nanette was struggling to get away. She did not invite his attentions." Nathan watched Francois face pale. "Calvert wanted to ruin her happiness because she'd refused to marry him. Your lack of trust made it easy for him to destroy your marriage."

"That's a lie." Francois whispered. "She never mentioned Calvert's proposal."

"Did you give her a chance?" Nathan started down the stairs. "If I were you, I'd get down on my knees and beg her forgiveness. Something tells me she loves you enough to take you back."

Nathan climbed into the carriage. He'd done all he could to help Francois. Hopefully, it was enough. Now, all he wanted to think about was Madalyn and how happy she'd be when she saw William.

The journey to Charleston passed quickly. During that time, Nathan came to appreciate his new brother-in-law. The boy had been thrust into manhood, but was handling it. One day his ordeal would be a barely remembered adventure, but now it was too fresh to be considered objectively.

William wanted to know how Madalyn had come to America, but Nathan refused to tell the story. William would have to ask his sister for that. The only thing he said was that Madalyn had faced difficulties. He knew that had only fired William's curiosity, but it was up to Madalyn to disclose how much of the truth she wanted her brother to know.

The coach drove up to the house and the men descended together. Nathan let them into the house. The only noise he could hear was at the rear of the house. The servants were packing for the move to Briars. He walked into the drawing room, but Madalyn wasn't there. He motioned William to sit.

"I'll find Madalyn and bring her down to you."

Next he checked the library. When he found that empty he started up the stairs.

She must be taking a nap. A grin spread across his face. It was his fault that she wasn't getting any sleep at night, but he couldn't get enough of his wonderful wife. He took the stairs two at a time and after a quick knock at the door, walked into the bedchamber.

The room was empty.

His heart stood still.

He took another step into the room. The scent of roses filled the air. The bedcovers were in a tangle at the end of the bed and a tray with an empty plate sat near the pillows.

Nathan's eye settled on the open trunk. Gowns and undergarments hung from the sides, satin and silk trailed onto the floor. His heart beat in a furious staccato. Someone had left in a hurry.

There was only one explanation.

Madalyn had left him.

Chapter 29

He leaned against the bedpost and forced himself to breath. Madalyn had run away. That didn't make sense, unless she'd been lying to him. He'd been an idiot to believe that she loved him. She'd bolted the first opportunity she had.

Nathan dropped his head into his hands. His mind refused to work. Everything was muddled. Madalyn's desertion was the only thought that kept replaying over and over. He'd been a fool to believe she loved him.

It was just as he'd feared. Madalyn had come to her senses and left. Nathan looked up and took a deep breath. A sharp pain stabbed his heart. He moved away from the bed, his steps faltering as he tried to regain his balance.

How could he go on?

Madalyn was as vital as breathing to him.

His eyes scanned the room again and stopped at the tub. It was full. The water was strewn with rose petals. They floated undisturbed on the surface. Nathan frowned and walked over to the bath. His fingers fluttered in the now cold water. It was clear and fresh.

Unused.

He glanced once more around the room and saw Madalyn's dressing gown lying in a heap on the floor by the fireplace. He picked it up. It was in two pieces, silk threads ripped and hanging from jagged edges. Nathan inhaled a quick breath. Why would Madalyn have been in such a hurry to dress? His eyes scanned the room again, a suspicion slowly surfacing in his thoughts.

Madalyn hadn't left willingly.

"Dupuy." Nathan swore aloud.

He remembered the message Jackson had given him. Was this the revenge? The man was a scoundrel, but Nathan would have sworn that kidnapping was beneath even him. Still, Madalyn was missing and Dupuy had made threats.

Nathan threw the torn robe to the floor and ran down the stairs shouting for Isaac. When he reached the kitchen, all the staff were looking at him as if he were mad.

"Did anyone see or hear anything unusual this morning?"

"No." Isaac straightened up from the trunk he'd been packing.

Nathan turned to Annie. "Did you help Madalyn dress?"

"She's not rung yet." Annie shook her apron out. "I've been listening."

A couple of the maids agreed with Annie and then others joined in until the room was loud with voices.

"She's gone. Someone has taken her."

Nathan's words silenced the staff. They stared; their mouths open in surprise and their heads shaking denial.

"When?" Isaac was the first to speak.

"I don't know. Did anyone see or hear anything out of the usual?"

"I saw a man yesterday," a small voice said from behind the others.

Nathan motioned for young Tom to come forward. "Where?"

"He was outside looking at the house, but when I asks him if I could help, he yelled at me." Tom glanced at Nathan and then his gaze skittered away. "When I went to get Isaac, the man had left."

"What did he look like?"

"He was a large man with gray hair." Tom patted his chest. "He made a noise when he breathed."

Nathan frowned. He'd expected Tom to describe Dupuy, but this man was different. He racked his memory, but no one came to mind.

"This was the first time you'd seen the man?"

"Yes sir." Tom pointed at Nathan. "He was dressed like you."

Nathan frowned and looked at his chest. Suddenly he understood. The man was a gentleman with money. That would narrow his search.

"Annie, you search Madalyn's room to see if there is a clue as to where she's been taken. Isaac, you make certain that someone watches for any strangers outside. Have the footmen check with the neighbors to see if they saw anything unusual. Before you do anything, have someone send refreshments to the drawing room. We have a guest."

Isaac nodded and motioned to the footmen. "Where will you be?"

"At Monsieur Dupuy's house." Nathan paused in the doorway. "Send for me if Madalyn returns."

Nathan went to the drawing room. William was standing by the window, his hands behind his back. Nathan rubbed his chin. This wasn't going to be easy. He was expecting his sister.

"Madalyn is not here."

William turned and glared at Nathan. "What has happened? Is this another plot to keep me a prisoner?"

Nathan brought up his hands in a conciliatory gesture. "No. When I left this morning she was still in bed. It looks as if she may have been forced to leave."

William tilted his head. "Who would do such a thing?"

Nathan cleared his throat. "I don't know, but I'm going to see a man who made threats this morning."

"I'm coming with you."

"Stay." Nathan turned to leave. "If Madalyn returns, she needs someone here."

Nathan didn't wait for William's agreement before he left the house. He ran to the stables. Once his horse was saddled, he raced to Dupuy's house on the outskirts of the city. The only thing he could think about was Madalyn. He rode as fast as his horse would take him, arriving disheveled and out of breath fifteen minutes later.

Nathan pounded on the door and when it was opened, he barged into the hall. "Get me Dupuy," he shouted. His chest heaved as he struggled to catch his breath.

"What the hell?" Dupuy's angry words came from beyond the hall.

Nathan moved in the direction of the voice and confronted Dupuy at the door of his library. He pushed the man in and shut the door.

"How dare you come into my home uninvited?" Dupuy glared daggers at Nathan.

"I don't have time for your sensibilities." Nathan leaned against the library door, blocking Dupuy's escape. "Where is my wife?"

Dupuy tilted his head and then his lips turned up in a slight smile. "Have you misplaced her?"

"You bastard." Nathan grabbed Dupuy by the shoulders and lifted him into the air. "Speak."

Dupuy's eyes widened. "Put me down."

"Where is she?" Nathan gave Dupuy a shake before throwing him into a chair. He leaned over him, his arms on either side of the chair to imprison him.

"I will have you arrested." Dupuy spat the words at Nathan.

"Try." Nathan's anger rose as Dupuy struggled to be free. "Who kidnapped my wife?"

"How would I know?"

"You threatened her yesterday. You left me a message saying you had your revenge." Nathan forced his voice to remain calm. "Now she is missing."

"Perhaps you did not suit her." Dupuy sneered.

Nathan clenched his jaw and leaned closer to Dupuy. "I know there is a stranger watching my house. Who is he?"

"That is a problem with marrying in haste." Dupuy eyes darted away from Nathan. "One never really knows the other's family."

Nathan's eyes narrowed. The man was terrified. Something in his words struck a chord in Nathan's memory. Madalyn's uncle had tried to force her to marry her cousin. He'd also probably been responsible for William's abduction. Surely he wouldn't have followed her to Charleston? That was a possible explanation for her disappearance, though.

"What family?"

Dupuy shrugged his shoulders. "Despite your wife's actions and sullied reputation, her uncle took great pains to find her."

"Helped by you?" Nathan spat the words through clenched teeth.

Dupuy shook his head. "Unfortunately, all I could do was recount the sad facts of your marriage to him. He didn't need my aid."

"So he refused to pay you." Nathan smirked before pushing away from Dupuy. "The man has more intelligence than I thought."

Dupuy straightened his jacket and wiped the sweat from his brow with a shaking hand. Nathan shook his head. Dupuy was contemptible. He made his way in the world on the fear and guilt of his victims. He was without honor. Still, he might prove useful.

"When did you speak with this man?"

"I warned your wife yesterday, but she wouldn't listen."

"So you met with him yesterday."

Dupuy shook his head. "I saw him last week. A well-heeled stranger in Charleston is hard to miss, unless one is otherwise occupied."

Nathan clenched his jaw. He'd spent all of his time with Madalyn last week.

"Does this stranger have a name?"

"For a price." Dupuy smirked and walked to his desk. He pulled out a piece of paper and threw it at Nathan.

"What's this?"

"It's a contract signing Briars over to me." Dupuy pushed his inkwell closer to Nathan. "For that, I will give you the information you need."

Nathan looked down at the paper and then at Dupuy. If he signed over Briars, Dupuy would be able to pull himself out of arrears. The thought of rewarding a bounder like Dupuy was revolting, but what choice did he have? He needed to find Madalyn.

He picked up the quill and dipped it in the ink. He pulled the paper to him and was about to sign his name when he remembered William. William would be able to identify his uncle. He still needed to know where the man was staying.

"I don't need his name." Nathan put the quill down. "I need to know his whereabouts."

A muscle twitched at the side of Dupuy's mouth. "I can give you that."

Nathan narrowed his eyes. "You lie."

Dupuy shrugged and pulled the contract away. "It's your wife's life."

The image of Bertram Harden came into his mind. Madalyn's uncle was his partner. All he had to do was find Bertram. He threw the quill down on the desk.

"Where are you going?" Dupuy's voice was shrill.

"I'll think about your proposition." Nathan jerked open the library door and looked back at Dupuy. "I'm not without resources myself."

"You won't find her without my help." Dupuy's voice shook.

"We shall see."

Nathan slammed the door and raced out of the house. He had already wasted enough time on that sniffling coward. When he reached the harbor, he sprinted to the rear of the Exchange building to where the slave auctions were held. He pushed through the crowd that was gathered. Bertram Harden was nowhere in sight.

"Where is Harden?" he shouted into the crowd.

Silence followed his words as a multitude of eyes turned in his direction. Nathan inhaled a slow breath, trying to control his ragged breathing. He must look a wild man, his hair and clothes strewn about from his ride, but he didn't care.

"Bertram Harden," he repeated. "Has anyone seen him?"

"He's left Charleston," a hesitant voice said from behind.

Nathan turned. "Come forward."

A slight built man with dark hair moved through the crowd. Nathan recognized him. He was the man who'd been with Bertram the day Madalyn had visited the Exchange.

"You are?" Nathan's voice was clipped.

"Frank Milford." The man held his hand out tentatively. "I was Bertram's partner."

Nathan shook hands. "Where is Harden?"

"He left for New York." Frank cleared his throat. "An old friend from England visited him last week. He set him up in business in New York."

"What did Bertram have to do?"

Frank adjusted his collar. "He didn't tell me. Only said that everyone gets what he deserves. I took that to mean Bertram had done the man a favor."

"Or me a disservice?"

Frank's eyes shifted away from Nathan. "He didn't say that."

Nathan grunted. "Does this friend have a name?"

"Lord Phillip Montgomery."

"Montgomery," Nathan repeated under his breath. So her uncle was responsible. "Where is Montgomery now?"

Frank's eyes bulged. "He's gone."

Nathan leaned in closer. "Where?"

Frank motioned to the harbor. "He left on a ship this morning."

Chapter 30

Nathan looked over the railing and watched the ship pulled into the Liverpool harbor. His foot tapped against the deck and he gripped the railing to prevent himself from jumping overboard. Time had crawled in the last three weeks.

"We'll be docked shortly."

Nathan turned to the man who stood beside him. "I've waited long enough."

"We made good time in the crossing." The captain leaned on the railing beside Nathan. "There was a wind behind us the whole way."

"The same wind was behind the ship Madalyn was in."

The Captain sighed and pushed away from Nathan. "I'll see that the men are ready to disembark as soon as we land."

Nathan put his hand out and stopped the captain. "My apologies Eddowes. I'm in a foul mood, but that is no excuse."

"You're worried. Everyone on ship knows that. Soon you can begin your search."

"I'm surprised you didn't barricade me in my room for the whole voyage." Nathan forced a smile. "I've been a bear to deal with. Even my brother-in-law has stayed clear of me."

Eddowes squeezed Nathan's shoulder. "I'd do anything in my power to ease your mind. You were the only one to give me a chance when I thought my life was over."

"You've always been a damn good sailor." Nathan moved from the railing. "I knew you wouldn't fail me."

"I understand what you are going through." The captain looked down at his feet before glancing back at Nathan. "There's nothing worse than losing the woman you love. You'll find her."

"Thanks."

Nathan turned back to the harbor. The ship seemed to be inching its way closer to land, each second of waiting, an agony of despair. His journey had been pure hell as he tortured himself with every imaginable horror that could have befallen Madalyn, after her uncle had kidnapped her.

A vice had gripped his heart, until he thought he'd die of the pain. He'd never known such a gnawing emptiness. The pain when Heloise had died was pale in comparison.

His anguish seared him until he could barely breathe. The image of Madalyn haunted him. His body craved her touch, his mind her voice, his soul her presence. For the first time in his life, he truly loved. He only prayed he wasn't too late.

He'd never felt anything like this for Heloise. His love for her had been a chaste, boyish worship. Now he loved and hungered as a man. He wouldn't allow it to be snatched from him. He had no intention of letting another man destroy his life.

An hour later the ship's gangplank was lowered to the pier, and Nathan was the first man down it. William followed close behind.

Nathan had picked a group of sailors to come with them. When they were all assembled, he sent them off to the nearest inns to see if anyone fitting Madalyn or her uncle's description had stayed there.

Nathan made arrangements to have horses for his men and a carriage for Madalyn readied. He didn't want to waste any time once they'd found her. He sent a rider off with a note to his brother Alex, the Marquess of Caldern. Once Madalyn was safely in his arms, he'd take her and William to Caldern.

William was stomping his feet behind him. "Do you think this will take long?"

"No." Nathan scanned the dock. "If we're lucky, they're still here."

"He'll probably take her to his estate in Acton."

"We can't risk missing them."

"Sir," a deep voice spoke behind him.

It was one of his men. "What news?"

"They were at the Boar's Arm, but left early this morning."

Nathan pushed back his impatience. They'd been so close. "Where did they go?"

"The landlord wouldn't say, sir." The sailor gulped and straightened his shoulders. "He said the gentleman was too powerful to cross."

Nathan took a deep breath. Anger and frustration threatened to consume him, but he needed a clear head. Obviously Montgomery thought he was above the law. Nathan would soon destroy that illusion.

"Lead me to this inn."

When they arrived, they were greeted by a flurry of activity. Horses, coaches and grooms seemed to fill the courtyard. The constant traffic and noise was overwhelming after the quiet of the sea.

The inn was several hundred years old, its brick walls weathered by the salt air. Inside the oak beams and walls were darkened with age and soot. A fire burned in the common room.

Nathan scanned the room and spied a door leading to the back. He pushed his way past the small crowd of men, and thrust open the door. It was the kitchen. There was a short round man yelling orders at a surly looking lad. Nathan cleared his throat.

"Are you the landlord?"

The man stopped midsentence and turned to Nathan with a scowl. He replaced it with a smile when he realized who'd interrupted him. "What can I do for you, sir?"

Nathan stepped close to the man. "Do you know a Lord Phillip Montgomery?"

The innkeeper's eyes grew wide and he pursed his lips. "Yer the second person asking today"

"I will be the last." Nathan leaned close to the landlord. "Where did he go?"

"He's a might powerful." The man wiped his brow with the sleeve of his shirt. "I can't say where he went."

"I can fer a price." The surly lad held out his hand.

The innkeeper swatted the young boy on the head. "You best be keeping quiet."

Nathan ignored the innkeeper. "Where?"

"Fenton. Now me money."

Nathan tossed the lad a couple of coins and turned to leave when the innkeeper's voice stopped him.

"It'd be safer if you didn't go alone." The innkeeper cleared his throat. "Lord Phillip's a man who takes the law into his own hands, if you understand my meaning."

"He chose the wrong man to threaten. I don't scare, or back away from a fight."

Nathan did not wait for the innkeeper's reply. He slammed through the kitchen door to the outside and raced back to the pier. He gave orders to the coachman and the sailors who were waiting.

"We go to Fenton." He pointed to two other men. "Find the magistrate and tell him to meet us there."

"I can't believe he had the nerve to go to my estate." William ran beside Nathan.

"He thinks you're as good as dead." Nathan grabbed a horse and motioned for the rest of the men to mount. "The man stops at nothing."

"Then we best get there before he harms Madalyn."

He waved the coach on ahead of them. "We'll travel quicker on horseback. I expect you to get there as soon as possible."

The coach started off and Nathan mounted his horse. "We should be there in under an hour."

Madalyn tried to pull her arm away from her uncle, but he tightened his hold. She winced as pain shot through her. With one quick tug, he wrenched her from the coach and dragged her up the stairs of her brother's house.

The face of Adams, the butler, was a blur as Madalyn was hurried into the library. Her uncle threw her into a chair with such force that it leaned back on two legs before righting itself.

Her head ached, and she rubbed it to try and ease the pain. She'd been a prisoner aboard her uncle's ship for the last three weeks, forced to stay in her cabin except for meals. The last couple of days had been pure hell. She'd been seasick and her body was still racked by chills.

"You can't hold me here."

Her heart beat at frantic pace, and fear held her in its grip. She wouldn't let her uncle know how terrified she was, though. She was a grown woman, not a child. It was past time that she stood up to him.

Lord Phillip shook a finger at her. "You're my property. You always have been."

"I'm not one of your slaves." The words were out of her mouth before she had a chance to think.

Lord Phillip's lips narrowed to a thin seam. "It would be easier if you were. I could have rid myself of you years ago."

Madalyn's heart constricted at the venom in her uncle's voice. She'd tried to please this man, to show gratitude for the home he'd provided after her parents' death. She knew that he had acted out of a sense of duty, not love. She'd never realized until now, that he hated her.

"I took care of you and your brother. You owe this family loyalty and you will marry your cousin."

"I'm already married."

"A hole in the wall ceremony onboard a ship. It won't be long before that is annulled." Lord Phillip snorted. "I offered you a wonderful life and you threw it away."

"You offered me a prison." Madalyn thrust her chin out and glared at her uncle.

Lord Phillip's eyebrow rose. "You'll soon understand what prison is. You'll be under lock and key until I say otherwise."

There was a sharp rap on the door and then it opened to admit her cousin Horace. Madalyn noticed that he looked paler than usual and his lips seemed locked into a permanent frown. The thought of Horace becoming her husband sent a shiver of revulsion through her.

"Where have you been?" Lord Phillip snarled. "I told you to be waiting when I returned."

"I was outside reading." Horace plopped down in a chair. "I came when I heard the carriage drive up."

"I've brought your bride." Lord Phillip waved his hand in Madalyn's direction. "She'll stay here until we can settle the matter of her colonial marriage."

Madalyn leaned forward in her chair and touched her cousin's hand. "Surely you don't desire this marriage?"

Horace shrugged his shoulder. "It's what father wants."

"Don't you want to choose your wife?" Her cousin was her last hope. If she could make him see reason then this nightmare would be over.

"I have to marry someday." Horace picked a piece of fluff off his pantaloons.

"You should wait until you fall in love."

"Is that what you have?" Uncle Phillip's voice was thick with sarcasm. "Do you expect me to believe that a man bought and married you for love?"

Madalyn stuck her chin out and glared at her uncle. "I love Nathan."

"You would love any man that looked at you twice."

Lord Phillip leaned over her chair. His face was inches away, and she could see the vein pulsing in his neck. She swallowed her fear, forcing herself to look him in the eye.

"I didn't always love him."

"You think that makes it real? What a fool." Her uncle pushed away from the chair. "Has he ever said he loved you?"

Her uncle's words hit Madalyn like a slap. She opened her mouth to deny them, but realized they were true. Nathan had never promised her love. He showed her respect and consideration, but that wasn't love.

She'd known that when she agreed to make the marriage real. She'd just assumed over time Nathan would come to love her. He desired her, but that wasn't love. A shiver of uncertainty raced up her spine.

She loved Nathan with her whole being, but was that enough? When she truly needed him, would he be there for her? Did he even care that she was gone from his life?

Nathan was a gentleman, and honor was a part of him as much as breathing, he would adhere to their marriage vows, but at what cost? Her uncle wouldn't rest until he had what he wanted, even if that meant destroying Nathan. Had she trapped him into a marriage he would regret?

"He married you for your money."

"No." Madalyn was still reeling, but she knew this was false. "Nathan had no idea of my inheritance when he married me."

"Then it should be easy to convince him to return the money and annul the marriage."

Chapter 31

"Why on earth would I do that?"

Madalyn's breath caught in her throat as the familiar voice of Nathan boomed through the library. She turned and saw him standing in the doorway. His beloved face was as hard as granite and his blue eyes icy with contempt.

"Ah the mysterious Mr. Carter." Montgomery's voice was cold, each word a threat. "You surprise me."

Nathan walked into the room, his steps measured and exact. Madalyn's stomach fluttered at his nearness and she tried to stand up, but her legs wouldn't hold her. The world started to spin and she leaned back in her chair to catch her breath.

"There's nothing surprising about my visit." Nathan slapped a glove against his hand. "I have come for my wife."

"Your bought bride?" Lord Phillip's words were an insult.

Nathan's eyes narrowed. "I have no wish to bandy words with one who is beneath contempt. You will release Madalyn."

"She is my niece." Montgomery's hands curled into a fist. "You've no rights here. Leave."

Nathan's mouth tightened and he took a step nearer Lord Phillip. Madalyn was spellbound as she watched a sense of authority and suppressed power, suddenly come to life within her husband. It was as if the cool veneer of a gentleman had been stripped away to reveal a fierce warrior.

"Not without my wife." Nathan's voice was cold, each word a measured stab of fierceness.

"No man comes into my home and makes demands." Lord Phillip's face twisted with anger. "I will have the servants throw you out."

"That might be difficult." Nathan's voice held contempt. "My men have ensured that your servants will remain below stairs."

"You're insane," Lord Phillip spluttered. "My power is far reaching."

"So is mine." Nathan snapped his finger and a man suddenly appeared at the door. "Ah Jenkins. Has the magistrate arrived yet?"

"No sir, but Smith has returned. Lord Rochedale should be here shortly." Jenkins made a slight bow and left the room.

"The magistrate?" Lord Phillip's eyes bulged with fury. "You cannot mean to make this public?"

"If need be." Nathan's lips curled into a sneer. "Now you must decide whether you made a mistake, or do I have you arrested for kidnapping?"

"Who the hell do you think you are?"

"I am Madalyn's husband. I thought I had already made that clear."

"No." Lord Phillip's face turned a bright red. "Your marriage is not valid. I have taken steps to have it annulled."

"The marriage is legal and there is nothing you can do to change that."

"No court will uphold a colonial ceremony aboard a ship." Lord Phillip waved his hand dismissively.

"There was a clergyman and witnesses. The marriage is binding." Nathan's voice was steady and unhurried. "You've no grounds for kidnapping. Once the magistrate arrives, you will no longer have any standing in the neighborhood either."

"Your threats are useless. I own this county."

"Perhaps." Nathan voice held a hint of impatience. "But my brother, the Marquess of Caldern, knows the Magistrate, Lord Rochedale. They're particular friends. Rochedale will do as the Norward family wants."

"Caldern?" Horace's voice came out as a squeak.

Nathan raised an eyebrow. "You know him?"

"We were at Eton together." Horace tugged at his cravat. "He was several years ahead of me. I thought he was in India."

"He returned last year." Nathan gestured toward Lord Phillip. "You should explain to your father how far reaching my family's power is."

Horace nodded and turned to his father. "It might be prudent to reconsider."

"You want me to let go of what is rightly ours because this upstart is related to some nobleman?" Lord Phillip shook his head. "Thank God you never took to gambling. The man is bluffing."

"I don't wish to marry Madalyn." Horace cleared his throat and turned to Nathan. "Perhaps we could discuss this?"

"No discussion." Nathan's voice boomed out. "Release my wife."

"I have gone to a great deal of trouble to bring the chit back. She stays," Lord Phillip roared.

"Then you will go to jail." Nathan turned to leave the room, his hand on the doorknob. "Rochedale will be here shortly. I will wait in the hallway."

The sound of horses' hooves pounding on the gravel drive reverberated through the room. Nathan inclined his head to the window, his mouth tilted in a slight smile.

"I believe my wait is over."

Lord Phillip ran to the window and peered out. His hand shook as he rested it against the window jamb. Madalyn's heart began to soar as she saw her uncle's shoulders sag.

Lord Phillip turned to Nathan, his eyes wide, his mouth gaping. "It's Rochedale."

He jabbed his finger at Nathan. "You can have the ingrate, but her money stays here."

Madalyn's hands tightened on the chair's arm. Her breath stopped in her throat as she waited for Nathan's reply. Her whole being willed him to deny that he wanted her money, but a part of her knew it was insane. No man would willingly walk away from a fortune.

"It's Madalyn's money." Nathan walked over to her and held out his hand. "No man will take it from her."

Madalyn's hand shook as she put it in Nathan's. He squeezed it and she took strength from his reassurance. Whatever he thought about the money, he meant for her to be with him. She stood and was pulled into Nathan's protective embrace.

"We're leaving now."

"Not with my money." Montgomery's voice rose hysterically.

Madalyn watched her uncle's tirade for the first time without fear. His anger and threats could not hurt her as long as Nathan held her close. Her uncle was a bully and a coward.

"You have no legal standing." Nathan rubbed a hand across Madalyn's arm and walked her toward the door. "Madalyn is of age."

"She owes me." Lord Phillip's words came out as a whimper.

Just then the door opened and William walked in. "It is you who owe us."

"William." Madalyn's voice was a whisper. "You're alive."

"Thanks to your husband." William clasped her outstretched hands. "I am well despite our uncle's attempt to kill me."

"I did no such thing," Lord Phillip sputtered. "We were concerned when you disappeared."

"No need for lies. I've already had the truth from Bertram Harden's partner. You arranged to have me kidnapped and indentured as a servant."

Madalyn gasped. "You have proof?"

Nathan's arm tightened around her. "I'm afraid it's true. Your brother is lucky to be alive after the treatment he suffered aboard ship. All of it, at your uncle's orders."

"I'm going to give you a choice, uncle." William walked towards Lord Phillip. "That's more than you gave me."

Madalyn felt tears prick her eyes. William had grown in stature and behavior since she'd last seen him. His ordeal had changed him. Gone was the schoolboy. She sagged back against Nathan and shivered. Her brother didn't need her to watch over him anymore. She'd done all that her mother had asked.

"I'm innocent." Lord Phillip backed away from William. "I gave you a home when your parents died."

"You coveted Fenton." William shook his head. "You had money and an estate that grandfather left you, but you wanted mine."

Lord Phillip's back hit a bookcase. There was no escape. He straightened his shoulders and lifted his chin.

"You were too young to appreciate Fenton. You took it for granted, but I care about it."

"I was a boy." William crossed his arms. "You tried to kill me."

"I did no such thing." Lord Phillip's voice was indignant.

"You made it highly probably that I would die." William shook his head. "I don't need you in my life any longer. Madalyn is married. She and her husband can be my guardians, until I'm of age."

"What does that commoner know about running an estate?" Lord Phillip's jaw clenched. "Their marriage isn't valid."

"It is valid." Nathan boomed. "I built up my own business. I can show William how to manage an estate."

William grinned. "Now uncle, you can leave quietly or Lord Rochedale will remove you with force. Either way, you will be off my estate within the hour."

"And if you come near Madalyn or William again, I will have you thrown in prison." Nathan's voice was a menace.

He didn't wait for her uncle's reply as he led her out of the library and house. Once outside, Madalyn took a breath of air and leaned against Nathan. The world seemed to stop spinning and the ache in her head lessened.

"That went well." Nathan said with a nod of his head.

When they reached the bottom of the stairs a well-dressed gentleman in riding coat and breeches met them. He held out his hand to Nathan.

"What a pleasant surprise Carter. I thought you were in America."

"Sorry to drag you into this mess Rochedale, but Lord Phillip left us little recourse."

Lord Rochedale grinned. "The man likes to take the law into his own hands. Usually his victims have no connections."

Nathan nodded his head. "Your timely arrival put an end to Lord Phillip's plans. Thank you."

"Happy to oblige." Rochedale glanced over at Madalyn. "Your wife?"

"How remiss of me. Let me introduce Lady Madalyn." Nathan inclined his head to Lord Rochedale. "Madalyn, this is Gavin, Lord Rochedale."

Madalyn curtsied, surprised at the seriousness of the green eyes that looked back at her. Lord Rochedale brushed back a lock of light brown hair that had fallen onto his forehead and bowed.

"Pleasure." His voice was sincere. "I spent many a summer at Caldern with Alex and Nathan."

Madalyn felt her strength slipping. The sun was high in the sky, its searing heat beating down on her. With trembling hand, she wiped away the beads of perspiration on her forehead. Nathan looked down at her and frowned.

"Madalyn is exhausted." Nathan motioned to his coachman. "I'll let her rest in the coach, while we settle up with Lord Phillip. There's still the matter of his servants that my men are holding and of course Fenton wants his uncle removed from the estate."

Nathan handed Madalyn into the carriage and she leaned back against the squabs and closed her eyes. She could hear the crunch of gravel under the men's feet, and the stomping of the horses, and then the world faded away. Her stomach churned uneasily.

Nathan seemed to be gone for hours before she heard his voice. He yelled some orders to his men and then jumped into the carriage.

"You've had a rough go of it." Nathan's voice was low. "I'll take better care of you in the future."

Madalyn swallowed back her tears. "Even I didn't think my uncle would do anything so rash. He must be insane."

"Greed can make people do evil things." Nathan turned her face to him and ran a finger down the side of her cheek. "The man is a monster."

"He almost killed William." Madalyn's voice shook with emotion.

"I'm certain he intended the same for you, once he had your inheritance secured."

"How could I have been so blind to his character?" Her words ended on a sob.

Madalyn couldn't control her tears. Everything that had happened over the last couple of weeks came crashing in on her. Her weeping filled the carriage. The dam that had held back her fears, humiliations, and anxieties had finally broken.

Nathan gathered her in his arms, stroking her back as he held her close. His warmth melted the block of ice that had settled around her heart. He had come for her, despite everything her uncle had said.

"This is unlike you." Nathan's voice was gruff. "I'd expected shouts and anger, but not tears."

"I was so afraid," Madalyn cried. "My uncle was determined you would never find me."

"What kind of husband loses his wife?" Nathan's tone was light, but his arms tightened about her.

Madalyn sniffed. "You never wanted to be married. I thought you'd breathe a sigh of relieve when you found me gone."

"I've never been so crazy with fear in my whole life." Nathan's hoarse whisper tickled her cheek. "I tore through Charleston looking for you."

Madalyn hiccupped and lifted her face. She looked into Nathan's eyes and saw the truth there. "I tried to fight him, but he was too strong."

"I'd no idea he was in Charleston." Nathan's lips tightened into a grim smile. "I had to squeeze the information out of Dupuy."

Madalyn wiped her cheeks with her hand. "What did he have to do with Uncle Phillip?"

"Dupuy threatened you the day before your disappearance, so I went to him first."

Nathan took out his handkerchief and began to wipe Madalyn's damp cheeks. His hand shook and Madalyn's mouth went dry at the look of tenderness in his eyes.

"Did he help my uncle?"

Nathan shook his head. "Your uncle already had his plans in place. Still, Dupuy had every intention of betraying you to him."

A shiver went through Madalyn. "That man is wicked."

"He won't be causing any trouble in the future." Nathan feathered a kiss across Madalyn's forehead. "I've taken steps to ensure he stays away from Charleston."

A sigh escaped Madalyn. Nathan's lips had sent a quiver of sensation throughout her body. For the last weeks, he had seemed no more than a dream; a thirst that would never be quenched again. Her body burned with need, and she felt lightheaded with happiness.

Nathan tapped his finger against her lips. "Just the sight of you has me hungering for a taste, but this is not the place. William will be joining us."

Madalyn straightened her shoulders. "Is he coming back to Charleston?"

"No. I am taking both of you to my brother's house, Caldern." Nathan brushed his hand through Madalyn's hair. "We should arrive in two days."

She frowned. Nathan had suggested she go to his brother when he'd thought she should marry someone else. Surely he didn't still want that? The joy and hope she'd felt now soured. Nathan hadn't rescued her for love. He hadn't been acting out of love. He'd rescued her because of a sense of pride and honor.

Madalyn pushed away from Nathan.

The world started to spin.

Nausea overwhelmed her, and she leaned forward in the coach. "I'm going to be sick," were the last words she said before the world went dark.

Chapter 32

Nathan strode around the library circumference. His hand fluttered against the spines of numerous books, stopping on one for a few seconds before continuing with his search.

"You'll wear the floor out with your pacing."

Nathan looked at his brother, Alex. He was sitting in a wingback chair by his desk. They had arrived at Caldern over an hour ago, and the first thing Madalyn had done upon leaving the coach, was faint.

"It's making the wait easier." Nathan turned back to the books.

"Pick one and sit down." Alex stretched his legs out in front of him. "You can do nothing until the doctor is finished."

"How long will Caruthers be?"

"He's only been up there fifteen minutes."

Nathan banged his hand down on a shelf. "It doesn't take that long to give her medicine."

Alex looked down at his hand. "It may not be that easy. How long has she been sick?"

"Since Liverpool." Nathan turned back to the bookcase, lowering his head against his outstretched arm. "I thought it was a reaction from her kidnapping, but the closer we got to Caldern, the sicker she became."

Alex cleared his throat. "Is it possible she's in an interesting way?"

"I hope it's that simple, but when I carried Madalyn upstairs she was burning up with fever."

Alex rubbed a hand across his face. "All of this is news to me. The last time we talked you weren't planning on ever marrying. You had better tell me everything."

Nathan sat down with a groan. "We were wed on board the Folly before she sank. Captain Galer and Reverend Willet performed the ceremony."

Alex rubbed his nose. "Was it a shipboard romance?"

"Somewhat." Nathan looked out the window and grimaced, as he remembered the details of his wedding. "I was forced to marry Madalyn to protect her reputation."

Alex's eyes narrowed. "But you loved her."

"I do now." Nathan dropped his head into his hands. "I tried to help her, but I failed."

Alex held up his hand. "You'd better start at the beginning."

Nathan took a deep breath. He'd always been the steady one. Alex's tone suggested that his senses were addled. A part of Nathan believed that was the case. Ever since he had met Madalyn, nothing in his life had been the same.

"Madalyn had the foolhardy notion of finding her brother in America. She'd seen him abducted and the ship sailed before she could rescue him. The Folly was the next ship to sail, so she hid aboard and when Galer found her, he auctioned her off to the highest bidder."

Alex crossed his arms. "You bought her?"

Nathan leaned forward and stared at his brother intently. "She was terrified, but stood there undefeated and proud. I couldn't bear to think of her being abused and passed around the crew. I know it was crazy, but what choice did I have? I intended to set her free."

Alex nodded and relaxed his arms. "That doesn't explain marrying her."

"Galer told the reverend's wife that I had compromised Madalyn and they insisted that we marry."

"You compromised the chit?"

"No." Nathan's voice rose defensively. "I never laid a hand on her."

"You would never have married without love."

Nathan rubbed his neck. "There was the added persuasion of Captain Galer's pistol."

Alex whistled. "So why stay married?"

"Madalyn had to find her brother, so initially we stayed married because it was easier. I had every intention of having the marriage annulled. Things changed. Madalyn wanted to make our marriage real. I agreed."

"And you fell in love." Alex nodded his head. "Does Madalyn return your love?"

Before Nathan could reply to his brother's question, the door opened. Doctor Caruthers stood there with his bag in hand, his face a picture of weariness. William followed the doctor into the room. Nathan stood up on shaky legs.

"Well?" Nathan's voice boomed in the silence.

The doctor frowned and looked down at the floor. "She has an unusually high fever. All I can suggest is keeping the fever down and hope it breaks."

Nathan slumped back into his chair. His chest constricted as he considered the possibility of yellow fever, or as some called it, stranger's fever. It claimed numerous lives in Charleston every year, and it attacked mainly newcomers.

Some thought the change in climate was too much for those newly arrived in Charleston. Others thought it had something to do with the heat of summer because the disease was worse in August.

Some doctors believed that biting insects were responsible. He clenched his jaw tightly when he remembered the time they had spent in the marshes before being rescued. The woods near the beach had been teeming with flying insects.

"She has yellow fever." Nathan felt as if he were giving a death sentence.

"Of course!" The doctor dropped his bag on the desk. "I have never seen a case of it before. It is usually only seen in warmer climes."

"We came from Charleston."

"I see." Dr. Caruthers cleared his throat. "She's strong. With enough care, and time, I'm certain she'll recover."

"Oh God." Nathan's words were barely a whisper.

"You need to keep the fever down. Hopefully she has only a mild bout." Dr. Caruthers stood with his hands behind his back. "It is imperative that the disease not reach her liver."

Nathan forced himself to focus on the doctor's words. If Madalyn were to survive, he needed to be strong. He stood and straightened his shoulders.

"We'll do everything necessary."

"Good." Dr. Caruthers shook Nathan's hand and nodded to Alex and William. "I'll go and leave instructions with the Marchioness. I have some medicine that will help."

"I'm certain my wife will have some ideas of her own." Alex led the doctor from the library.

Nathan went to the window and stared out at the gardens. Everywhere flowers were in bloom, the world was alive, but he could only think about Madalyn. She was young, but the past few months had been harrowing. Would she be able to fight the fever?

Alex returned a few minutes later. "The doctor has left and Sarah has sent for her medicines."

Nathan nodded. "I need to see her."

Without another word Nathan, brushed by Alex. He took the stairs two at a time and paused for a second at Madalyn's bedroom. What if Madalyn couldn't fight the fever? Nathan shook off his fears and opened the door.

Sarah was busy folding linen next to the bed. The curtains were drawn and the only light was a single candle that stood on the bedside table. The room was shrouded in darkness.

"How is she?" Nathan's voice was low.

"Burning up." Sarah put the linen on the bedside table. A bowl of water stood there. "The doctor says she needs to be kept cool and left some medicine. I have ordered a tea of willow bark to be prepared also."

Nathan gave Sarah's arm a squeeze. "Thank you."

"I'm only sorry I don't have better news for you." Sarah brushed her hand over Madalyn's forehead.

Nathan nodded and sat on the bed. He picked up Madalyn's hand. Her face was flushed and her head moved restlessly against the pillow.

"I'll stay with her tonight." Nathan reached a hand for the cloth that Sarah was holding.

"I can tend to her."

"You can stay during the day." Nathan took the wet cloth. "Alex would never forgive me if I let you get overworked in your condition."

Sarah rubbed a protective hand over her abdomen. "I'm used to tending the sick."

"You do it very well, but I need to be with her." Nathan wiped Madalyn's forehead with the damp cloth.

Sarah nodded. "I'll take over in the morning."

A low moan escaped Madalyn's lips and Nathan's chest tightened. He took a deep breath and continued with his bathing. "I'll sleep then."

"She needs her medicine every six hours." Sarah pointed to the bottle on the table. "One spoonful."

Nathan's lips felt weighted down, but he forced a smile. "I have tended a sick bed before."

"Call me if you need help."

"Get some rest." Nathan turned back to Madalyn.

A deafening silence descended when Sarah left the room. Nathan brushed strands of Madalyn's damp hair from her face with his finger, lingering at her neck. He refused to consider the possibility of her not surviving.

He started to bathe her forehead again. Her body was still burning with the fever. If she didn't survive he would never forgive himself. In such a short time, she had become precious to him. He couldn't imagine life without her.

His love for Madalyn was all consuming. She made his blood sing; his passions boil; and gave meaning to his life. In the quiet moments of the night, Nathan made a vow. If Madalyn lived he would make certain she would be safe. He would never again take chances with her life.

Madalyn moved her head and winced. Her body felt as if she had suffered a severe beating. She caught her breath as she moved her arm and pushed back the blanket.

"Let me do that."

Madalyn didn't recognize the voice. She opened her eyes and then closed them quickly. The bright sunlight was blinding. She opened them again, this time allowing them to adjust to the light gradually.

"Try and sit." The voice was soft and encouraging.

Madalyn put her weight on her arms, but her body refused to move. She would have fallen backwards, but for the arm that supported her. Adept hands held her upright while arranging the pillows behind her back.

"I'm so weak." Madalyn struggled to catch her breath.

"You've been ill for over a week." A cup was held up to her lips. It was warm broth.

Madalyn took a sip, surprised at how dry her throat felt. She leaned back into the pillows and finished the cup of liquid. Her stomach was hollow, but the heat from the broth seeped into her bones.

"Who are you?" Madalyn watched as the dark haired woman put the cup down on the table.

The woman turned and smiled. "Sarah."

Madalyn struggled to remember the name, but her head was foggy. Sarah was too well dressed to be a servant, and her manner was of one gently bred. Madalyn felt reassured by the understanding she saw in her dark blue eyes, though.

"Is there any more broth? My throat is dry."

"I'll have cook send some up." Sarah straightened the bedcovers before leaving the room.

Madalyn pushed away the covers and swung her legs over the side of the bed.

The room spun.

She waited until everything had righted itself before standing up. Her legs shook. She stretched her arm out to the table to balance herself.

"What the hell are you doing?"

Chapter 33

Nathan's roar startled Madalyn. She lost her balance and began to sway. She would have fallen if Nathan hadn't rushed to her. He lifted her against his chest and then put her back in the bed.

"You've just woken up." Nathan tucked the covers under Madalyn's chin. "Gain some strength before you start wandering off on your own."

"I can't just lie here."

"Why not?"

Nathan glared down at her and the urge to cry was overwhelming. Tears welled up in her eyes and she turned from him to wipe them away with her hand.

"Here." Nathan handed her a clean handkerchief.

Madalyn took it and blew her nose. "I never cry."

"You've been ill." Nathan's voice softened. "It's a miracle you survived the fever."

"The last thing I remember is traveling in a coach." Madalyn frowned. "Where am I?"

"Caldern." Nathan sat down on the bed. "Try not to strain yourself. The doctor says you need to rest if you're going to recover fully."

"Recover from what?"

"Yellow fever." Nathan brushed Madalyn's hair from her forehead. "You were one of the lucky ones. Most people die."

Madalyn gripped her bedcovers. "I'm sorry if I was a burden."

Nathan's eyes softened. "You could never be that. The whole household was relieved when your fever broke."

Madalyn relaxed. Nathan's tone soothed her. She leaned back into her pillows. Nathan looked drawn, his skin pale. He seemed to have aged overnight. If only she could wipe the weariness from his face.

"I don't remember."

Nathan squeezed her hand. "The illness takes its toll. That's why I want you to regain your strength."

"I feel useless lying here."

"In a couple of days, you'll be walking." Nathan cleared his throat. "The doctor says it will be weeks before you are fully recovered, though."

"Weeks?" Madalyn pushed away from the pillows. "Nonsense. As soon as I get some food, I'll feel better."

"The fever weakens your whole body." Nathan's voice was low and steady. "Most people die because it leaves them too feeble to survive. It's important for you to take the time to heal fully."

"I can't stay in bed all the time." Madalyn could hear the panic in her own voice and took a deep breath. "There has to be something for me to do."

"I expect you to ease yourself back into activity."

Nathan's jaw was rigid and set and she didn't have the energy to fight him. She sagged back against the pillows.

"I'll try."

"Good." Nathan stood. "I'm not the enemy. Save your energy for your recovery."

Nathan leaned over and kissed her forehead before walking to the door. "Let me worry about your welfare. Trust me."

Madalyn took a deep breath and nodded. Nathan wasn't demanding anything difficult. She barely had enough energy to talk, much less fight him.

"Good," Nathan opened the door. "I'll take care of everything."

Nathan left the room and Madalyn closed her eyes. What had happened during the time she'd been ill. Before she had a chance to worry about her lost week, Sarah knocked at the door and entered. Behind her was a servant carrying a tray.

"Cook prepared gruel." Sarah motioned for the servant to put the tray on a table. "That should help you regain some of your strength."

"It doesn't look very appetizing"

"Doctor's orders." Sarah put a napkin against Madalyn's chest and picked up the bowl of gruel. "We don't want a relapse."

Madalyn took a small nibble. It tasted bland, but was edible. Once she started to eat, her strength improved. When she was finished, Sarah handed her another cup of broth.

Madalyn sipped the broth. "I feel better already."

"I've ordered a bath." Sarah pulled back the covers. "You'll feel more yourself, once everything is clean."

"Maybe you can convince Nathan." Madalyn swung her legs over the side of the bed.

"He's been very concerned about you. He did most of the nursing." Sarah helped Madalyn to a chair. "He spent every evening with you and most of the days. I had to force him to leave for a few hours of sleep."

The pale, tired Nathan she'd seen earlier flashed before her. He must have some feelings for her. Then, the cold steel of reason dashed her joy. Nathan was a man who was serious about his responsibilities. He was a man who felt duty bound to care for another. An overwhelming sense of weariness flooded her. Once she was bathed, dressed, and into bed, she was asleep.

The days passed in much the same way. Sarah lingered longer each visit and the two women became friends. Nathan spent a short time with her each day, but they never seemed to be alone. One day he brought his mother Mary to visit and Madalyn felt an immediate connection. How could there not be when they both loved Nathan.

On the fifth day of her recovery, Madalyn woke long after the rest of the house had gone to bed. She'd spent the better part of the day sleeping, so it was no surprise that sleep escaped her now. She lit a candle and sat up in bed. She picked up her book to read, but the soft click of the door handle interrupted her before she could open the book. She looked up to find Nathan standing there. He was magnificent in candlelight.

Her heart beat quickened as she watched Nathan walk into the room. He'd never looked so handsome, or strong, or beloved. Her body trembled with need.

"I thought you'd be asleep." Nathan closed the door.

Madalyn put her book down on the table. "We need to talk."

"Is something amiss? Are you feeling worse?"

Madalyn would have smiled at the note of concern in Nathan's voice if she hadn't been so nervous. Instead, she shook her head and patted the bed. "I want to talk about us."

Nathan ignored her invitation and sat in the chair beside the bed. "I thought everything was settled."

She took a deep breath. "I need you to be honest with me."

"You sound serious."

She nodded. "I know you were forced to marry me and I am thankful."

Nathan's lips narrowed and he leaned back in the chair. "But?"

"My uncle said something that I can't forget. He made me realize that perhaps I had made a mistake."

"I see." Nathan's tone was cold, his eyes devoid of expression. "You've realized that you could do better than me."

"No," Madalyn denied. "You misunderstand."

"There's no need to explain." Nathan stood up and walked toward the door. "I'll make the arrangements for a divorce."

"Stop." Her voice was weak, but loud enough to be heard.

Nathan paused with his hand on the doorknob. He didn't turn to look at her. Madalyn took a deep breath.

"A marriage cannot survive when love is one-sided."

Nathan leaned his head against the door before turning back to the room. His body was tense, every muscle straining against his clothes. "Why would you believe that?"

"My uncle said that I forced you to marry me, and that's true." Madalyn faltered as she looked into Nathan's icy blue eyes. "I don't want you to feel obligated."

"Is that how you feel?"

Madalyn's mouth went dry. Nathan's tone suggested that he didn't believe her. She'd begged him to take her as his wife, professing her love over and over again, and yet he still doubted her.

"I love you," she said in a soft voice. "But I won't force you to stay married to me."

"You want me to release you from the marriage." Nathan's lips tightened into a sneer. "I warned you this would happen."

Madalyn slammed her hand against the covers. "I'm concerned about you."

"It's difficult to see how this is in my best interest."

"You're deliberately misunderstanding me." Madalyn's voice rose.

"Then what do you want?"

"I want you to love me." The words were out of Madalyn's mouth before she had a chance to think. "Will you ever be able to do that?"

Nathan moved back to the bed and sat down. He took Madalyn's hands in his, gently massaging her fingers with his thumb. "Why is my love so important now?"

"You were honest about not loving me." Madalyn's voice trembled. "I thought that you'd grow to love me, but my uncle made me see how foolish I was."

Nathan's hand shook slightly as he brushed it against her cheek and then gathered her close to him. His lips feathered against hers, before capturing her mouth in a searing kiss.

Madalyn's doubts melted as Nathan lips caressed and aroused her until she was burning with desire. All that mattered was the feel of Nathan holding her. She moved to pull Nathan closer, but he ended the kiss.

"I couldn't grow to love you because I already do." Nathan's voice was hoarse. "My actions should have shown how much you meant to me."

Madalyn's heart beat raced and her mind was still in a fog of desire, but she couldn't deny the love that shone from Nathan's eyes. She'd been crazy to let her uncle's words nearly destroy her marriage.

Madalyn tapped Nathan's lips with a finger. "I need to hear the words."

"I love you." Nathan kissed her finger. "From the first moment I saw you standing on that table, bravely facing that crowd of sailors. I tried to ignore it, to convince myself that it was a marriage of convenience and the attraction between us was merely physical. I thought I could make love to you and walk away without feeling anything. I was a fool."

"Why didn't you tell me sooner?"

"I didn't realize it myself until you were gone." Nathan closed his eyes briefly. "I thought I'd die of the pain."

She looked into his eyes, imploring him for a second chance. "Can you forgive me for doubting what we had?"

"On one condition." Nathan tilted his head, a wicked gleam shone in his eyes. "You let me show you every day how much I love you."

A slow smile crept across her lips. "Agreed."

Nathan eased them down onto the pillows and pulled the covers up. Madalyn rested her head on his chest, the sound of Nathan's beating heart soothing to her ears. His arms encircled her with love and warmth. She felt complete.

"I do have one request, though," Nathan whispered.

"Anything." Madalyn's body melt into Nathan's.

"Marry me."

Chapter 34

Madalyn adjusted the golden silk dress on her shoulder. It was truly a piece of beauty, with cream lace cascading from the three-quarter sleeves and falling to her wrist. She turned to look in the mirror, the rustle of silk loud in the silent room.

"Well," an impatient voice asked. "Do you like it?"

"It's wonderful." Madalyn swished the small train back and forth before turning to Sarah. "How did you manage this?"

"I found it in one of the trunks yesterday. I thought of you immediately." Sarah straightened the skirt so that it draped smoothly to the floor. "I know it's not in the current style, but the narrow cut of the waist is perfect for your figure."

Madalyn could find no fault with Sarah's choice. It fit her like a second skin. Sarah had been wonderful, throwing herself joyfully into the preparations for the wedding. She was as beautiful in personality as she was physically. Happiness and love shone in her eyes.

The last two days had been a whirlwind of activity in preparation for the wedding in the chapel. Nathan and his brother Alex had ridden to Carlisle yesterday and obtained a license. Nathan's half-brother Samuel had been sent for and had arrived late last night. Everything was in place for the wedding this morning.

Sarah stood up as the clock chimed ten. "It's time."

A knock at the door signaled her brother's arrival. Sarah let him in and then left the two of them alone. Madalyn took William's hands in hers and smiled.

"Be happy for me."

"I am." William grinned. "I don't think he can wait much longer. He was a bear on the voyage over here, but that didn't come close to how he suffered through your illness."

"I love him."

"He's a man worthy of your love." William kissed her cheek. "I wouldn't have agreed to give you away if I didn't believe that."

Madalyn picked up the bouquet of roses Nathan had sent up earlier and heaved a sigh. She was marrying the man she loved. Eager anticipation coursed through her veins and she took William's arm.

Together they made their way through the halls until they reached the original section of the house. It was here that the small ancient chapel built by the first baron was located. Large oak doors stood open and inside Nathan's family were gathered.

Nathan's half-brother Samuel stood at the altar, prayer book in hand and a smile on his face. He had the same dark coloring as Nathan and Alex, but his hair had begun to turn gray. He was also thinner in stature, almost gaunt in comparison to Nathan.

Sarah was standing beside her husband, Alex. Nathan was at the front of the chapel. When she and William reached him, he took her hand. He raised it to his mouth for a kiss before placing it on his arm.

They turned to Samuel and stood before God to make their vows. Madalyn was overwhelmed with happiness as she listened to the words of the marriage ceremony.

Nathan's love, his family's good wishes, and the spectacular beauty of their surroundings were a stark contrast to their first wedding aboard the Folly. She knew in her heart that their lives together would be blessed.

After Samuel pronounced them man and wife, a cheer went up from the others. With tears of joy in her eyes, Madalyn turned to face Nathan's family. Nathan pulled her into his arms and together they greeted the others.

Nathan walked over to his mother, Mary, in the first pew. "Mother, may I present my wife."

Mary gave her a hug.

Mary's eyes were misted with unshed tears, and her face shone with delight. She embraced Madalyn tightly before kissing her on the cheek.

"It's wonderful to see my son so happy. Thank you."

Before Madalyn could reply, she found herself embraced by Sarah and then Alex.

"All Norwards who marry in the family chapel are blessed with a long and happy life together." Alex grinned at his brother. "You two are a match made in heaven."

William shook Nathan's hand. "I know you'll take care of her."

The last to approach them was Samuel. "It's time Nathan settled down."

Nathan grinned and patted Samuel on the back. "It's your turn next."

Alex chuckled. "You're a little overdue Samuel. When will you be announcing your wedding?"

Samuel paled and shook his head. "I gave up hopes of love and marriage years ago."

"That doesn't mean it won't happen." Alex pulled his wife Sarah into his arms. "Love happens when you least expect it."

"And in the most unusual way," Nathan added as he kissed Madalyn's hand.

Later that day, after a festive luncheon and numerous well wishes from their families, Madalyn and Nathan were finally alone. They were to stay their first night at Caldern and then tomorrow travel to the small estate Nathan had accepted from Alex. They would spend a few months there before traveling to Charleston. They still hadn't decided where they would call home, but Madalyn suspected Nathan wanted to be closer to his mother.

"Everything was wonderful."

"And a ceremony we can tell our children about." Nathan gathered Madalyn in his arms.

"You don't think a shipboard wedding is romantic?"

"I think we were very lucky."

"Mrs. Willet would insist that God's hand was involved." Madalyn curled her arms around Nathan's neck.

Nathan touched Madalyn's nose with his. "Then I will be forever grateful to Him."

His lips brushed against her nose and trailed down to her lips. Her body tightened in anticipation. Nathan captured her mouth in a kiss that ignited flames of desire. She clung to him, as her body moved against him.

Nathan groaned and then stooped to pick Madalyn up in his arms. He carried her to the bed and placed her onto it. Madalyn stretched her arms out and Nathan didn't hesitate to accept her invitation. Within seconds, they were lying beside each other, their bodies entwined, their lips locked in a duel of passion.

The kiss ended with both of them gasping for breath. Nathan's hands stroked Madalyn's hair and then he pulled the pins from it, using his fingers as a comb to arrange her brown tresses about the pillow. His eyes scanned her face before raising her hand to his lips. His lips caressed each finger with slow and seductive kisses, sending shivers of delight throughout her.

She wrapped her arms around his neck and pulled him close to her. She arched her back, showing him she could wait no longer, but Nathan didn't give her the relief she wanted. Instead, he ran his hand down the side of her body, stroking every curve, every valley. Madalyn groaned with need.

Only then did Nathan move to unfasten her dress, caressing her bare skin, as inch by inch, it was exposed. A slow ache built within her. She reached a fevered pitch when the last shred of her clothing was stripped from her. The cool air against her heated skin only increased the urgency of her desire.

"You're perfect," Nathan whispered, his voice hoarse with desire. "Every inch, every thought, every deed."

Madalyn tugged at Nathan's coat. "Help me."

Nathan grinned and sat up. With deft fingers he disposed of his clothing and within seconds was naked. Madalyn's breath caught in her throat at the sheer wonder of her husband. She let her hands roam across his broad chest, relishing the feel of the harnessed strength beneath her fingers.

Nathan growled and captured her hand. "I can't wait."

His lips trailed heated kisses across Madalyn's face, neck, and shoulders. When he reached her breasts, his mouth moved in a slow circular motion around each one until he reached the center. His tongue darted across the erect nipple before his lips enclosed around it. Sharp splinters of hot lava shot through Madalyn.

She arched against him, begging him to ease her ache. He entered her with a swift thrust, letting Madalyn's body accept him before beginning to move. His strokes were slow and steady, building their passion until it reached a blinding crescendo.

The world shattered as spasms of ecstasy rolled through her body. Nathan thrust deep once more before collapsing in his own release. Together, they floated back to reality.

Nathan gave her a quick kiss and moved off her. He gathered her in his arms and nuzzled her neck. Her body hummed with contentment and she put her head next to his, inhaling deeply of his scent. She was complete for the first time in her life.

"I love you." Nathan's voice was low and sincere. "You invade my dreams, my thoughts, my very being."

Madalyn's heart was full. "Knowing you love me is more wonderful than I ever imagined."

"You've shown me what love is when shared. Together, our love will carry us through anything."

A surge of happiness brought fresh tears to her eyes. She had set out on a voyage to find her brother and succeeded in finding her love. Now, the real adventure began. Life with Nathan would be an exciting exploration with twists and turns, but at every corner he'd be waiting for her.

Author's Note

While researching my family genealogy I came upon some fascinating information. One of my ancestors was kidnapped in the 1670's. He was 21 and living in London. He was brought to Virginia, where he was sold and forced to work as an indentured servant for five years. This man came from an upper class family in Sweden, and was well-educated. He was spending a year in London to finish his education before embarking on the life of a statesman. He never returned to Sweden. When he was free, he walked north until he found a community of other Swedish immigrants and settled there.

I thought this was an isolated incident, until I found another ancestor, on a different family branch that was kidnapped in the 1730's. He was abducted at the age of eight, from the Netherlands by pirates. When his family was unable to pay the ransom, he was taken to Virginia, and sold. His papers were bought by a Virginian plantation owner. He spent fifteen years there and found favor with the family. He eventually married one of the owner's daughters and they settled on 700 acres in Maryland.

Despite my ancestors' experiences, many people arrived in the colonies as willing indentured servants. Unable to pay for their passage to America, they signed papers agreeing to work a number of years as servants, in exchange for their fare. When these contracts were signed with ships' Captains, the papers would be sold to others once they landed.

About the Author

Cynthia spent most of her childhood with her nose in a book. She began writing stories in her teens, but it wasn't until her forties that she took her writing seriously. Cynthia has an eclectic range of interests that includes reading, ghost hunting, exploring paranormal phenomena, history, quilting, gardening, and great conversation. She has a BSc in Biology, a BA in anthropology, and recently graduated from nursing. Cynthia enjoys writing the type of books she reads.

She writes historical and paranormal romances with a dash of honor, suspense, and intrigue. She lives in Northern Ontario with her husband of thirty years, her teenage son, and their two dachshunds.

Books by Cynthia Clement

Science Fiction

aHunter4Hire Series
aHunter4Rescue
aHunter4Saken
aHunter4Life
aHunter4Ever
aHunter4Trust

Historical

The Seduction of Sarah
The Seduction of Madalyn

Novellas
Pleasuring Emily
Christmas Kisses